Marguerite's Redemption

TROUBLE IN TIMBISHA TOWNSHIP
BOOK FOUR

ELISE MANION

For my writing buddy, Dianna—or Drea—or whatever name
you're using these days!
I hope Marguerite makes you smile.

Contents

Marguerite's Redemption

Prologue

DELETED SCENE/EXCERPT
FROM JOSH'S CHALLENGE...

Summer - *Timbisha Township, Nevada*

"SHIT!" DECLAN SAID OUT LOUD TO NOBODY AS HE checked the time. He'd set up a meeting with Marguerite to discuss what he discovered from his research on Timbisha's stalker case. As a US marshal, he spent his life hunting down fugitives, but since his most recent prey had been found dead, he'd decided to stay in this small rural town to help local authorities sniff out the unsub bothering Marguerite's sister.

Marguerite Theroux. Damn, he'd never met a woman like her—a mixture of beauty, brains, and a smart mouth he found hard to ignore. Half the time he either wanted to tell her off, or kiss her. She worked as the administrative assistant to the Timbisha County Sheriff, and she was definitely too young for his weathered old ass. He had no business meeting with her, except he had questions about her sister's roommate.

And now I'm running late.

By the time he made it to Blue's Whisky Bar, vehicles were packed into the crowded parking lot. As he drove around looking for a space, he spied Marguerite's little red sports car on the second pass. A glance at the clock told him she'd been waiting for at least thirty minutes. Finally, he spied tail lights, and he drummed his thumbs on his steering wheel while a pickup took its damn time backing out of a spot near the bar's entrance. Declan wasted no time claiming the space.

Music blared through the open front doors before he even entered Blue's. He maneuvered his way through the crowd trying to find Marguerite. Instead of preparing to make his apologies for being late, Declan saw red. She'd definitely been waiting a long time and she'd definitely made use of the bar's liquor menu.

A drunker woman he'd never seen before...

...and, she hung in another man's arms—the town bachelor, no less—who was supposed to be dating Marguerite's sister.

Declan marched to the couple who kept knocking into people on the dance floor. "You two have had enough." He reached for Marguerite, who squealed out a little giggle before falling to the ground, while Josh King took a swing at Declan.

He ducked and the momentum made Josh stumble, then try to reach for Marguerite on the ground. "I'm helpin' her."

"To do what, exactly?" Declan pulled Marguerite from the floor and her head flopped onto his shoulder. He turned toward the door when the bouncer blocked his path. "Move."

"Not til they pay for the damages."

At the bouncer's words Declan noticed a turned over table, a broken chair, and a waitress sweeping broken glass into a dustpan.

"I don't feel so good," Marguerite whispered before becoming a limp rag in his arms.

Josh slurred, "'s okay Magpie. I'll take ya home," before tripping on his own two feet. The bouncer thankfully caught him before he face-planted.

Declan whipped out his cell and called the sheriff, who also happened to be Josh's brother; and then called Marguerite's uncle because her breathing had become labored.

Sweat covered her pale skin.

"What did they take?" he asked the crowd of disgruntled patrons. Cell phones pointed in their direction but no one would talk to him.

"Everyone step back, and damn it, turn off the music!" Sheriff King yelled, who'd already been on his way to the bar because of complaints from the owner. "Josh, what the hell do you think you're doing?"

Declan looked up to see Josh standing on a pool table taking off his shirt. "It's hot in here."

"Oh, for the love of all things holy," the sheriff grumbled as he wrestled his little brother from the table.

"I'm gonna take Marguerite to the ER. She's gettin' worse." Declan lifted her into his arms. "Someone get the door."

Sheriff King struggled with Josh, who slurred, "Wha'z wrong with 'er?"

"Same thing that's wrong with you, idiot." The sheriff pulled Josh outside while the bouncer held the door for them.

"Here," the man said, who'd changed his attitude after the sheriff arrived. He opened the passenger door of Declan's pickup. "Is she gonna be all right?"

"I sure as hell hope so." Declan placed her in the passenger seat, buckled her belt and ran to the driver side and hopped in.

He cranked the ignition key a litter harder than he should've, and backed out a lot faster than was safe, then headed for the hospital.

Declan slowed down at the first red light, looked in all directions, then pressed his foot to the floorboard and blew through the intersection. He reached a hand to Marguerite who remained slumped against the window.

Shit, shit, shit!

He gunned it up the road to the ER entrance. A security guard gave him a warning finger-wag but Declan couldn't have cared less. The second the truck stopped, he jumped out and hurried around to the passenger side. He shouted for help and two orderlies rushed to him with a gurney.

"I think she's overdosed on something. She's not breathing, sweaty, clammy..." His voice trailed off as he followed the men inside. A doctor in blue scrubs checked her vitals once they'd placed her in a bay.

"Pupils fixed and dilated, weak heart rate."

"Sir, you'll need to step back." A nurse pushed on his chest to draw a curtain.

"I'm stayin'." He flashed his United States Marshals badge and dared the woman to make him leave. "I'll stay out of your way."

"She's coding."

"CLEAR."

Everyone moved away from the gurney.

Declan jumped when Marguerite's small body jerked from the defibrillator. At the sound of a rhythm from one of the machines Declan counted Marguerite's breaths.

One...two...three...Thank God.

"Will she be all right?"

"Are you family?"

Knowing what was coming, Declan mustered up all the authority he owned by once again flashing his badge. "US Marshal Declan McKinley. I brought her in. I'm working with Sheriff King on a case and I believe this woman is another victim."

The doctor took his measure. "She needs fluids and we'll run her blood work to find out what she took. We're waiting for the cardiologist but she'll definitely need to be monitored overnight. Once we know more we'll let her family know."

He didn't bother correcting the doctor about her taking drugs on purpose. For one, he didn't know what happened. Two, a murderer walked the town, and three, the killer knew their way around pharmacology.

"I've already called her family and I'll need to see the results of those tests. Will you be moving her soon?"

"You can wait in the waiting room until her family arrives. We'll let them know more once the tests are back and I hear from cardiology." With that the doctor closed the curtain.

Declan took in his surroundings. The rest of the emergency room remained quiet, just a rushing nurse here or there. He wandered back the way he'd come and found Marguerite's uncle and mother in the hallway outside the waiting room.

"The nurse at the desk said you'd brought her in. How is she?" the frail woman in the wheelchair asked.

He'd heard Darla Theroux was battling cancer but seeing what the disease had done to her made Declan sick. Dane Bainbridge, Marguerite's uncle and an ex-FBI agent, *and* the reason Declan had come to Timbisha Township in the first place, stood stoic waiting for an answer.

"Unconscious. She flatlined once but her heart's beating now. They're waiting for a room so they can monitor her overnight."

Mrs. Theroux began to cry.

"We're gonna do things my way now." Bainbridge turned and wheeled his sister inside of the waiting room leaving Declan with one choice. He followed along.

EVERYTHING HURT BUT THAT WAS NOTHING compared to the thirst drying up Marguerite's mouth and throat. She opened her eyes to find her mother holding up a cup with a straw.

"Careful, you've been out awhile."

"What's with the peanut gallery?" Marguerite rasped as she pushed her sore body into a sitting position.

The whole room sighed in relief at her sarcastic tone. That's when she realized almost everyone she knew surrounded her hospital bed, including the marshal who did funny things to her heart rate.

"We just wanted to see what you looked like hungover," Jarod said.

Marguerite's eyes widened before a hand went to her hair, and then an embarrassed groan issued from her mouth. "Get out so I can get dressed, will ya?"

"Not a chance," Mom said.

"Fine." She closed her eyes with resignation before asking her boss—who also happened to be the sheriff, "Jarod, please tell me you caught the driver of the truck that ran me over."

Everyone chuckled then. "No." He shook his head once. "There was no truck, but maybe you can fill in some blanks for us."

Her thoughts were cloudy. "I'll try." Her eyes went to

McKinley. "You called me and wanted to meet at Blue's Whiskey Bar, right?"

"Right," he said quietly, and Marguerite frowned at the regret on his face.

"I remember Josh was there playing darts." She looked to Josh for confirmation. "Jeez, you look like shit." He had black circles under his eyes and his naturally tan skin appeared sallow.

"Feel like it, too. Go on, because I don't remember seeing you at all. I barely remember the darts."

The admission frightened her. She looked at everyone in the room, then the IV in her arm, and a tear fell. "What's happened, guys?"

"You and Josh were drugged, honey." Her mother reached for her hand and squeezed. "If it weren't for the marshal, God only knows what would've happened to you."

Chapter One

THE MISSION

Fugitive Task Force, *three months later...*

DECLAN DRUMMED HIS THUMBS ON THE STEERING wheel as he scanned the New Mexico horizon for the drug mule's silver Toyota Avalon. He hoped the son of a bitch would stop soon. The surveillance van rattled, and its engine was a gutless wonder.

At least the radio works.

Music helped drown out the noise—and the complaints coming from his two road weary companions.

Declan felt, more than heard, a sigh coming from the inexperienced analyst sitting in the passenger seat.

"What are we listening to?" Marguerite's question held annoyance, amping up his irritation.

He glared her way, still wondering how the hell she ended up on the task force. He tapped the volume-up button, filling the cabin with Phil Collins' ode to the 1984 movie *Against All Odds*. "Don't blaspheme the classics, Blondie."

Marguerite scrunched her forehead. "How old *are* you?"

Ignoring the beautiful brat, he studied the road. "None of your business, Blondie."

"Stop calling me that," she gritted out between clenched teeth.

"Children," came a warning voice from the back.

In the rearview mirror, Declan met Dane Bainbridge's eyes before returning them the road. Technically, both the analyst and the ex-FBI man acted as consultants on this assignment but Bainbridge was a mentor and friend.

Marguerite adjusted her seatbelt to glare behind her. "Not funny, Uncle Dane."

Dane grunted, his equivalent to a laugh while flipping through pages.

Probably an atlas. The man was definitely old school.

"How many towns are between us and Pueblo?"

Marguerite readjusted her seat to consult her tablet. "Four, assuming that's the subject's destination."

"Crosscheck any known safe houses in those towns. Sun's setting. He's gotta stop for a piss somewhere. Hopefully, he'll stick with his pattern, and find a place to hole up for the night."

Declan asked Marguerite, "Where's he pinging?"

"Still heading north. Wait...he's pulling off in Raton."

"About time. What's in Raton?" The team needed a break, and Declan prayed for a motel with multiple room vacancies, preferably on opposite sides of the building from one another.

Marguerite tapped the screen. "Not much, only one motel...couple of gas stations...population six thousand." She looked his way. "I can't believe how far ahead he got. Getting caught in the construction zone really screwed us over."

Declan drummed his thumbs again, agitated at their bad luck. The task force had assembled in Reno, Nevada to follow Rocco Monti, a known drug mule and fugitive. They'd almost had him in Las Vegas but the task force commanders wanted to wait until they knew his routes, contacts, and drops. They wanted the whole organization from top to bottom and they believed following Monti's route would reveal the entire cartel. Declan had his doubts. Local police were on notice, and other task force teams had been implemented to arrest buyers and associates along the way but only after Monti made the drops and left town. The task force hadn't picked up any chatter among the cartel about their mule being followed and no attempts to hide any drop points from the law had been made.

Too easy.

Declan didn't like it.

Bainbridge's phone rang. After a couple of grunts, Dane leaned forward. "A CI's just confirmed their contact that Monti's stopped for the night. Marguerite, honey, why don't you see if the motel has vacancy. We'll get some shut-eye and start this madness again in the morning."

"Sounds like deja-vu, but you got it, Uncle Dane."

By the time they rolled into Raton, New Mexico, Declan was ready to collapse. Marguerite, usually put-together and professional, now sported droopy hair and wrinkled clothes. They pulled into the motel's parking lot and began the process of cleaning out the van and gathering their things. Bainbridge went inside to get the key cards, while Marguerite collected her electronics, make-up bag, and the dozen or so fashion magazines strewn about the van.

"Here." Marguerite handed him an armload of magazines. "I don't need these anymore."

Declan chuckled because, as far as he knew, she hadn't purchased anything from them so what did she need them for in the first place? Rolling his eyes, he stuffed the magazines inside a trash bag, along with a myriad of used coffee cups, empty snack wrappers and other refuse accumulated along the way. Then he found a dumpster and made the deposit.

"Got everything?" he asked when he returned.

She hitched a purse and other bags over her shoulders. "Yes, I think so. Uncle Dane's coming out."

Declan turned to see the grumpiest man in the world. "What's wrong?"

"Couldn't get two rooms. We have to bunk together."

Declan's shoulders fell when he surveyed the crowded parking lot. He'd offer to sleep in the van but, at forty-two, his battered bones needed a hot shower, and a softer place to lay his head. By the looks of Dane and his niece, they were in the same boat. He was about to offer to sleep on the motel floor when Marguerite surprised the hell out of him.

"No worries. I brought my sleeping bag. I'll take the floor."

Declan shared a look with Bainbridge, who beamed with pride. "Okay, honey. Let me know if you change your mind."

Declan wondered where she packed a damn sleeping bag in those totes.

"Trust me, I won't. Uncle Dane, you have a bad back and, Declan, you've been a grouch all day. I think you both need your beauty sleep."

Declan followed the sway of her hips as she led them to their room. Even loaded down with bags and dragging a rolling case, she oozed sex appeal. In the beginning of this adventure, he'd tried to be a gentleman by offering to help her but she'd rebuffed his chivalry. Bainbridge explained she didn't need to be coddled, so Declan hadn't offered assistance since.

Bainbridge opened the door. The room had seen better days. Declan didn't comment on the "cleaning" crew meeting minimum requirements, nor the fact there was barely enough room for the three of them to sleep. Marguerite dumped her computer crap on the only table—situated just inside the door next to the window on the right—while Bainbridge made a beeline for the toilet.

Declan picked up the TV remote and surfed until he found a news channel. He'd been bunking with Bainbridge for a while and knew the man wanted the bed closest to the bathroom, which was pushed up against the opposite wall. One nightstand was sandwiched between the beds. Declan leaned back on "his" bed and frowned at the narrow space between the two doubles and wondered where Marguerite would make a pallet.

His eyes left the news broadcast and landed on her. Even wilted and road weary, she made a pretty vision, which only irritated him.

What is she, twenty-six? Twenty-seven? So full of herself and yet she strived to please her uncle, who'd encouraged her to come along. Marguerite had no field training which worried Declan. He respected Bainbridge as a lawman, but the uncle indulged the niece in things she had no business doing.

I gotta bad *feeling about this assignment.*

"Think he'll stick with the same schedule?" She'd opened up her laptop and began searching whatever database she used to find people.

"I see no reason why he wouldn't."

She nodded, never taking her eyes from the screen. "If he continues on this path, it leads to Denver. Has to be his drop point, right?" She turned in her seat. The same thump in the chest he got every time their eyes collided had him taking a swift breath.

He swallowed. "Probably."

She turned back around. Her job included mapping out routes, looking for construction and possible stops Monti might make, and gathering information online. According to Dane, Marguerite was supposed to be a wiz on the computer, and had great people skills. Her previous undercover work had led to the leader of a meth ring, but not before the ringleader kidnapped the sheriff's wife and daughter—and then committed suicide by cop. None of that had been Marguerite's fault and, to her credit, she'd been instrumental in the investigation, but Declan was uncomfortable with the tactics. According to small-town gossip, she'd damaged her reputation within the Timbisha community in the process, whatever the hell that meant.

He wondered how far she'd gone to earn trust with the ringleader. Bainbridge remained closed-mouthed about it, and so did Marguerite.

Declan had never asked.

As his mind wandered, Marguerite stood and stretched. "What?"

Damn it, he'd been staring. Before he could defend himself, Bainbridge finally emerged from the bathroom. "All yours." He'd changed into sweats and a t-shirt. "You think the diner will deliver?"

"Probably not," Declan said. "I'll get some takeout." He took their orders and escaped the room to get some sustenance.

MARGUERITE TOOK A CURSORY GLANCE AT THE WORN out carpet and grimaced with distaste.

It's gonna be a long night.

With no room between the two double beds, she'd have to make her pallet between Declan's bed and the outside wall under the window. Oh well, this wasn't the worst thing she'd had to do for her job.

Don't go there, her mind whispered and she immediately stuffed the memory of her undercover work back in the locked box—which held all of her shortcomings and regrets—where it belonged.

Urgent need for a shower propelled her into the bathroom. The only thing that mattered was the current case; keeping tabs on Rocco Monti. Easily done with the tracking device placed on the Avalon in Vegas the day before yesterday. Since then, she'd been trapped in a noisy mobile office with Uncle Dane and the marshal.

Declan McKinley. God, he'd made her feel inadequate since the day he walked into the sheriff's station a few months ago. Growing up in a small town taught her the crueler side of people and she was used to being looked down upon. Doing the undercover stint hadn't helped much. When Uncle Dane asked for her help with this task force she jumped at the chance to leave Timbisha Township. However, three days on the road with McKinley had worn her nerves to their nubs.

Cussing when the tub's drain began to back up, she kicked the soapy water around while rinsing shampoo from her hair, then added a little conditioner. She rinsed again before twisting the shower knob to the off position and escaped the tub to dry herself and put on jammies. Once done, she let her hair air dry to avoid another McKinley rant about her taking too long in the bathroom.

He'd already made wisecracks about her appearance and, therefore, she didn't want to fan the flames. Yes, there were times when she was vain, but she also knew how to be practical.

She opened the bathroom door to find Uncle Dane on the bed, fingers tapping on his tablet. A notebook sat next to him and he kept referencing it. "How was your shower, honey?"

She raised an eyebrow and he grunted.

"Wouldn't it be easier to type your report on the laptop?"

He glanced up, eyeglasses low on his nose. "I didn't want to bother you."

She chuckled as she opened up the report program the FBI used and pulled out the chair at the table. "Sit. It's better for your back, anyway."

Just as her uncle's butt hit the seat, McKinley arrived carrying fast-food sacks. "Diner was closed."

Marguerite hurried to clear a space on the other side of Uncle Dane at the tiny table, which was meant for two people —max.

McKinley let out a sigh. "If the bathroom's free I'll clean up and eat after."

Pulling out the burgers and fries for herself and her uncle, she made sure McKinley's sandwich was wrapped tight to keep it warm. Why she cared if he ate a hot meal or not was a mystery, but she didn't want to dwell on her actions too closely with regard to the marshal.

Uncle Dane click-clacked his report until he'd finished, taking bites every now and again, neither of them talking. She finished her food long before he did, and prepared her pallet on the floor. It was only when she'd lowered herself into her sleeping bag did Uncle Dane ask, "Are you sure you'll be all right down there?"

"Yes, don't worry about me. Sleep well." Using the wall and

her pillow as a headboard, she put her earbuds in, found some relaxation music, and accessed the DEA database. Monti's associates were easy to find if you followed the breadcrumbs. She cross referenced names with social media accounts and followed his digital trail along the southwestern states. From the pictures she found it was clear Monti was an idiot. Dangerous, but still stupid enough to let his picture float all over the internet. The cartel couldn't be happy with him.

The bathroom door opened and McKinley stepped out shirtless, wearing only a ragged pair of lounge pants.

Marguerite's eyes lingered on well-defined abs and a spattering of chest hair before escaping back into her laptop.

I'm not attracted to him. Not. At. All.

The mantra ran in a loop inside her mind while she pretended she hadn't lost her place on the screen. Bare feet entered her peripheral. Her nose twitched.

My god.

Her eyes drifted closed as his heavenly scent assailed her... fresh from a shower, all woodsy masculinity...

Until his big foot bumped into hers as he rummaged around the table, amping up her irritability again.

She pulled out an earbud and pointed to the bag right in from of him. "You're burger is there."

"Thanks." But instead of sitting in the chair, he stepped over her outstretched legs, and climbed onto his bed. Soft crunching, and the occasional slurp from his cup, were the only sounds competing with the news droning in the background.

Ignoring both Declan and Uncle Dane, she considered using the noise cancelling function on her ear buds but immediately dismissed the idea in case Monti made a move and they had to leave right away. So, she continued her research until finally, into the quiet, came the smashing of paper.

Without warning, Declan leaned over her to deposit his empty wrappers into the wastebasket, which she'd pushed against the wall under the window to make room for her gear. Once again, her nose twitched and her eyes got a fantastic shot of his derrière, the tops of both gluteus maximi exposed from the sagging waistband of his sleepwear.

It most certainly is not the cutest plumber's butt I've ever seen. No sirree.

"Mind if I turn out this light? Your uncle's already asleep." He clicked off the bedside lamp before she had a chance to reply, confirming that yes, Declan McKinley was an ass.

At 4:00 am, the laptop she'd set on the floor next to her to charge, pinged loud and clear into the dark motel room. She grappled with her sleeping bag, cursing the thin twisted material's zipper until she could open the screen.

Monti's tracker had activated.

"Shit." McKinley flipped off his blankets and leaned over her to look at the screen. "Is he out of town yet?"

Ignoring the heat of his chest near her shoulder she shook her head. "Not yet. Looks like he's at a trailer park not far from here," she mumbled.

McKinley turned on the light, waking Uncle Dane. "Rise and shine. Monti's making a drop."

Her uncle groaned. "God, this guy's a prick."

Marguerite chuckled while McKinley made his bed. She began rolling up her compact sleeping bag and travel pillow while Dane used the bathroom again. She turned to stuff the bedding into one of her totes and caught McKinley watching her. "What?"

Whatever he'd had on his mind left when Monti's tracker alerted them he was done with his business and now on the move, this time to the interstate.

Chapter Two

THE MISTAKE

"He's never left this early before." Marguerite rushed around the room cramming all of her crap into her bags. Declan shook his head, threw on a t-shirt and headed for the van in disgust.

She was right. Monti had stuck to a tight schedule so far. Either the cartel was putting pressure on him, or he knew he was being followed.

Probably both.

Declan threw a pair of jeans over his shoulder then left uncle and niece to collect themselves while he moved the van closer to their room. He'd changed his pants in the parking lot.

Thirty minutes later they were crossing the border into Colorado. He'd hoped to catch up with Monti in Pueblo when they caught a break. Only Monti didn't meet with anyone. It was a pit stop for breakfast at a mom-and-pop diner on the outskirts of town just off I-25 North where he took his time. Declan pulled into a truck stop for some much needed coffee across the street from the diner.

By the time Monti got back on the road, Bainbridge had called the Denver field office to alert them they were headed their way. Four days in and Declan was sick of documenting the mule's route.

"Is it always this tedious?" Marguerite asked from the backseat.

"Whatsa matter, Blondie? Not enough action for ya?" Declan caught her glare in the rearview mirror.

She narrowed her eyes but Dane intervened before they could get into another row. "Surveillance was never my favorite detail, honey. Fortunately, the information we gather is crucial for convictions. Sometimes the unexpected happens. Until then, you two care to make a wager?"

Declan squinted at Bainbridge. "On what?"

"Whether or not he'll change directions at Denver."

Marguerite tapped on some keys. "Okay, I'll bite. From Denver he could continue north to Cheyenne, or take I-70 east," there was more clicking, "through the plains to Kansas City."

"West would take him back through the mountains to Grand Junction. He'd hit Vail. There's money there," Declan pondered.

"What's the prize, Uncle Dane?"

"Bragging rights."

Declan met Marguerite's eyes again in the mirror. One of her eyebrows raised in challenge, making him chuckle. "You first, Bainbridge."

"He'll head east. Just to piss me off."

Marguerite laughed. "Okay, then I'll take west to Vail, then hit all the other little ski towns hidden in the mountains. Tourist attractions always have side action."

Declan shrugged. "That leaves me north to Cheyenne. If I win, double or nothing he heads west on I-80 back to Reno."

"You're on," grunted Bainbridge.

"Double bragging rights? That's just what we need." Marguerite shook her head, disgust dripping off her words.

Declan wondered what the hell she meant by it. He wasn't arrogant and he didn't brag.

Do I?

"Okay, Blondie, if I'm right, and Cheyenne is the turnaround point, you have to forego make-up the rest of the trip."

"I'm only wearing eyeliner and mascara now."

Really? Damn, she's pretty. "And we have to wait for you to apply it every damn day."

"Whatever, McKinley. Fine. If you win the double-or-nothing, I'll leave my make-up bag closed." He caught another eye roll while Bainbridge let out another grunt.

They followed Monti north on I-25, a hazardous freeway fraught with potholes, construction zones, and people too impatient to deal with any of it. By the time they reached Denver, Monti had made thirty stops scattered between Pueblo, Fountain, Colorado Springs, and Monument. Marguerite documented the drop locations and called local authorities while Bainbridge took photos.

On the outskirts of Denver, Monti pulled off at a convenience store. Declan kept driving.

"What are you doing? You just passed him." Marguerite leaned up from the back to point at the Avalon.

Declan shared a look with Bainbridge, who'd just hung up with the Denver field office. "They picked up chatter which alerted Monti he's got a tail. Cover's blown, honey. They want us to come in."

"Damn it," Declan muttered. Making sure he drove as far from the convenience store as possible, he took an alternate route to the office.

"What happens now?" This from the brat in the backseat.

"If we're lucky, they'll arrest the son of a bitch and we can go home. We've got enough evidence to lock him away until he's ninety." This grunted from Bainbridge.

"What happens if we aren't lucky?"

Declan didn't want to think about it. Bainbridge gave the bad news. "They still want us on him. They've arrested buyers only, no one key to the cartel. The drop points were cleared faster than it took for authorities to intervene. They don't have anyone in the network."

Marguerite leaned up further. "And?"

Declan sighed. "They'll give us a different vehicle. As long as Monti hasn't found the tracker, or he hasn't exchanged cars, we can still follow him."

She scooted back into her seat and picked up the tablet. "He's pinging on I-25, still heading north."

Declan cursed and hit the gas pedal. *Please let him head back to Reno.*

The vehicle exchange took an hour, but he gladly traded the van for the new Chevy crew cab. Less obvious than the van, and it had a bigger engine. By the time they were back on his trail, Monti had made three stops, this time all for sellers in the network, but too low in the ranks to amount to anything.

"Where is he?" Agitated, Declan scanned the freeway while drumming a fast rhythm on the steering wheel.

"Pulling off in Loveland."

"Good. Maybe his stops will give us time to catch up. Road conditions?"

Keys clicked. "No accidents, no construction. Traffic is

light." She caught his eyes in the mirror, eyebrows raised in surprise. Yeah, he couldn't believe their luck would last either as he set the cruise control to eighty-two.

He ignored how his heart pounded every time he looked into those hazel eyes. Declan hadn't slept a wink knowing she'd been right there, in the same room, next to his bed in her flimsy sleeping bag. Hell, he'd snuck peeks at her all night, her hair askew over the pillow, eyelashes fanned across the flawless skin of her cheeks. Visions of kissing her lips, tasting her neck—and other places—kept him wound tighter than a spring. He couldn't survive much more of her proximity. It made him edgy, and edgy made him sloppy. The bad feeling he'd had since the day they left Reno crept up his spine, momentarily wiping out his lust for Marguerite. Again, he scanned the road for danger.

As the miles sped by, her voice would float up to report Monti's location, and traffic conditions. Bainbridge stayed silent, and soon Declan couldn't stand the tension in the cab.

"Damn it!" Marguerite slammed her tablet on the seat next to her.

"What?" Declan's heart lurched at her sudden curse.

Pinching the bridge of her nose, she said, "Declan won. He just turned west onto I-80 at Cheyenne."

Bainbridge chuckled and Declan sagged in relief. If the bastard was heading home, this farce of an assignment was almost over.

Declan caught Marguerite's glare in the rearview mirror, as if she were waiting for him to gloat. His shoulders relaxed and the tap, tap, tap of his thumbs stopped.

"How far ahead did he get?"

She picked up the tablet again and made a few calculations. "We've made up thirty minutes. There's nothing between

Cheyenne and Laramie but wind farms, grass, and antelope. We should catch up to him by then." The note of disgust in her voice made him chuckle.

"In the mean time," her uncle chimed in, "maybe we should stay back so as not to give ourselves away again."

"Good plan." Declan fiddled with the radio until he landed on Eddie Rabbitt's *Drivin' My Life Away.*

He glanced in the review mirror. Marguerite had closed her eyes, but he heard the unmistakable "Ugh," drift from her lips.

MARGUERITE REGRETTED HER CHOICE TO COME along. Never one for a long ride, this job had lost its luster somewhere in Arizona. Puzzling out how the bad guys got away with bad shit intrigued her but the confines of a vehicle made sleuthing a bore.

That, and the incredibly poor music choices from both Declan and Uncle Dane. Apparently, the 80s were calling them home and Marguerite just wanted out of the damn truck and off the damn road.

I'm losing my damn mind.

The tracker pinged an alert. "Shocker. He's pulling off in Rock Springs," she deadpanned. Monti the Mule, as she'd started calling him, had stopped at every stupid village and town, no matter the size, since hitting I-80. Some of the locales had no law enforcement to speak of, therefore no arrests had been made.

"Perfect," Declan drawled, not sounding any happier.

"Rock Springs police have been notified," Uncle Dane growled. "Hopefully, this is the end of his route. My ass hurts sittin' here."

Marguerite checked the time. 7:30 pm. The sun had long been set and her stomach grumbled with hunger. "He's stopped at a trailer park on the outskirts."

"Finally."

"Any place to stay nearby?" Declan asked.

"Yeah, a few. Diners and gas stations too." She tapped on one off the interstate and made reservations. "We're set. Two rooms. Take the next exit."

Glad no one questioned her, they pulled into the parking lot of a new motel. She'd picked it because of the diner next door, but it was closed for renovations, which hadn't been on their website. The convenience store on the other side of the diner claimed they sold broasted chicken.

"I need to stretch my legs." She pointed at the store. "Any requests or do you want me to see if they do full meals?"

"I'm hungry enough to eat a damn horse, Blondie. I trust you." With that comment, which might've been the first compliment Declan had ever given her, he began unloading her personal gear.

She met Uncle Dane's expression with raised eyebrows and he grunt-chuckled. "Like he said, we trust you, honey."

She held up her cell. "Text me if anything strikes you."

"Will do. Meet us in our room when you get back."

She lifted a hand in acknowledgement as she trekked across the parking lot toward the store.

Autumn had hit Wyoming hard. Marguerite wrapped her sweater tighter to ward off the crisp air. Few people were out and about, and she attributed it to the town's size and it being a weeknight. The store was well lit and, for the most part, empty. She smiled at the man behind the chicken case, did a cursory perusal of the menu before heading for the restrooms located in the back of the store. There were three doors in the alcove; the men's and women's restroom opposite each other, and the stockroom straight ahead. Through the stock room was a small area she assumed to be the loading dock. The rolling door stood open revealing the dark alley in the back. Marguerite took it all in before entering the ladies' room.

After completing her business, she stared at herself in the scratched mirror while she washed her hands. *He can keep the damned mascara*, she thought before drying her hands and pulling out a tube of tinted Chapstick from her pocket to smear onto her dry lips.

Thinking she'd won over Declan, she stepped out of the restroom.

A grimy hand covered her mouth and the point of a gun jabbed into her side.

"Don't make a sound or I'll end you right here."

Marguerite pinched her lips closed to show she'd cooperate, as the man—she assumed to be Monti—dragged her through the storeroom and out the rolling door.

Once they hit the asphalt, he yanked her around and shoved her inside a gold Buick made sometime in the last century. Marguerite panicked for a minute before she realized he hadn't taken her cell.

Without the Avalon to track, Declan could still find her, hopefully before either he or Uncle Dane crashed for the night.

Monti said nothing as he squealed tires out of the alley, into the parking lot, and down a dirt road toward the trailer park he'd stopped at earlier. He didn't stop there though. He drove through a gate leading to storage facilities.

"Get out. Don't even think about running because I'll shoot you before I chase ya, bitch."

He waved his gun toward a larger RV unit. As she

approached the empty unit, he shoved her inside to the farthest wall, not bothering to roll the door closed.

"Who sent you?"

"No one."

A hard punch landed into her stomach. "Who. Sent. You?"

Cough. "No one."

"Wrong answer, bitch."

A hard slap to the face. "We can do this all night."

"No one sent me."

"You and those two cowboys have been following me since Reno. Who. Are. You?"

"My uncle and I are on vacation."

A large fist grabbed a handful of hair and ripped it from her skull. She sucked air between her teeth as he held his prize up as a warning in front of her face. "Who's the prick with you. I don't see no ring on your finger. He ain't your husband."

"My brother."

A punch to the other side of her face dropped her to her knees, and she saw stars.

"You're a lyin' skank. He's a US marshal."

A kick to the stomach.

"I hate feds. But you ain't no cop, are ya?"

He'd taken her air with the last impact to her gut. She could only cough, which made him angrier. He yanked her arm back, and up, until she heard the pop of her shoulder but he'd brought her back to her feet, which she swayed upon.

Pain screamed.

She screamed.

"Tell me who you are, you lyin' c—"

"M-Marguerite!" Ready to blackout, saying her name helped to ground her to reality.

Monti took hold of her chin and squeezed between his fat fingers and thumb. "That means nuthin' to me, sweet cakes."

He moved in close enough for his foul breath to fan her face. She fought the urge to puke.

Through swelling eyes she saw lights flash. At first she thought they came from pain but realized they were blue and red, coming from outside.

He cursed again and aimed his gun at the door.

"You should give up now." Marguerite hoped his agitation would bring on his downfall.

Another sucker punch to the face knocked her to the ground. She landed hard on her wounded shoulder. Darkness clouded the perimeter of what was left of her vision.

"How'd they find us?" Monti screamed. Rough hands searched her until he found the cell. He chucked her phone across the unit at the same time he slammed his foot into her gut.

Tires crunched.

Two car doors slammed.

The only two men she cared about shouted her name. The edges of her vision clouded. She tried to rub her eyes but her arm hung useless at her side. Her vision wavered now as breath grew harder to draw.

Monti slunk into the shadows.

She opened her mouth to warn them about the gun.

Can't speak.

Can't breathe.

"Marguerite!" Uncle Dane yelled as he ran to her.

Took her hand.

Monti fired off a round and Uncle Dane lurched forward.

Declan shouted. "NO!"

Another round went off and Marguerite's side caught fire.

Bodies fought, bones cracked, voices bellowed.

Everything went black.

———

TWENTY-FIVE MINUTES AGO...

DECLAN'S NECK HAIR STOOD ON END, NOT FROM THE sharp wind, but in warning. He scanned the area for danger as Marguerite sashayed away but found none.

Filling his lungs with the night air, he hefted her totes from the truck bed—*how is she lugging these around every night?*—and followed Bainbridge into her room. The man had secured Marguerite's electronics and proceeded to unceremoniously dump them onto the bed.

"Is that the rest of her things?"

Declan nodded, then set the totes next the mess on her bed before making sure her room was locked when he left. She'd have to get her keycard when she returned with the chicken.

Outside, the bad feeling continued and something made him glance around towards the convenience store which was blocked by the motel's office. "Is she still in view?"

Bainbridge stopped in his tracks to survey the parking lot as well. "No. But..." He didn't finish his thought and Declan pulled out his phone to check the team's GPS tracking app. Satisfied with Marguerite's red dot glowing from inside the building, he went to his own room to relieve himself, making sure to flip the metal security flap into the door jamb to prevent locking out his teammates.

Finished with the john, he flicked on the television,

knowing Bainbridge would want to watch the news while they ate.

Declan checked the time.

She'd been gone fifteen minutes since he'd tracked her phone.

This time when he opened up the GPS, he flew out his door and yelled at Bainbridge. "Get your ass in gear! She's on the move!"

They hustled across the lot and he threw himself into the truck. Thank God it was new as it fired up right away. Pounding his hands against the steering wheel, Declan roared, "I knew it!" as Bainbridge slammed the passenger door.

Declan burned rubber flying out of the parking lot onto the street. "It was a mistake to bring her, Bainbridge!" Declan's phone bounced in the cupholder he'd tossed it into, but he could still make out Marguerite's red dot.

"Shut up and drive, McKinley," the man growled before finishing his call to dispatch for more units.

The storage sheds weren't far and before they'd even stopped the truck, blue lights and sirens flashed behind them.

McKinley's heart skipped a beat when Marguerite's cry of pain hit his ears.

"Marguerite!" Faster than he'd seen the man move before, Bainbridge was out of the truck and charging toward the unit, Declan hot on tail.

A gunshot fired and Declan watched in horror as Bainbridge fell to the ground. Declan swung his firearm in Monti's direction but the son of a bitch caught him off guard and clipped him with a round to the arm.

With adrenaline flooding his body, the bullet didn't stop Declan from twisting Monti's wrist until bones cracked while his screams filled the dark space.

"Goddamn feds! I'll kill you! I'll kill you all!"

Declan didn't wait but continued to pummel the piece of shit until rough hands pulled him off Monti's limp body.

"Sir, he's done," one of Rock Spring's finest said.

"My team?" Declan searched to find Marguerite unconscious, and Dane being worked on by EMS.

"Bastard shot him in the back," said a uniformed officer.

Not wanting to interfere with the life-saving measures being done, Declan skirted around them to kneel by Marguerite, who remained unconscious. He'd seen dislocated shoulders before. Her's was the worst he'd seen yet. She'd need major physical therapy, if not surgery to repair what that animal had done to her. With gentle hands, he searched her form, needing to touch her.

To feel her breathing.

Her face swelled around her eyes, and part of her hair had been torn out.

Oh, my beautiful girl, what did he do to you?

Anger ripped through Declan.

This is what he'd been afraid of from the beginning. She'd had no business being on this mission, this stupid, useless tracking of a man who everyone knew was a mule.

Who everyone knew worked for the cartel.

None of this had been necessary.

He tracked fugitives and brought them in, not *this*, and it made him sick to have participated in it.

He should've never let her go to the store alone, not with Monti on the loose.

Hell, Monti had made them once already. Declan should've known he'd do it again, for God's sake.

"Sir, you're bleeding."

"What?" Declan snapped.

Intimidated, but not giving up, the young med tech repeated his claim.

Declan looked down and, yes, he was most definitely bleeding at the same time burning pain seared his bicep. "Her shoulder's dislocated. Be careful with her."

Declan marched outside and was immediately rounded up by another EMS technician, this one brooking no argument. He tolerated the tech's ministrations a moment before two gurneys were wheeled out of the building and into ambulances.

Declan opened his mouth, but the medical technician held up a hand. "Everyone's going in the same direction. Sit back, please, so we can close the doors and head out."

Not one for coddling, he tolerated the ride to Rock Springs trauma center, refusing to lay down. His bleeding had stopped but Declan was forced to endure being cleared and released by a physician before he could check on Bainbridge and Marguerite.

Marguerite.

She'd been pale, unresponsive, and badly battered. He couldn't get her bruised and bloodied face out of his head. He worried about Bainbridge but knew the man to be a tough old fart, so he wasn't nearly as concerned as he should've been.

"Still alive, I see."

At the smooth voice, Declan found Special Agent Roland Lightfoot leaning against the wall outside the waiting room. "How bad is he?"

Lightfoot shrugged. "They're stabilizing him for trauma flight to Salt Lake City. Bullet nicked an artery, possibly pierced a lung. They won't know until they get him to Utah."

Shit.

"What about his niece?"

"She's in surgery to retrieve the bullet. Her shoulder's

pretty bad. They wanna make sure no blood vessels were torn. She's got some bruised ribs. The bastard broke her orbital socket, too, but they didn't find any stray fragments near her eye or sinus, which is good."

Declan closed his eyes and sat in a plastic chair, trying to process everything he'd just heard. "What bullet?"

Lightfoot sighed. "Probably the same one that nicked your arm. It's lodged above her hip bone. Missed anything serious... they think."

Several swear words floated through his head. A woman with a child walked by looking shaken, so he held his tongue.

"What's your status? Been too busy checking on the other two to inquire about you, McKinley."

"I'll live. You call next of kin?"

"Yep. Mrs. Theroux is torn between flying into Rock Springs, or meeting us in Utah."

"What'd you say?"

"Told her to meet us in Salt Lake. Closer for her, and I think Marguerite's gonna need better care than what the fine folks of Rock Springs can offer."

Declan drummed his thumb on his thigh. "Where's Monti?"

"Upstairs getting his nose put back into place. He's in federal custody, now. We'll fly him east once he's been discharged."

"What about me?"

"That's up to you."

"How so?"

"You can help us get the rest of the cartel, or go home."

"*McKinley!*"

"I'm right here, honey." Large, warm hands eased her back to her pillow.

Marguerite groaned as a dull ache coursed from her face to her shoulder, then down through her torso, ending at her side. She blinked one eye open since the other wasn't cooperating. McKinley fussed over her blankets until he sat next to the bed.

"Where's Uncle Dane?"

"ICU."

"Is...he awake?"

He shook his head. "No."

Dread made everything hurt worse. She peeked around and noted her arm firmly packed into an immobilizing sling. Her gaze swung to McKinley to see he wore something similar, though not as padded. "Are you all right?"

Even as she asked, she knew he wasn't. Whiskers covered his cheeks and chin. His clothes were wrinkled as if he'd slept in them. Dark shadows of exhaustion lived under his eyes, yet he continued to just stare at her. "Where are we?"

Finally, he blinked. "University Medical Center." When she didn't respond, he clarified, "Salt Lake City."

"How long have I been out?" She didn't remember traveling here, or how she'd gotten the damn sling. God, was she wearing her clothes and, if not, where were they? Did her mother know?

Where's Monti?

The heart monitor started beeping and McKinley stood again. "Hey, you're okay. You've been out for thirty-six hours. Your family should be here any minute. I made sure to get your things brought in, and your purse is there." He pointed to a cupboard across the room.

"Thank you." She swallowed, not liking the dryness in her mouth and throat. "Why've I been out so long?"

He moved some hair from her forehead but grimaced before sitting down again. "Combination of post-surgery to remove a bullet and concussion." He soughed out a halting breath. "You gotta stop ending up in a hospital bed, honey."

Not wanting to think about how she got shot—or Declan's misplaced endearment—Marguerite steered the topic back to Monti.

"He got me when I left the bathroom. Thank God he didn't search for my phone. That's how you tracked me, right?"

Again, he nodded, and she noted his eyes were tight, lips pinched.

"I'm sorry, McKinley. It's all my fault. I should've paid more attention—"

"Don't. It's mine. I shoulda never let ya walk off alone." The twang in his voice she hadn't heard in a while came through loud and clear.

She wanted to argue but whatever they'd put in the IV kept her brain foggy. To fill the silence, he described everything she'd missed while unconscious. After he finished, she dozed off as her mind wondered what would happen now. Thank God they got Monti but surely, there'd be inquiries. Most likely she'd be released from her duties and sent home.

As she began to envision all the tongues wagging in Timbisha Township, familiar voices and the constant dull ache called her back to reality.

"Marguerite!"

She grimaced at Missy's attempt to hug her and jostled her shoulder. "Ow."

"Oh, no! I'm sorry!"

Josh, never far from her sister, pulled Missy back. "Careful, sweetheart. Here, hold her hand. Is this okay, Magpie?"

"Yeah. And will you stop calling me that?"

"No." But his handsome smile didn't reach his eyes, telling her he'd been as worried as the rest of her family.

Missy sniffed. "Uncle Dane's in a coma. Have you seen him yet?"

"With my one good eye?" Her little sister frowned at Marguerite's lousy attempt at levity so Marguerite opted for truth. "No, not yet. I haven't been out of this stupid bed. Which reminds me..." She looked at the wires and tubes because her bladder screamed to be emptied.

"I'll get the nurse." McKinley left her alone with her family.

"Mom, are you all right?"

Her mother had taken McKinley's seat, a tissue clutched in her hands. "No, but I will be. Will you please come home now?"

It hurt to chuckle. "Yeah, I'm pretty sure I don't have a choice in the matter."

"Well, good because Jarod still wants you back, so you have a job. Isn't that right Josh?" Missy said as she leaned into her husband.

Josh rubbed Missy's swollen belly. "He hasn't quit bitchin' about you leaving."

"Sounds about right," Marguerite muttered.

God, where's the nurse? She pressed the buttons on the side of the bed, trying to find the one to help her into a sitting position, which made her wince in pain.

God, I hurt.

Finally, the door swung open.

"Oh, wait, dear. Let me clear these IV lines out of your way."

Everyone stood back while Marguerite and her helpful nurse made their careful way to the toilet. There wasn't any sweeter relief when she finally sat down and let go.

Afterward, as the nurse helped her back to bed, Marguerite refused to acknowledge just how awful her face looked. Instead, she asked, "When the hell can I get out of here?"

"I'll check your chart, but don't count on leaving until tomorrow or the next day. You did a number on your shoulder, and the orthopedist needs to clear you. Are you hungry?"

On cue, her stomach growled.

"I could eat."

Unfortunately, she tried to shrug at her own comment but ended up groaning in pain, just as McKinley returned with Special Agent Lightfoot, who Marguerite had met at the beginning of this fiasco.

"I'm sorry to break up the party," Lightfoot said, "but now that Marguerite is awake, we need to clear up some business."

Everyone said their goodbyes and filed out. When the door closed Agent Lightfoot began his debriefing. Afterward, Marguerite signed her exit papers. Agent Lightfoot confiscated her electronics, wished her well, and left with McKinley at his side.

He shut the door without a backward glance.

Without saying goodbye.

Shoulder throbbing, and her heart now broken at her stupidity, she let the tears fall. Wallowing in self-pity proved cathartic and allowed her time to think.

In her heart, she knew she'd bounce back as always, but this time her arrogance had gotten people hurt, and ended her future in law enforcement. Of course, Jarod would always take her back as his personal assistant at the sheriff's station, but did she want to end up where she'd started? She supposed she could become a deputy in order to advance her career, but after her abysmal freshman launch into the field, the very last thing she wanted to do was go back out there with crazy-assed criminals, wearing a god-awful heavy uniform.

She glanced at her IV bag.

The drugs made me think it.

Closing her eyes, she dreamed of home in the fall, her new baby niece waiting to be born, and a life without danger.

A life without US Marshal Declan McKinley.

Chapter Three

BLUE'S WHISKEY BAR

Two years later in a suburban cul-de-sac in Reno, Nevada...

"She's crashing!"
"What happened?"
"Does she have an allergy?"
"She's coding, get the paddles!"
"Save her!"
"Tell the chopper they're taking two."

Declan woke with a gasp. Breathing heavy, he mopped a hand over his brow and threw off the covers. His nightmares were never the same but always about losing *her*. Some were filled with her beaten and bruised face, others a confused jumble of reality and fiction.

He sat up, disoriented, not recognizing his surroundings

until he flicked on the bedside lamp and swore at the blurry numbers on the nightstand.

4:08 a.m.

A few bones creaked as he swung his legs over the mattress, then padded to the bathroom.

I'm too old for this shit.

His body had seen some miles. Faded scars and mended bones kept him moving slower than he liked. He flexed his fists. Only dumb luck saved him from broken knuckles when he'd bashed in Monti's face.

After he'd kidnapped Marguerite.

After the coward shot Bainbridge in the back, a wound that would eventually kill the man.

Now, as he let the hot water burn the memories from his brain he realized something crucial. He wouldn't get any real sleep until he saw the woman who drove him nuts again.

Beautiful, headstrong, Marguerite.

Too young, and too inexperienced for field work.

Too eager to impress her uncle.

He closed his eyes to block out what his mind replayed without permission—Marguerite sprawled on the cement floor, beaten, bloodied, and her arm dislocated. Dane rushing to her only to catch a bullet in the back from Monti. The satisfying crunch as he, Declan, tackled the son of a bitch to the ground and beat him within an inch of his life.

Because of Declan's monumental screw up he'd been given two choices; round up the remaining targets in the cartel before retiring, or leave immediately without his pension.

It had taken almost two years to track down every last scumbag and bring them into custody. Declan turned in his badge and gun the same day.

Now, he couldn't stop the nightmares, or thinking about...

...Marguerite Theroux.

He made quick work of his shower and got dressed. Time to get his life in order. He'd kept in touch with the Timbisha County Sheriff, Jarod King, to inquire on Marguerite's new life while simultaneously looking for his own place to live in Timbisha Township.

But first he had charges to feed, a.k.a. his niece and nephews.

Morning sun filtered through a tiny window in the silent hallway leading to the stairs. Since retiring from the U.S. Marshals Service a month ago he'd been crashing with his sister, Sonja, to lick his wounds and regroup. To give himself some credit, he hadn't been a total waste of space. He'd tried to pay his sister rent, but she refused out of stubbornness. So, he played nanny as a form of payment.

As the coffee brewed, a thunder of foot stomps hit the stairs. He braced himself when his niece flung her arms around his knees for the first hug of the day.

"Good morning, Uncle Declan!"

"Mornin', Rosie." He gave her a soft pat on the back before the seven-year-old let go to climb onto a barstool. "Hungry?"

"Nuh-uh." She swung her legs back and forth while she rubbed the sleep from her eyes. "Can I have some orange juice, please?"

"'Course, sweetheart." Just as he set a cup in front of her, Rodney, her twin brother, yelled into the ethos from upstairs and they both jumped.

"THERE'S NO TOILET PAPER!"

The twins' rooms were divided by a jack-n-jill bathroom. Declan caught Rosie's smirk before a door slammed above, and their mother's scolding voice murmured above the ceiling.

Declan raised an eyebrow at Rosie. "You emptied the canister next to the toilet, didn't ya?"

The innocent child shrugged as she sipped her juice. "He put a cricket in my bed."

Stifling a chuckle, Declan offered his fist for a bump. "Well, played." Then he placed bacon in the microwave to thaw.

Ryan, the eleven-year-old, flopped onto the stool next to Rosie and thunked his forehead onto the granite countertop. "I hate Mondays."

Declan silently agreed while he whipped the eggs he'd cracked into a bowl and added some milk.

"Ow!" Rosie screeched as Rodney ran by and slugged her in the back on his way into the family room.

"Serves you right, booger-head."

Declan set the bowl down and hurried after his nephew before the boy could turn on morning cartoons. Palm around the back of Rodney's neck, he commanded, "Never hit girls."

"But Uncle Declan—"

"No buts, Rodney. Real men never hit women. Now apologize to your sister."

"Sorry," he spit out, anything but.

Rosie stuck out her tongue and Declan sighed before returning to his egg mixture.

By the time Sonja finally made her appearance, dressed and perfectly coiffed, all three kids were fed and on their way back up the stairs to get ready for school.

"Thanks," she said, as Declan handed her a mug. "I hate Mondays."

"Ryan must get it from you." Declan leaned on the counter sipping his second cup and eyed his sister. "I'm headin' out today after I drop off the kids."

"What?" She slammed her mug on the counter, sloshing some coffee over the side. "It's too soon. You need time."

Though Declan was the oldest of his siblings, he felt closest with Sonja, who treated him like a friend—and a mother hen. "I've been moochin' off you for three months."

"So?"

"It's time, Sonja."

When she looked on the verge of tears he wrapped his arm around her shoulders. "I know."

When she continued to pout he added, "I have unfinished business I need to take care of."

She took another drink and raised an eyebrow. "Dane's niece?"

He nodded.

"She's a pretty thing," she stated, always the matchmaker.

He wasn't ready to talk about his feelings, therefore he kept to the facts. "Yes, she is."

"Have you talked to her since—"

"No."

"I see." She sighed. "You sure you want to go back to Timbisha Township?"

"Yup." He hadn't spoken to Marguerite since he left her hospital room in Salt Lake City. She lived with her mother, again. He knew she worked as a bartender, which didn't make him happy, but he wasn't going to share those details with his sister either.

"I'll see her soon. Anyway, Jarod said he'd like some advice tracking down a suspect."

She narrowed her eyes. "What about your retirement?"

He raised an eyebrow. "It's just a consultation is all." After he was shot Sonja worried nonstop. When he'd finally returned home, retired and "safe"—her word, not his—she kept reminding him that the days of hunting fugitives were over.

"You promise you won't get involved with anything dangerous?"

"Of course I won't promise." He added a wink to keep from getting smacked. He wasn't stupid, after all. "Mr. King, however, also asked for a meeting."

She cocked her head. "The sheriff's father? Whatever for?"

He shrugged. "He said he needs help with the ranching side of his business but I suspect he's trying to replace his body-guard." Declan choked back the grief of losing Dane Bain-bridge, his mentor and friend.

Out of nowhere, Sonja reached over and hugged him. "I'll call you tonight. I want to hear all about your new digs." She wiped a tear from her eye and left the room as abruptly as she'd entered.

Declan waited for Sonja's morning ritual yell up the stairs...

"HAVE A GOOD DAY AT SCHOOL, MY LOVES!"

I-love-you-toos floated down and then the door to the garage slammed shut.

I'm gonna miss living here.

He passed Ryan on the stairwell on his way to corral the twins and grab his meager belongings. Bickering from the jack-n-jill bathroom met his ears and he rethought the missing-living-here part. "You two ready?"

Rosie stood at her sink with a hand out in a give-it-back gesture while Rodney stood on the toilet seat with a pink toothbrush in the air.

"Rodney," Declan warned.

"She stole Bear!"

"He spit bacon at me!"

"ENOUGH." Declan scooped Rodney off the toilet while

simultaneously taking the toothbrush from his hand and handing it back to Rosie. "You two finish gettin' ready. Rosie, give Bear back to your brother."

Saying goodbye to the kids was harder than he expected—especially when Rosie refused to let go from their hug goodbye—but once they were delivered to school, Declan hopped on the highway for Timbisha Township. Music set to his favorite 80s playlist, he spent the next couple of hours letting his thoughts conjure up an image of Marguerite.

Would she be happy to see him or turn taciturn? If it was the latter, he was willing to work for her trust again.

Two years without her had been hell.

If she wasn't willing to forgive him, well—he'd burn that bridge when he got there.

"WHAT'RE THOSE?"

Marguerite didn't stop arranging the chocolates on the three-tiered display. "What do they look like?"

"Heaven, Mags. They look like my mouth is about to taste heaven."

Trey, the 18-year-old high school senior who worked as a bus boy at Blue's Whiskey Bar, lived to flirt. Apparently, he was addicted to chocolate too. However, rules were rules, and Marguerite couldn't let his slip go unnoticed. She spun around to stare the man-child in the eyes.

"Call me that again, and I'll break your nose."

Trey gave blank face before his mouth split into a giant grin. "No you won't. You love me too much."

Shaking her head as she flipped back around to hide her

own smile, she continued building the chocolate display. "They're turtles. I couldn't take your nagging any longer."

"Really?" He snagged a piece from the box holding the latest batch and popped it into his mouth. "Oh. My. God. These are the best. You're a wizard, *Marguerite*."

Trey patted her shoulder as he moved off to clear a recently vacated table while she placed the last piece on the top, wincing when the constant ache in her shoulder reminded her of—

Don't go there.

Marguerite's shift behind the bar started in thirty minutes but she liked to get in early, especially when she had a new selection of treats for the customers. She didn't sell the chocolates. They sat on the bar along with random bowls of peanuts and Chex mix for patrons not ordering food to munch on while they savored their adult beverages.

Trey snagged another treat on his way to dump his dirty dishes in the kitchen, wiggling his eyebrows in appreciation before disappearing behind the swinging door. Marguerite gathered her purse and the empty container then headed to the employee lockers. As she passed the restrooms, Sheriff Jarod King exited the men's.

Without preamble he launched into his oft-repeated plea for her to come back to work for him.

"The job's yours when you're ready, Marguerite. The station isn't the same without you."

Which was his way of saying, *Just stop with this bartending nonsense. You're wasting your talents.*

Yeah, they'd had the conversation many times but she wouldn't go back. Never again would she risk herself, or someone else getting injured...or worse. As long as she worked at Blue's, everyone was safe.

Bartending allowed her to talk to people, hear gossip. It

made her comfortable and felt...familiar. At least, that's what her therapist had said.

Whatever.

After she'd finally been released from the hospital, she'd rented a room in Salt Lake City while Uncle Dane's coma waged on. It gave her time to focus on physical therapy for her shoulder, and counseling for her soul. Unfortunately, Uncle Dane never woke from his coma. He was eventually moved to the long-term care wing at Timbisha Township's hospital where he wasted away for a year.

It was all her fault.

Since her move back home, she'd found solace living with her mother, and making chocolates for people to enjoy. There'd be no going back to any kind of criminal investigations, or tailing drug mules, or compromising herself with jerks to gain information.

I am so done with that life.

"Marguerite?" Jarod touched her shoulder.

"Oh, geez, sorry. Must've been in the clouds." She laughed a bit as she rolled the ache away, before repeating her oft-replied answer. "No thanks, Jarod. I'm happy right where I am."

To temper her refusal, she placed a small kiss on his cheek and sauntered into the locker room away from anyone else who dared remind her of the life she'd once led, the plans she'd once made, or the person she'd once been.

After securing her jacket and purse in a locker, she checked her sparse make-up, tightened her ponytail and swished her butt behind the bar. It was Two Buck Pint Night, the normal for a Thursday at Blue's Whiskey Bar, where ranchers, miners and construction workers, and the occasional trucker came to kick off Friday Eve.

Since it was the middle of August, Marguerite grabbed the

remote and found the app broadcasting a preseason football game. She switched most of the TVs over, with the exception of a few smaller screens for the weirdos who enjoyed soccer and some who still had an interest in baseball.

Jarod sat in his normal spot with a glass in front of him, which contained ice water with a slice of lemon. The sheriff never drank in public, and never while wearing his uniform, which he still donned. "You waiting for Jason?"

"Lauren, actually. Jessica's got a church recital and I said I'd follow them."

She topped off his water. "Who's watching Joey?"

"Mom. Jessica has to be at the parish hall early, so the whole crew's coming later. Lauren and I are saving seats."

The "whole crew," Marguerite knew, referred to his large family. Parents, brothers and sisters-in-law—one of which was Marguerite's sister, Missy—and all their children. Joey was Jarod and Lauren's three-year-old son.

"Oh, that's right. She texted me about it last week, but I'm stuck here."

"Jessica?"

Marguerite nodded. The second grade beauty was a firecracker and Marguerite hated to miss her sing. "Yeah, why? Was she not supposed to?"

He choked on his water. "No, of course you're invited. I didn't mean it like that. She wasn't supposed to have her phone last week, is all."

Marguerite busied herself prepping beer glasses for the coming rush. "What'd she do this time?"

Jarod looked chagrined. "Snuck into Charlie's room to play video games when she was supposed to be cleaning her own."

"He's still in Reno attending UNR, right?"

"Yes, which is why she snuck in there. He left last week and she misses him."

Marguerite chuckled before pouring a couple beers for some regulars who'd just arrived. Jarod waved goodbye after checking an alert on his cell, which she assumed was from Lauren to let him know she waited in the parking lot.

The night picked up its pace after that as Blue's filled with thirsty customers clamoring for Marguerite's chocolates and two-dollar pints of beer.

"Marguerite, darlin', you are lookin' mighty fine tonight, honey!"

"Why thank you, Frank. Your wife know you're flirting with me again?" Marguerite turned around to put cash in the till as she waited for Frank, a regular, to finish his Jameson.

"Hell, what she don't know won't hurt her!" He slammed his glass on the bar, along with a generous tip, and waved goodbye. His ride waited outside.

"How do you stand it?" Cheryl, the 23-year-old waitress who irritated Marguerite to no end, griped as she counted out her meager tips. Closing bell had been rung and Frank had been the last customer to leave.

"Stand what? Stuffing my pockets with cash? I like it just fine." Marguerite turned off the TVs, switched Pandora from country to rock, and began the long process of cleaning up.

Cheryl tsk. "I mean the sexist comments all night! You bark at anyone who doesn't call you by your legal first name, but you let *men* objectify you like a piece of meat."

Instead of defending herself, Marguerite asked a bold question purely for the shock value because she was sick and tired of this young women running off customers. "Are you a lesbian?"

"What?" Cheryl gasped. "No! I have a boyfriend. I—"

"Are you a member of some feminist man-hating group looking to push your activism all over Timbisha Township, or in this case, Blue's Whiskey Bar?"

Cheryl crossed her arms over her chest, narrowed eyes aimed at Marguerite as if to melt her. "I'm simply asking why *you* let them treat you that way. It's uncivilized and hurts women."

Marguerite shook her head. "You need to lighten up. This is a bar, sweetness. Get used to it. You catch more flies with honey, and I'll tell you something else. If anyone grabs you, or touches you, Dusty will make sure they spend a night or two in the hospital. There's a big difference between sexual harassment and being friendly. If you don't like the service industry, you should get out now."

"But they're so denigrating."

Marguerite rolled her eyes. "No, they're not. The majority of our patrons have wives or girlfriends who also come along and wouldn't let their men be sexist assholes. Just because Frank calls me "darling" or "honey" doesn't make him a pig. And, since I've known him forever, I can also tell you I'd trust him with my life if push came to shove. My advice is for you to pull your head out of your ass and figure out the difference between a real sexist and our patrons who're just looking for a friendly place to unwind after work. Got it?"

"Yeah." Cheryl picked up a rag to take her aggressions out on the tables. "I get you're a massive hypocrite."

Marguerite ignored the little idiot, not wanting to spend another minute on Cheryl's confused ideas. The waitress was young, with no life experience and a serious bad attitude. If she wasn't careful, Dusty would step in and remind his waitress of the benefits of treating his customers with kindness.

Raised by a gruff, ex-FBI agent uncle, Marguerite had a unique perspective on men and how to deal with them.

Deal with them? Hell, maybe I'm *the sexist.*

Dismissing the thought, Marguerite finished up behind the bar to help Cheryl put chairs on top of the tables for the cleaning crew. Trey's shift had ended right after dinner service to accommodate his varsity football practices.

Marguerite said goodbye to everyone and slid out the back door to the parking lot, and her pretty red convertible. Nights in August were warm but not enough for her to drop the top in this part of Nevada. The engine roared to life and Marguerite leaned her head against the rest, letting the engine warm up before putting it in gear. She used to love driving her car but now it gave her too much time to think. She wished she could forget about the past, wished she'd made better decisions —well, maybe not better just...different. She'd wanted to impress her uncle, to bring down people who hurt others in her town, to stop the cartels from trafficking meth and every other horrible drug into Timbisha Township.

How naive she'd been to think her efforts wouldn't come at a cost—her uncle's life, and before that, her reputation for being associated with a dirty cop.

She turned the corner onto her street. The bright driveway waiting for her baby pulled Marguerite back to the present. She parked it in her usual spot to the right of her Mom's old Lexus. Once she locked up and headed inside, she frowned at the lights coming from the eat-in kitchen.

"What are doing still awake?"

Her mom sipped on something warm in a mug. "Couldn't sleep. How was work?"

"Busy." Marguerite sighed as she plopped into the chair opposite her mother and waited for Darla Theroux to come clean about whatever weighed on her mind.

After her third slurp of hot chocolate—the heavenly aroma had finally wafted over Marguerite's nose—Darla said, "Camille called. They found another body. James is getting involved, much to Jarod's chagrin."

Marguerite closed her eyes. "How involved?"

"I think he's gonna call *him*."

Marguerite knew whom her mother referred to. None of the Kings held a grudge against Declan McKinley, and to be honest, neither did Marguerite nor Darla, but...

"He's going to, or he already did?"

"Already did."

"Thanks for the warning." Marguerite pushed her chair back, careful not to let it drag on the linoleum. "I love you, Mom, but I'm beat. Thanks for waiting up. I'll see you at breakfast." She didn't wait for a response, though Darla didn't offer one. If they got into it again about Marguerite settling down, or any other nonsense, she'd lose her mind.

After a quick shower to wash the bar from her hair and skin, she threw on a t-shirt and undies, and slid into bed.

She tossed and turned for ten minutes before curiosity got the better of her and she reached for her MacBook. It didn't take long to find the news report of the second body found. Instead of off the highway like the first body, this one was found by dirt bikers a few miles outside of Timbisha Township up a hill; a young woman found wrapped in shrink wrap from head to foot. Other than being female, the victims had nothing else in common. At least, none the journalists were privy to.

Marguerite's naturally curious mind begged her to do some research but she wouldn't.

Curiosity killed the cat after all.

She set her computer aside and flopped back onto her pillows. She couldn't help those women, and even if she could, she'd probably screw it up anyway. Nope, she wasn't going there. Instead, she focused her mind on the chocolate warmer and new ingredients waiting for her in the morning. She wanted to spice things up—maybe with cayenne—to see what people thought of the combination of flavors.

As her mind tempered chocolate, her muscles relaxed and she slowly drifted into oblivion.

Chapter Four
BAD MANNERS

"Thanks for meeting with us," James King said, as Declan took the bench across the booth from him. "Jarod's running late, oh, hold on…here he is now."

Declan waited as the Sheriff said hello to people he knew sitting at the counter of Molly's Diner—Timbisha Township's premiere spot for who's who in their little community—until the man finally slid in next to his father."

"Good to see you again, marshal." Jarod offered a hand.

"It's just Declan now, Sheriff," he corrected, while shaking hands. "I don't have the backing of the marshals service anymore, but I'll try to help any way I can. Tell me about your case." Declan didn't want to waste time. Clues and leads grew cold the longer it took to investigate.

James and Jarod shared a look.

"What?"

"Nothing. Have you seen Marguerite yet?" This from Jarod.

"No."

"But you plan to, right?" James asked.

Declan prayed for patience. "Yeah." He didn't elaborate on when because he wasn't sure himself. Working up courage to face a woman wasn't something he was used to, especially Marguerite. Not to mention that he'd only gotten into town the night before, later than he expected, and missed an appointment with a property manager. He lost the rental he'd been interested in and had to scramble to find a room. "Back to the bodies," he prompted to get them on track again.

"Right." Jarod nodded once. "There's two women, one found within three miles of Timbisha Township just off I-80; the other up an old dirt bike trail. Age and ethnicity are the same and C.O.D is roughly the same, strangulation, but the second victim suffered multiple stab wounds and was badly beaten. The official report on the second vic hasn't come in yet because the medical examiner has been out sick."

"He wraps them in plastic film, like industrial shrink wrap," James added. "The killer, not the M.E."

Declan noticed Jarod's grimace of annoyance at his father's knowledge of the case but chose to ignore it for the moment. "Sexual assault?" Declan directed his question to Jarod.

"Definitely on the first victim."

Something familiar about the murders tugged at Declan's memory. He'd seen this before but he couldn't remember when or where.

"I need you to help me convince Marguerite to do some digging," Jarod stated.

"No."

Jarod shook his head in disgust. "On the computer, McKinley. She has a skill unmatched—"

"I said no."

Jarod leaned away and pinched the bridge of his nose. "She's wasting her talents at Blue's."

"You know she's a grown woman, right?"

"Of course. But she won't lis—"

James leaned in and lowered his voice, cutting off his son. "Camille says Darla's concerned about her daughter. I'm with you, McKinley. I don't want her working a murder case. Not after..." He leaned back letting his words whither. Bainbridge and James King had been more than boss and employee, but close friends. Declan's heart went out to the older man.

Jarod said, "I'd appreciate your help on the case, McKinley, in whatever capacity you're allowed now. You're one helluva tracker, but I hope you reconsider talking to Marguerite because she's just as good with a computer as you are on the hunt."

A waitress came by to pour coffee. "Sorry. Super busy. What can I get you boys?"

"The usual, Cathy." James offered a smile as he handed back his menu.

"Same," Jarod said.

Declan perused the menu a moment before handing it to the young woman. "Pancakes and eggs." Bainbridge always got pancakes and eggs.

He took a sip of coffee while waiting for the other two men to gather their thoughts. He hadn't revealed his plan to set up residence in Timbisha Township. He didn't want to make promises he couldn't keep. And, it was no one's business exactly why he'd come other than at Jarod's request. At the very least, he needed to make amends with Dane's niece. At most, well, he couldn't see a future beyond that yet. For now, he wouldn't admit to wanting to set down roots. Whether it was here or somewhere else was anyone's guess, including his own.

Making amends with Marguerite is my first priority.

"I contacted Roland," Jarod said, interrupting Declan's

thoughts. "Shrink-wrapped bodies have been found all over the US for decades. Apparently, it's a favorite countermeasure with the nut jobs out there. He doesn't think there's a link to our vics but he said he'd do some research. Honestly, I don't want the feds here. Which is why I need Marguerite."

Yeah, that's why it sounded familiar.

Ten years ago, Declan had worked an unsolved series of murders in Texas. To his knowledge, it was still a cold case.

He squinted. "Why?"

He noted Jarod's blank face, the one he used when he was in "cop mode" and James rolled his eyes.

Jarod stared him in the eyes. "Because I like to do things my own way," through gritted teeth. "And my way is to have Marguerite do a little online digging from the safety of the station house."

Though Timbisha Township was a growing town it'd had trouble in the past, and it looked like it continued to do so. The community consisted mainly of ranchers and churchgoers. Because of Timbisha county's low tax rate, many industrial businesses were building new warehouses and processing plants around the township proper, which brought more employees to the area. And new people moving in meant a bigger suspect pool, and...

"Are the mines running again?"

Jarod nodded. "Yeah, I thought about that. Most of those folks work long shifts, though. Not much time off."

"They still housed by the companies near the mines?"

"Mostly," James said.

Jarod and James moved their arms from the table when Cathy brought their platters. "Enjoy, fellas."

Declan nodded his thanks before they tucked in for a few bites. "Damn, I forgot how good the food is here."

"It's just as good at Blue's," Jarod admitted, "but don't tell anyone here I said so."

Declan knew what the sheriff was doing. "I'm going to see her, damn it."

"I know. When you do, don't be surprised if she rips your head off."

"That bad, huh?"

James offered, "Call it a hunch but that girl's been suppressing her emotions for two years."

Declan didn't blame her. He'd been doing the same but the older he got, the more his brain wouldn't let it go, hence the nightmares.

They ate in companionable silence for a while before a thought occurred to Declan. "If it's a miner, they could be using the monthly time off to indulge some killing-urges, so to speak."

"Yeah," Jarod nodded. "I thought of that and requested background information on the mine's employees but they're taking their sweet-assed time getting back to me. Plus, they cycle them in groups of twenty or thirty. It's a big suspect pool."

Made sense. Though the mines offered good money, the work was difficult and it was hard to fill positions. Not everyone wanted to work round the clock shifts with limited access to the outside world, or relocate to Timbisha Township.

When they'd finished breakfast and paid the check, James and Jarod followed Declan to his pickup.

"Where're you staying?"

"Cottonwood Grove, down by the river."

"Follow Dad to The Estate," Jarod said. "Most of my files and notes are out there. I'd like you to take a look at them, maybe you can see a pattern I don't. I need to stop at the station first and then I'll be out."

The Estate, Declan knew, belonged to James and Camille King. James had built a small construction empire in Timbisha Township decades ago. Their three sons were also vital to the community; Jarod was the sheriff, of course; Jason ran the business end of King construction, and Josh's architectural engineering and real estate savvy helped gain and improve properties. Josh was also married to Marguerite's little sister making Marguerite a part of the King family—which is why Declan wasn't surprised by their concern for her.

The ride into rural Timbisha didn't take long, and Declan appreciated the beautiful desert landscape, especially with the bright, blue sky above. Knowing he wouldn't be running into Marguerite out here any time soon only added relief to his jangled nerves about seeing her again.

His assumption was obliterated when he parked his pickup next to her little red convertible.

He sighed—*just sighed*—at both Kings' manipulation. James wore a smirk when Declan climbed out of the cab.

"Better now than never. Besides, with everyone here, she'll be on her best behavior."

Declan snorted. "What's she doing out here, anyway?"

"You'll see soon enough."

Curious, he followed the man through a side entrance which led through some sort of utility room and into a combination kitchen and dining room. Voices drifted to his ears and when he crossed the threshold, five sets of eyes belonging to three King wives, Marguerite's mother, Darla, and of course, Marguerite, all met his with mixed reactions.

"Marshal, so nice to see you again."

"Hey, Declan!"

"What the hell is he doing *here*?"

Well, so much for holding her tongue.

MARGUERITE REGRETTED THE WORDS BEFORE THEY left her lips, especially after she met her mother's censuring expression—head tilted down, eyes narrowed over the rim of her glasses. She hadn't had an outburst in a while and she hated for the Kings to see it firsthand.

Camille, Master of Manners, stood to greet Declan.

"Marshal McKinley. It's so good to see you again. Please, have a seat."

And, of course, the chair next to Marguerite had been left empty, except for the box holding her latest creations.

The bastard purposefully moved it to the tabletop and sat.

They hadn't laid eyes on each other in two long years, not since he left her in the hospital after being released from the team. Marguerite forced the image of him walking out the door —out of her life—from her mind, and tried to squelch the conflicting emotions vying for attention.

"You look good."

His gruff voice raised goosebumps on her arms. Thankfully, she wore long sleeves. She eyed him after his quiet comment, and pinched her lips for a moment to keep from blurting out another tantrum. "Thanks."

He looked amazing, and smelled even better than she remembered, but she couldn't bring herself to say it out loud.

Two years was a long time to let bitterness fester.

The room held its breath waiting for her to explode.

She swallowed, giving her tongue time to be civil before repeating her question. "What are you doing here, McKinley?"

"James wants to speak with me, and Jarod needs some help with a case."

Marguerite rolled her eyes. "I meant, what are you doing here, at The Estate, specifically."

His mouth ticked to the side as if he wanted to smile, and she narrowed her eyes at the movement. Nonplussed, he repeated, "To help Jarod with the case, and to talk to James."

So, it's like that, then. She wanted to remind him who she was, but...

Breath escaped his lips, as if in resignation, and he leaned closer, putting goosebumps on goosebumps. "I didn't know you'd be here. I think we've both been set up."

She met his tobacco-colored eyes and friggin melted.

Resigned, she nodded. "Yeah, that sounds about right." She offered him a brief smile and it eased the tension clogging the room.

Camille set out the plate of chocolate samples Marguerite brought with her for the meeting. "Have a taste. The round ones are delicious."

Marguerite followed Declan's hand as he reached for one she'd named *Sweet Kickin'*. She noted the bent fingers, and large knuckles covered by weathered skin. They evoked memories she'd worked hard to forget; bruised hands and a bruised face fresh from taking out Monti.

Suddenly, Declan's face lit up as he looked at her. "You made these?"

"Surprised?" She decided to let the past go for a now.

He responded by popping another in his mouth. "Damn, they're good."

"Poblano peppers," Julie said. "What made you think to add them, Marguerite?"

Honestly, she didn't know. Trying to come up with something intelligent rattled her for a moment. "An old movie came on about a chocolatier adding cayenne, and then I remembered a spicy cheese soup I love with poblanos, and well," she pointed at the plate, "voila."

The side door opened revealing Jarod. "Hey, are those the peppery ones?"

Lauren, Jarod's wife, turned to her husband. "When did you taste them?"

"I'm sorry, but that's privileged information."

"You didn't say anything about them," Lauren accused, her eyebrows wrinkled in a 'you will pay' way.

Jarod leaned down to kiss her, but she backed away clearly wanting an answer for his betrayal.

"I knew you had to try one for yourself to understand."

Satisfied, she leaned up for the kiss. "You were right."

Camille inquired, "What are you doing home?"

"Needed to bring McKinley the new information on the case before I head out again." He lifted the papers he carried at Declan. "Wanna follow me?"

Marguerite felt the loss when McKinley vacated the room.

Someone cleared their throat.

She turned back to the women at the table, who openly stared at her. "What?"

All four of them grinned, as Lauren said with a shrug, "He's handsome, Marguerite."

Julie nodded. "Very."

Marguerite widened her eyes in innocence. "What would Jarod and Jason think of your infatuation with Marshal McKinley?"

Lauren and Julie, who'd been best friends most of their lives and both married to a King brother, grinned at each other.

Camille looked at Marguerite with a raised eyebrow. "My

sons would know it was strictly an observation. Now, let's get down to business. If we catered a wedding, how many of these wonderful confections could you produce?"

Marguerite consulted a spreadsheet on her tablet. "As long as I had ample time, depending on the number of guests, I could produce enough for a King sized wedding."

Darla laughed at her pun, along with Camille. Marguerite relaxed a bit after her recent censure from both older women.

Camille said, "Perfect. Do you have a menu of what you've created so far?"

Marguerite produced a list of items she'd made. As Julie and Camille studied the list, Darla got up to get a pitcher filled with iced tea and refreshed their glasses. Marguerite contemplated what it would be like to work with these women, and got nervous, something that'd been happening more and more lately. She hated the fact her confidence had been broken.

Meanwhile, Lauren popped a praline into her mouth while staring at Marguerite. Finally, she swallowed. "Has he stopped nagging about you coming back to work yet?"

Marguerite's mouth ticked to the side. Lauren knew her husband well. "No. In fact, Jarod asked me again the other night while he waited for you. How bad are things at the station?"

Being Jarod's first administrative assistant before they fell in love, Lauren knew the ins and outs of the sheriff's office. Marguerite had replaced Lauren after the two love birds eloped. Now, Jarod needed help, and didn't miss a chance to whine about it either.

Lauren answered, "They aren't as busy now that the crime element has been cleaned up, but things still happen. I'm not supposed to talk about it but I know they're all worried about the murders."

"Jason thinks the killer is a mining employee because of the timing," Julie said, no longer looking at Marguerite's list.

"How so?" Lauren asked.

"He spoke with one of the foremen at Blue's the other night. He told Jason there's a lot of turnaround because of the shifts, but sometimes they get repeat workers."

Camille said, "Seasonal workers, you mean?"

Julie raised her eyebrows in thought. "Could be."

"I'm sure the mines keep good background checks. Don't they?" Lauren looked around the table.

Darla said, "Most likely. With heavy equipment, they'll at least do drug testing and want to know if anyone's been convicted of drug or alcohol offenses."

Marguerite listened, wondering if the ladies were in cahoots with Jarod to get her to come back to work by triggering her curiosity. She immediately dismissed the idea because her mother never wanted her to go back into criminal justice of any kind.

As the conversation ebbed and flowed over various suspects, Marguerite knew they wouldn't solve anything without proper data.

Data currently being shared in another room of the mansion.

Which she wasn't willing to search out.

No, siree.

She needed to get this meeting back on track.

"What do you think of the menu?"

"Oh, we love it, dear." Camille wore an easy smile. "Can you help out with the Harvest dinner at church? If all goes well, we'll need you for Thanksgiving and Christmas too."

"I'd be honored. I've got a chocolate and candy cane recipe I'm playing with. I could have it perfected by Christmas."

The Harvest dinner, followed by the Kings annual Halloween bash, were famous events in Timbisha Township, and being part of the prep would give her little chocolate operation the boost it needed. That is, if she wanted to go into business for herself. For now, she didn't want to commit. She loved working for Dusty at Blue's but the hours lately had started wearing on her. She wasn't a teenager anymore, and even then she hadn't been one to stay up all night and party.

She had a lot of decisions to make.

"THE SECOND BODY'S STILL IN THE MORGUE. Coroner won't get to it until tomorrow. Backlogged," Jarod said without preamble as they stepped into a large office opposite the family room.

"How the hell can it be backed up?" James asked. "There's only two victims. How many suspicious deaths could there be around here?"

"More than you'd think, Dad."

Declan scanned the report. "Found in different locations, shrink wrapped and nude, with differing injuries. Forensics concluded rape, no semen found on victim one."

"Bastard used a condom." Jarod verified.

James growled in disgust.

Declan read further down the report. "Bleach found on the skin of the first victim. Forensic counter measure?"

"Probably," Jarod admitted. "There's no fingerprints or any other physical evidence found on the plastic wrap. However, the second victim is dirty, and it appears no bleach was used on her. She looked to have been dug up, like animals had scavenged her remains, but the body's intact. We'll know more when the forensic report comes in."

"Homeless?" James asked.

Jarod raised his eyebrows, considering the theory. "Maybe. Neither have been identified."

Declan shook his head. "I'm not sure how you think I can help you if there's no one to chase. I don't want to waste anyone's time."

Jarod and James shared a look. "You're not," they said in unison, causing Declan's bullshit meter to go off.

He put down the folder. "Why, exactly, am I here?" He fixed them both with his no nonsense face and James puffed out a sigh.

Declan closed his eyes, knowing what was coming.

"We do need your help with these murders," Jarod admitted. "Once we have more to go on we're sure we can point you in the right direction. Can you stay another week?"

He'd planned on at least that much time to work things out with Marguerite. He'd moved out of his sister's house with the assumption he'd either be working on the case, or pleading with Marguerite to forgive him for screwing up so bad. "I can't sit around twiddling my thumbs waiting for another body, or for someone to come forward."

James nodded. "We understand, which is why I'd like to offer you a position with me here at The Estate."

"Replacing Bainbridge as your bodyguard, correct?"

"Yes."

Shit. How was he supposed to fill his mentor's shoes when it was his fault Dane was dead? If it wasn't for his lack of attention to details—if he hadn't been distracted by Marguerite—Dane Bainbridge would be alive today. As it was, James and

Jarod were already playing matchmaker. He'd be no good to either of them if they kept this up.

Distractions get you killed.

"Look," James interrupted his internal analysis of why he shouldn't be working in this capacity, "I know you're handy around a ranch. While we're waiting on the rest of the coroner's findings, my sons and I could use your help around The Estate with the livestock. You could get a feel of what it's like to live here. I don't need an answer right away."

Declan chuckled. "Bainbridge told you I grew up on a ranch?"

"Of course."

Declan opened his mouth—

"Just think about it." Jarod raised his hands up in a plea. "It'll give you time to mull over what you're going to do about Marguerite."

And just like that, Declan heard enough and stood. "I'll see myself out."

"Oh, come on, McKinley." Jarod followed right behind him. "We really do need help around here. I'm busy with work, and Jason and Josh are running the construction business, helping Dad keep his business empire strong. Meanwhile, Dad's overseeing everything and not getting any younger."

"Now wait just a damn minute, son," James said outraged by the insult.

Declan and Jarod turned, the latter facing his father, this time one hand up in a stop motion.

James sighed placing his hands on his hips, resigned. "I've looked over your record with the marshals service. Dane spoke highly of you, and frankly, I miss having my right hand man. Dane always lived in town but my sons are building a house specifically for whoever I hire. It'll be done soon. What'dya say?"

"To the bodyguard position, or running your ranch? I don't think I can do both."

"Dane did a lot of sitting around," Jarod said.

"That's not funny, Jarod," James countered.

No, Declan didn't appreciate Jarod's maligning of his mentor. In fact, he had a lot to say, mainly all words with four letters, but he ground his jaw shut looking for the exit. When he found the kitchen, he stopped in his tracks.

Marguerite's smile lit up the room as she conversed with the other women. It reminded him of her excitement when they'd first begun their journey tracking the drug mule. Only, a business venture in chocolate wouldn't end in danger or death.

As he stared, Darla passed by with a plate of sub sandwiches. "Oh, Declan, are you guys finished? Have a seat."

"I was just leaving, Mrs. Theroux."

"Darla," she corrected.

Declan nodded once. "You ladies have a good afternoon," he said before hurrying out the way he'd come. As he reached for the door handle on his pickup, Marguerite rushed outside.

"What'd they offer you?"

He closed his eyes, debating whether or not to just get in his truck and drive back to Reno.

"Declan."

Her soft voice and the use of his first name broke him. "A job. Here at The Estate."

Marguerite's forehead crinkled in adorable confusion, loosening the tense muscles in his neck. "Doing what?"

He crossed his arms over his chest and leaned against the truck. "They need a ranch manager."

The rest of her face bunched up to match her forehead. "Really? I thought for sure they needed help with the bodies."

Of course, she would know all about the murders. Her finger had been on the pulse of this community most of her life. "Yeah, Jarod needs some help with that too, and James is looking to replace," he stopped, cleared his throat and looked away.

Thankfully, Marguerite ignored his slip. "Why? There's no one to track. They haven't got a clue who's behind it or the identification of the victims."

Declan studied her for a moment. "But you have an idea, don't you, Blondie."

"Don't. Call. Me. That."

"Damn it, Marguerite, do not get involved."

Her face bloomed. "I'm not! I'm staying out of the crime business, remember?" She turned away but he reached out.

Spun her around to face him.

The momentum bumped her against his chest. Her breath fanned across his face, as he met her eyes and held on—getting lost in hazel flecked with blue, green and brown. All he wanted to do was kiss her until she made sense to him.

He leaned in.

She lifted a fraction.

A horn blared, and they broke apart, Marguerite looking as shocked as he felt.

Another pickup pulled in behind Declan's, blocking his exit. The youngest King brother got out with a little girl in his arms.

"Whatcha guys up to?" The gleam in Josh's eye told Declan he knew exactly what they'd been about to do.

When neither Declan, nor Marguerite answered, Josh

sighed. "Just take the job, Declan. If I know my family, they won't leave you alone until you do."

Chapter Five

JEALOUSY & BLAME

"Mar-Geet!"

Josh winked at Declan while Marguerite reached for her niece, Violet, kissing the sweetheart on both cheeks. "Hi, sugar. Where's Mommy?"

"Melissa got called out on an emergency," Josh said, "so me and the munchkin here thought we'd see what you guys were up to."

Marguerite glanced at Declan. "Just finishing up some business." She carried Violet into the house leaving Josh and Declan to their own devices.

As she walked away, Josh whined, "She's always stealing my baby."

Marguerite snickered to herself at this truth. Little Violet softened her heart like no one else could because the toddler had no preconceived notions about her aunt. Violet simply loved Marguerite, something she couldn't get from the others. Yes, Camille, Julie, and Lauren had invited Marguerite to talk about a business deal, but that's all. The other women tolerated her because of her relationship with Missy and Josh, people whom they love.

Missy's big sister.

Darla's daughter.

Dane's niece.

Marguerite knew her place among these King women—on the bottom rung.

Putting on a smile, Marguerite opened the door. "Look who I found."

She prepared herself for the emptiness she'd feel once she placed Violet on her feet, who made a beeline for Joey, Mikey, and Gabe, her three-year-old cousins.

"Come sit, honey." Darla patted the chair next to her. "Camille printed out mockups for the church festival."

"What do you think about harvest shaped candies, Marguerite? Have you ever made them?" Camille handed her a piece of paper with some ideas for fall leaves, a scarecrow, and some leafless trees.

"It shouldn't be a problem. I can find some recipes and tweak them. Molds are easy to find, and if I can't find what you want I can make them. What about Halloween stuff, like little witches, ghosts, and pumpkins?"

"Oh, that'd be cute," Julie said.

Marguerite made a note on the tablet she'd abandoned when she chased after Declan. Violet let out a screech that turned into belly laughs, followed by the other boys giggling.

"Well, MagPie, you ran him off," Josh said on a sigh as he wandered into the kitchen.

"I did not," she muttered. "He was leaving before you got here, idiot."

Behind her a round of "idiots" chorused.

Marguerite cringed. "Sorry."

"Don't worry about it, MagPie."

From behind her, angelic voices sang, "MagPie! MagPie!"

Marguerite glared at her brother-in-law, whose delight-filled grin encompassed most of his face.

Lovable jerk.

As the house became chaotic with people and voices, hugs and laughter, Marguerite felt more isolated. Jarod had returned to the station long ago, and Lauren left to pick up their daughter, Jessica, from bible school.

"I need to get going if I don't want to be late for my shift at Blue's." When she stood, Violet raced to her and demanded a hug. She clung to her niece before handing her off to Darla. "Mom, do you want me to take you home, or are you staying?"

Darla cuddled her granddaughter. "I can get a ride back with Josh and Violet."

Marguerite nodded. "Camille, thank you. I'll get some samples made and have Jarod bring them out for your approval."

Camille walked her to the door. "Sounds good, Marguerite. Drive safe."

The ride into town wasn't long but it gave her time to put her feelings into perspective.

Her attraction to Declan hadn't waned but grown stronger over time and...

... he still annoys the crap out of me.

She sighed.

I hope he stays.

She shook off the errant thought like a stray spider web she'd just walked into.

Once home, she started research on some fall themed confections, and built a grocery list. By the time she'd made it to Blue's, all thoughts of Declan had been replaced by ideas for the Fall festival.

Marguerite didn't consider herself a lapsed catholic but she hadn't exactly been a regular churchgoer either, especially when she went undercover for Uncle Dane. Then came her position at the sheriff's office with Jarod, and then her stint with the feds. At first, she skipped going to Mass here and there due to her work, until she stopped altogether.

When the rumors started about her "loose" reputation with Brad Anderson, and then the social media damage between her and Josh done by her sister's stalker, Marguerite wanted to leave Timbisha Township to get away from it all.

But everything went to hell.

When she returned home she'd found herself behind Blue's bar mixing drinks.

Again, the rumors flew.

Gossipy Marguerite.

Flirty Marguerite.

Can't keep a man, Marguerite.

People were people and she couldn't change them.

As Bonnie Raitt sang, "I can't make you love me if you don't."

The lyrics had become Marguerite's mantra. For whatever reason, she appreciated classic rock ballads now.

Friggin Declan.

Navigating through Blue's crowded lot, she found a spot and quickly parked before hustling inside the building to get her butt behind the mahogany bar. She slung drinks and filled the till for a couple of hours before Declan showed up.

"What are you doing here?"

"Checking out the local haunt. The better question is what are *you* doing here?"

She understood his meaning, but she wasn't taking the bait. "Working. What'll ya have?"

Declan's eyes lingered on her face before diving to the leather vest she wore as a top and the tight jeans she'd changed into for her shift. His eyes said *you* but his mouth said, "Bourbon."

Marguerite poured him an expensive double. "You're going to take James up on his job offer, aren't you?"

"Haven't decided yet."

She left him to his drink, filling orders, and cashing in more money. If he didn't want to talk to her civilly, that was fine. If he left town, she wouldn't have to worry about how she felt when he was around. With the luck she'd had lately, she knew without a doubt he'd string out the decision for as long as he could.

Making her life a living hell in the process.

"You all right, Marguerite?" Dusty asked, who'd snuck up on her.

"Yeah, I'm good, Soldier. The group by the darts, however, is looking a little rambunctious."

"I've got my eye on them. Who's the cop?"

Marguerite chuckled. "He's retired, supposedly. That's Declan McKinley, the US marshal I told you about. Jarod called him in."

"Hmm. Anything new with those bodies?"

She shook her head. "Not that I know of." Marguerite scanned the bar. The killer, she felt it in her bones, was among them but, damn it, she would not get involved.

Not again.

DECLAN TOOK A SIP OF HIS BOURBON, STUDYING THE man crowding Marguerite behind the bar. He'd done a little recon on her employer and knew he was looking at Dustin Boots, owner of Blue's Whiskey Bar.

He knew Dustin hailed from Timbisha Township.

Knew he'd served in the middle east until his unit was hit by enemy insurgents, and been honorably discharged afterwards.

However...

Declan certainly didn't like Dustin's assessment of Marguerite's attire.

Another sip.

He certainly didn't like the way Marguerite allowed the man's intimate proximity.

And another sip.

Definitely hated the way Marguerite smiled at Boots like he was the Messiah. She'd never looked at Declan that way.

He tossed back the rest of his bourbon, but he could still feel her sweet breath fanning his face.

God, he'd wanted to kiss her.

But it would've been a terrible idea.

Declan turned his back on the couple and scoured the establishment's open space. He liked the atmosphere, and it had nothing to do with the fact Marguerite worked the bar.

It didn't hurt either.

The far end held a small stage where Declan assumed local bands performed, and in front of it a patch of parquet hardwood indicated a dance floor, the same floor he'd found Josh and Marguerite drunkenly dancing on...

Don't go there.

...a neon jukebox stood against the wall to the side.

Someone had selected an old Brooks and Dunn tune, and a few people boot scooted.

The gaming space was made up of some dart boards, a shuffleboard, and a pool table. A few arcade games finished it off.

Patrons sat at small square tables eating, drinking and having casual conversation. Ceiling fans, beer signs, and animal mounts peppered the hardwood paneled walls, and interspersed were flat screen TVs showing various sports programs.

The mahogany bar made up the centerpiece, and of course, the bartender.

God, she's beautiful.

"Mighty fine, ain't she?" The man sitting next to him tipped back a long neck, eyeing Declan.

"Yup."

At first, Declan braced himself for an onslaught of vulgar comments but the man's face softened. "Marguerite's a good girl. People 'round here like to talk crap about her, but I know her family. She's good people."

"What do they say?" Declan subdued the anger bubbling up that people would trash talk Marguerite.

The man took another pull. "It's mostly the gals." He leaned in. "They're jealous, of course, because she's so gosh darn pretty. Smart, too. Did you know she helped get rid of all those crazy meth dealers?"

Declan smiled. "I did."

The man assessed Declan before sticking out his hand. "Name's Fred Wilkins. I'm a friend...well, used to be a friend of Dane's. You must be that hotshot marshal they took off with a couple years back. McKinley, right?"

"One and the same, although I'm retired. Nice to meet you."

"Spilling secrets again, Fred?" Marguerite replaced the man's empty beer bottle with a cold one.

"Never, Marguerite. I'm a vault."

"Not after round three," she countered, as she winked at Declan and meandered to the other side of the bar to fill an order from the waitress.

"Are you here about those dead girls?"

Declan sighed. He'd forgotten how loose-lipped a small town could be. "Not until I know who to track."

"What're you doin' until then?"

"Drinkin' at Blue's, I guess."

Fred eyed Declan before sliding his eyes toward Marguerite. "Don't go hurtin' my girl, now. I wouldn't like it."

Mentally, Declan sighed. Yeah, he'd hurt her when he'd left her in that damn hospital bed. The last thing he wanted to do was hurt her again.

Fred didn't need to know the truth.

Declan nodded in agreement before taking a sip of the new drink Marguerite causally placed in front of him on her way back from the other side of the bar.

A shout from the dart boards had Declan, and everyone else, turning in their seats. Boots hustled over to the ruckus but before he could get a handle on things, punches began to fly. On instinct, Declan rushed into the fray hoping to stop a bar brawl.

"You're out, Davie." Boots manhandled the instigator outside. Declan followed with his partner-in-crime.

"Get your damn hands off me, cop."

Declan tossed him to the gravel where he landed on his ass.

"Shut your mouth, Lance," Boots said. "You and Davie get the hell out of here. I don't want to see you boys for another month, understood?"

"A month?" they shouted in unison.

"You know the rules. Go on, now."

As the two grumbled off to their vehicles, Boots turned to Declan. "Thanks for the help, Mr. McKinley. My friends call me Dusty."

Declan took his hand. "Call me Declan." He took note of the firm handshake, the no nonsense way Boots handled himself and, though he'd wanted to smash his face in earlier, he discerned Dustin Boots to be a good man to know. "You have problems with those two often?"

"Only every other month when I allow them back in the building."

"Why not ban them permanently?"

"Too many friends." Boots opened the door for Declan inviting him to the bar again. "They'd sneak them in, or cause trouble in other ways. By banning them temporarily, it makes the whole thing seem silly."

Before Declan could reply, Marguerite cracked open a bottled water. "You all right?"

"Worried about me, Blondie?"

Marguerite's mouth ticked to the side in a smirk. "I wasn't talking to you." She handed the water to Boots.

"Be nice, Marguerite. Your friend here did me a favor. Get him another drink, please."

Marguerite nodded to Boots and handed Declan a water, which he appreciated. Two bourbons had been enough. However, he didn't like the silent conversation the two appeared to have. He drank half the bottle in one gulp.

"It's the low humidity this time of year." Boots nodded at the water before slugging down his own.

"I know." At Boots's questioning look, Declan explained, "I've been living in Reno with my sister for a while."

"What made you come to Timbisha Township?" Boots slid his eyes toward Marguerite.

Declan didn't take the bait. "Sheriff King asked for some assistance."

"Ah." Boots turned his body toward the dining area leaning on one elbow.

There was an edge to his voice and Declan wondered if Boots disapproved of Declan himself, Marguerite's career choices, or maybe the Kings in general.

Boots leaned closer to Declan. "Whatever you do, don't let her get hurt again. I wouldn't like it."

The man returned to the kitchen without a backward glance.

I wouldn't like it either, Dusty. Not one little bit.

MARGUERITE CHECKED THE TIME BEFORE RINGING the bell for last call. The few locals still hanging around began digging for their wallets to cash out. Declan had left a little while after helping Dusty throw out Davie and Lance.

He hadn't said goodbye.

Marguerite counted out her till and tips, stuffed the register receipts and cash in an envelope before dropping it into the safe.

"Headin' out?" Dusty pulled out his keys. Everyone else had gone home.

"Yeah, you?" She retrieved her purse from her locker and slung it over her shoulder.

"Alone as usual."

"What happened to Jasmine?"

"I don't want to talk about it."

Marguerite stopped. "Oh, come on. Not another one who couldn't stand your niece and nephew?"

Dusty sighed. "I don't get it. They aren't bad kids."

They're ornery little shits but she wouldn't say it to his face. "No, they aren't delinquents."

He narrowed his eyes but a dimple showed in his cheek. "They're a freaking handful. I guess I'm destined to fly solo until they're eighteen."

Laughing, they wandered into the parking lot.

"Declan was helpful."

Pressing her lips together, she nodded. "He can be."

"Seriously, what's the deal with you two? He obviously came here to see you."

She raised her eyebrow before repeating his words back to him. "I don't want to talk about it."

"You're a pain in my ass, you know that?"

"I'm your favorite hemorrhoid." She unlocked her door and slid in. "I'll see you later."

"Love ya, Girl."

"Love you, too, Soldier."

He waited for her engine to start before he got into his pickup and followed her out of the parking lot. Once they hit the city limit, she watched him via her rearview mirror. He turned right at the first intersection leading to his farmhouse while Marguerite continued into Timbisha Township.

The empty streets and green lights cut the drive time home to within a few minutes of leaving Blue's. Dane's pickup sat in its spot on the side of the house. Her mother hadn't the heart to sell it.

God, I miss you, Uncle Dane.

A light was on in the living room. Marguerite didn't want

to have another conversation about the life she'd chosen now that she wasn't working in law enforcement.

For once, she was happy.

Sort of.

She clicked the locks on the fob and jogged up the front steps. The storm door squeaked when she walked inside, her mother dozing in Uncle Dane's easy chair, the television playing a Rockford Files rerun.

She smiled to herself. James Garner sure was a handsome man, reminding her a little of Declan. The thought had her switching off the TV but the silence woke up Darla.

"About time you got home." She put a hand to her mouth to cover a yawn.

"You should go to bed, Mom. That chair can't be good for your back."

Marguerite turned to head upstairs.

"Wait, honey. I need to talk to you."

"Mom, there's nothing to say. I won't get involved with the case." She crossed her heart hoping to make her point. "Please don't worry about me."

"*I am so worried* with everything going on, and with your curiosity, that Jarod will eventually win you over."

Marguerite dropped her purse and sat on the couch. She reached across the end table between the sofa and recliner, turned her palm up and her mother took her hand. "He won't talk me into coming back. I've outlasted him for two years. I promise."

"Really? What about Declan?"

"What about him?"

"Just stop." Darla smiled. "You were never good at poker."

"I was pretty good undercover."

Marguerite regretted her words when she saw Darla's crestfallen expression. "I think your acting is better when motivated to catch criminals, not when you're in love. At least, that's what Dane used to say."

Marguerite swore under her breath. "I am most certainly... Not. In. Love."

Darla gripped her hand tighter. "Camille said he's staying at the Cottonwood Grove. James and the boys are going to make a hard pitch for Declan to work for them."

"Then that will be McKinley's decision and has nothing to do with me." She didn't understand where her mother was going with this until she said...

"Whether you like it or not, you have a rapport with Declan. What if they get him to persuade you back on the job?"

Here she released a small laugh and shook her head. "Declan would never ask me to come back, Mom. He never thought I was any good at it in the first place, especially after what happened. If anything, he'd dissuade Jarod from getting me involved now. You have nothing to worry about. I'm not going anywhere." She yawned and stood, helping her mother out of the old rocker recliner. "It's late."

"I think he's hurting, Marguerite. Just like you are. He's been living with his sister since he retired."

And I've lived with you since I came back.

Shame overcame her and her eyes welled, but she willed the tears not to fall—and won. She wouldn't blame herself for Declan's retirement. Hell, Marguerite was just now figuring out her own life. She didn't need to take on Declan's issues as well.

"What are you saying, Mom?"

"He's a good man. You should talk to him about what happened. At least get some resolution for both of you."

"Fine. I'll be nice."

Darla nodded. "As long as you talk to him. That's all I ask." She leaned in and hugged her. "Goodnight, honey."

Darla turned to the spare room downstairs. She'd been sleeping there since her cancer diagnosis. When she'd gotten the all-clear from the doctor, she decided she liked being downstairs and moved in permanently.

Marguerite schlepped upstairs to her own bedroom and landed face first on the bed.

Boy, she'd really messed up everyone's life. She drew a breath and her mind began replaying scene by scene the most massive screw up she'd ever committed.

Flipping over, she willed her body to relax before stripping down for bed. Though large, her childhood home had been built in the early 70s, and only partially updated over the decades. She stared at the glittery acoustic ceiling, glad she still had an imaginary starry sky to look at before falling asleep.

Suddenly, and without warning, her mind turned to figs, and how they tasted. Often, she'd be stewing on a profound subject, like what to do with the rest of her life, and an ingredient for a new recipe would pop right into her head. She sighed as she heaved herself upright and grabbed her notebook, and tablet. Sleep would have to wait because her research needed to be done now before she lost the idea. This one would be delicious, though she'd have to test it out. A play on fig newtons covered in chocolate in shapes for the harvest.

Camille was gonna love it.

Chapter Six

SONJA

"What the...?" Sonja thought as she stubbed her toe on the mountain bike blocking the stairwell. "Ryan!" she called upstairs for her oldest son, who'd obviously left it in the middle of the entryway.

"What?"

Rolling her eyes in exhaustion, she dropped her bags to the floor and prayed for patience. "Please come down here." Not in the mood for nonsense since she'd been informed her boss was under investigation for fraud, and her job would end by the end of the month. The news hit hard, and she wasn't sure what she was going to do. She had a decent savings but they couldn't live on it forever. She'd long given up on child support from her children's father.

They were on their own.

She checked her bank account app on her phone as Ryan came down the stairs. "Hey."

"Hey yourself. What's with leaving my bike here?"

Ryan shook his head. "I didn't. It was there when we got

home from practice. There's a couple of big bags in the kitchen filled with your stuff too."

"You're kidding," she said in disbelief. "Grant dumped off my things?" She didn't wait for Ryan to answer. Once in the kitchen she opened the first bag and, sure enough, it was crammed with clothes and other items she'd left at Grant's place over the last two and a half years.

Ryan began looking through the other bag and found an envelope. "Here, your name's on it."

"Thanks," Sonja mumbled as she ripped the flap open, cutting her finger in the process. This day would never end.

Sonja,

I know you said we should take a break to reevaluate where our relationship is going, and that's what I've done.

I'm sorry, but I can't be around your toxic kids anymore. The twins are a mess, and I can't stand the way Ryan looks at me. Maybe if you sent them to boarding school, or to live with their dad, we could make it work.

If you can't make our relationship the priority, then that tells me it's run its course, and we're finished.

Grant

He'd given back her house key along with all of her things —in garbage bags.

When the first tear fell, Ryan touched her shoulder. "The prick broke up with you, didn't he?"

For the first time, she didn't correct her oldest son's favorite nickname for the man she'd wasted over two years on. "Yup."

"Good. He didn't deserve you. And, I hated the way he treated Rodney."

She narrowed her eyes. "How do you think he treated your little brother?"

Nearly as tall as she was, Ryan stared right back. "Like a homeless orphan who deserved to be in juvenile detention. Grant sucked, Mom. I'm sorry you're sad, but the guy's bad news. Good riddance."

Ryan carefully tipped one of the bags onto the couch. "Need some help putting your stuff away?"

She watched her clothes, and some of the gifts she'd given Grant over the years, spill over the cushions. "Sure, honey. Thank you."

Grant's cologne permeated the first few items she touched. In anger, she wadded up a pair of pants and tossed them on the floor.

Ryan looked horrified.

"It's all going in the wash. Tonight."

Grinning, he ran to the laundry room for a basket. Once he'd returned, they sorted her things by color. Finished, Ryan began filling the basket. "I'll start the whites."

Why her son liked to do laundry was a mystery, but nevertheless, she thanked God for the small miracle. "I'll start dinner. Where are the twins?"

"Upstairs, doing homework."

Sonja gathered items in her arms while another tear fell. Not so much for Grant, but for the time she'd wasted trying to make their relationship work. His most appealing quality was his good looks. After she discovered the kids father had another family, Grant flattered her with a campaign to win her over.

He'd pursued her and she'd dropped all her walls to let him in, only to find out he didn't really like her.

He just didn't want to be alone.

Well, who did?

Over time, issues surfaced and they'd fought more than they'd laughed. She never could get him to warm up to her children. He never understood that they had to come first.

Why are men so stupid?

She put the myriad of gifts he'd returned, along with some pictures of both of them in the trash.

"The hamburger's thawed. Want me to start some sloppy joes?" Ryan returned from the laundry room and began breaking up the hamburger in a pan with an onion and some seasoning.

Ashamed of herself, she amended her thought to only include single men looking for bed partners. They weren't men.

Sonja gazed at Ryan and realized she was raising a real man. Jerks like Grant were nothing like her son and she'd never lump Ryan, or Rodney, into the same category.

Foot stomps came rolling down the staircase. Rosie appeared first.

"Smells good. Can I help?"

"Wanna spread the butter on the french bread?" Ryan said.

"Mommy, I need you to cut it in half."

Smiling, Sonja hugged Ryan, then Rosie, before cutting the loaf lengthwise for Rosie to butter the slices.

"Hey!" Rodney launched himself at Sonja for a hug, which turned into a wrestling match before he let go. "I get to put the parmesan cheese on, right?"

"Of course." Sonja knew Rodney wouldn't dump too

much on because he believed it didn't get crisp enough otherwise.

Without skipping a beat, Sonja made a green salad, set the table, and by the time the bread was out, the joes were ready to be served.

As one, they recited, *Bless us, O Lord, and these thy gifts, which we are about to receive from thy bounty, through Christ our Lord, Amen.*

They dug in at once, Sonja waiting for everyone to have a full mouth before breaking the news to them. "Well, kids. Mom lost her job."

Two mouths hung open, one mouth continued to chew with a scrunched up nose. Finally, Rodney said, "You hated your job, Mommy."

True. "I needed it, though."

"Are we moving again?" Ryan asked with trepidation. He'd made good friends in Reno and she hated to uproot him once again.

"I thought I'd start looking in Timbisha Township where Uncle Declan moved." God, she missed her brother. He'd been gone less than a week but with the loss of his help around the house, losing her job—and her stupid boyfriend—she was desperate for family. She refused to move back to Texas with her sisters.

"I love Uncle Declan." Rosie took a bite of buttery bread.

"Where's Timbisha Township?" Rodney asked.

"It's east, in the Nevada desert. There's lots of ranches there."

"Horses and cows?"

"Yes."

"Do they have peewee football?"

"I think so." She didn't but she also didn't feel like dealing with an emotional breakdown from any of her children at the moment.

Rodney nodded. "I'm in."

Sonja looked to Ryan. He'd just been put on a good team, too, damn it. "Are you okay?"

"When would we go?"

"I'll put the house on the market tomorrow. I made a few calls before I left work and applied for a job online." She kept it vague because she didn't want to pigeonhole herself.

Her children devoured their meals, even Ryan, though she knew he was troubled by the news. When all the plates were empty she began to clear the table.

"I'll put the clothes in the dryer. Then I have a report due." Ryan set his plate next to the sink and made a beeline for the laundry room.

"Thank you, honey."

As her son left the dining room, she wondered how much damage she was doing to her children by moving around so often.

Military families do it all the time. They'll be fine.

She said the mantra to herself but this time she had a hard time believing it.

DECLAN WANTED TO PUNCH A HOLE IN THE WALL. He'd known Grant wasn't good enough for his sister but she was a bum magnet of the first order.

Sonja thought her ex-husband left her for another woman, but Declan had put bracelets on the son of a bitch the moment he caught him dealing heroin, which also led to the discovery of another wife. He made sure the man gave up the kids, and let Sonja have the marriage annulled.

When she'd gotten involved with Grant, Declan had done a thorough background check and found it squeaky clean as far as criminal behavior went, but something about the prick made Declan want to body slam him into tomorrow.

His sister needed a job, though. Sonja was professional and organized. Trained as a paralegal, the vacancy at the Sheriff's office would be perfect for her, but Declan was loathe to suggest it. However, having a personality the exact opposite of Marguerite, Sonja's naiveté and lack of character judgement might work, guaranteeing she'd be impartial when dealing with suspects.

Damn it.

He hit Jarod's contact number and waited.

"It's late."

"You still need an administrative assistant?"

Jarod piped up. "You got Marguerite to change her mind?"

"Settle down. It's my sister, Sonja."

Silence on the other end.

"You still there?"

"Yeah, just debating whether or not I wanna break in another secretary."

Pissed, Declan snapped, "Do you want the help or not?"

"Are you going to help me convince Marguerite to help with the case?"

"Hell. No."

"Are you going to work for my father?"

Declan closed his eyes and pinched the bridge of nose. These people were like dogs with a dinosaur bone. But his sister and her children needed help. "I'm retired."

"A man's gotta stay busy."

"You're gonna use it against me, aren't you." It was a statement.

Jarod feigned innocence. "I mean, I don't even know your sister."

"Are you saying my reference isn't good enough? I wouldn't send an imbecile your way."

"Hmm, still..."

Declan shook his head in disbelief. "When do you need me?" he all but whined.

"Right away. When can your sister start?"

"She's got some things to clear up in Reno before she gets here. Next week, probably. I'll give her your information and she can give you call."

"Sounds good."

"Jarod," Declan warned, "She's got three children."

All kidding aside, Jarod said, "I'll expedite the paperwork as soon as she applies, Declan. Thanks for the reference."

Declan stared at the disconnected line.

Typical Jarod.

He called Sonja back to convey the new plan. He was stuck living in a motel until the ranch house was complete but the kids would need a home. They needed to get registered for school. Washoe County, where Reno is located, begins school the second week in August, but in Timbisha County, he knew school hadn't started yet, as Jessica was still in bible school at the Kings' church.

"I've got that part handled, Declan. There's a few decent houses for rent which fit my budget, too."

"How'd the kids take the news?"

"The twins are fine. Rosie can't wait to see you. Rodney's looking forward to seeing cows and horses."

"But?"

"It's harder for Ryan. His football team's doing really well this season."

"We'll figure it out for him. I'm sure there's teams here he can join."

"I better go. Thanks for putting in a good word for me. I'll let you know how my phone call goes with the sheriff."

After their call ended, Declan switched on the television.

Police are asking for help in identifying two bodies found outside Timbisha Township. If you have any information, please call the number on your screen. For Secret Witness, please call—

A vibrating hum from the nightstand caught his attention. He picked up his cell. "McKinley."

"How's small-town life?"

Declan's lips kicked to the side. "Small. What's up, Lightfoot?"

"Wondering if you've stuck your nose into those bodies found in your neck of the woods."

"I've been asked but there's nothing to follow. How'd the call with Sheriff King go?"

"It went. Seems those folks in Timbisha Township like to play matchmaker. How's that going, by the way?"

Declan rolled his eyes. "Shut up, asshole."

Agent Roland Lightfoot's laughter boomed before he turned serious. "FBI's sending a few of us out to help. Local law enforcement hasn't officially asked, so we have to play nice. It'd sure be helpful if we had an ally on our side. "

It was Declan's turn to chuckle. "I can try but you should know Sonja and the kids are on their way, and I bargained with King to give her a job."

Roland cussed. "Are you sure you don't want me to look into Grant?"

"No need. He dumped her. Didn't want to deal with the kids."

Declan heard the telltale gurgle of the longneck Roland sipped from. Quietly, his friend asked, "What kind of prick purposely involves himself with a woman who he knows has three children only to complain about them?"

"The kind Sonja seems to attract." Not wanting to betray his sister any further, Declan changed the subject.

"Listen, I'll do what I can with Jarod but understand, he and Bainbridge had a tenuous relationship when it came to authority. Dane stepped on the sheriff's toes more than once. Not to mention the FBI already stole his admin assistant, only to let her go months later and now she won't return to work for him. He's looking into hiring Sonja which is a good thing but I wouldn't try to stick it to him again, Roland."

"Noted. We'll see ya soon."

Again, Declan's line went dead before he was ready to say goodbye.

Declan tapped his fingers on his thighs, contemplating how to broach the subject with Jarod. The thumb on his right hand scrolled through his contact list. It stopped on Marguerite's number—or, at least the number she'd had two years ago.

Taking a chance she hadn't changed it, he clicked her name and waited...

"Someone better be dead." Her disgruntled, sleepy voice made him grin.

"We all die sometime, Blondie."

"What do you want, McKinley?"

Knowing a bad temper when he heard it, he got to the point and explained all the conversations he'd had tonight.

"How exactly am I supposed to help? I'm not involved with the Timbisha County Sheriff's department anymore."

"No, but you're related to the family. And, Jarod will probably ask you to help train Sonja. If the FBI shows up, maybe—"

"I haven't set foot in that building for over two years, McKinley."

Losing patience, Declan sucked air through his nostrils. "But this will be the first woman he'll have to train."

"Meaning?"

"Oh, come on, Marguerite. You know how he is!"

Declan waited so long for her answer he thought she'd fallen asleep. "Are you still there?"

"Where else would I be?"

That made him laugh, and he felt her surrender a tiny bit.

"Fine, but only if he asks for my help. If he doesn't, you're on your own." She huffed once and then asked, "Why the hell didn't you talk to James about this?"

"Because after everything that's happened I'm not sure anyone other than you could get Jarod to lighten up on the FBI."

A warm feeling overcame him when she let out one of her throaty chuckles. "Point taken."

When their comfortable silence was over, Marguerite sighed. "I'm beat so I'm going to hang up. Goodnight, McKinley."

She clicked off before he could wish her well.

What is with these people?

Disgusted, Declan tossed his phone onto the nightstand, flopped over and fell into a fitful asleep.

As predicted, Jarod had called and begged Marguerite to help him train McKinley's sister. The moment Marguerite stepped through the door, strong arms engulfed her from several deputies and a few staff.

"Are you coming back?"

"Jarod will be so relieved."

"The place hasn't been the same since you left."

"Thank God. I'm sick of Jarod's moods."

Laughing with each comment, Marguerite held up her hands. "Sorry, fellas. I'm only here to train the new administrative assistant."

"She hasn't arrived yet," Deputy Eli Wallace said. "I'm finishing up her personnel folder now." He turned, and Marguerite followed him to his desk. "Do you want to go over what I've got so far?"

"Eli, I don't need to inspect your work. I'm sure what you did is fine."

A sweetheart by nature, Eli grinned. "Yeah, but I've missed you pointing out all my mistakes in the paperwork."

"I wasn't that bad." *Was I?*

"No, you weren't, but will you pass the skill onto the new girl?"

Marguerite squinted at him before raising an eyebrow. "Do I need to?"

Eli laughed while shaking his head in the negative.

Marguerite looked around the small station, noting some changes but mostly it was how she'd left it two years prior. Jarod's office still boasted the oak armoire kept for an extra uniform, and her old desk and computer sat just outside the door. A partition offered some privacy from the rest of the squad room, and the desk appeared neat and tidy.

Jarod's work. She strolled to it and thumbed through the

files noting nothing was in order. He must've grabbed everything and shuffled them together with zero care. She hit a few keys on the computer and groaned. The calendar and schedules were a complete mess. The next click opened the admin's email inbox, revealing unopened correspondence and reports, and nothing had been filed in the last few months.

Sonja's got her work cut out for her.

"Excuse me? I'm looking for Sheriff King."

Marguerite turned and blinked. Before her stood a pretty mini-version of Declan McKinley. The resemblance was a little disconcerting but Marguerite smiled and stuck out her hand. "You must be Sonja. I'm Marguerite. Jarod's asked me to help get you settled."

"Oh." A big grin, not unlike the one Declan used to irritate Marguerite formed across the woman's face. "My brother's Marguerite? It's so nice to finally meet you."

"Uh…" Marguerite stumbled on Sonja's misconception of who she belonged to. However, she wasn't here to argue, she was here to train the woman and get the hell out before they sucked her back into the one place she didn't belong. To cover herself, she said, "Nice to meet you too. Shall we get started?"

After giving Sonja a tour of the station, the breakroom, locker rooms, and Jarod's office, she pulled out the desk chair.

"It's all yours so take a seat."

An outline of her duties had been printed, and Sonja made notes all over the document. Marguerite noted Sonja's focus and professionalism. Within a couple of hours, Marguerite was confident Sonja would work out just fine.

"Sorry, I'm late." Jarod held out his hand to Sonja. "I'm Sheriff King. We had a big rig jackknife and it took some time clearing the mess."

Sonja stood to shake his hand. "Nice to put a face to the voice. Thank you so much for giving me a chance here."

Marguerite looked at Jarod. "She's a natural. You two are going to get on just fine." She turned back to Sonja. "If you don't have any more questions for me, I need to go. My shift at Blue's starts in an hour."

"I think I'm good. Thank you for showing me the ropes. Everything else can be sorted out with Sheriff King." Sonja held her hand to Marguerite. "I hope to see you again soon. Declan said Blue's is family friendly. I'll have to bring the kids by to meet you."

"I look forward to it."

Marguerite was touched. Then her eyes collided with Jarod's. "I'm supposed to soften you up."

Jarod rolled his eyes. "McKinley called in the feds, didn't he?"

Marguerite chuckled. "The other way around, I'm afraid. Agent Lightfoot is on his way with a team. He's not going to get in the way. They just want to help. I suspect he's got some information to share so don't get your panties in a twist."

"My panties?"

Sonja giggled.

Marguerite turned to leave having completed her tasks but Jarod followed her out. "Panties? Really, in front of the new girl? How is she supposed to respect me now?"

"The same way everyone else respects you, Sheriff. You're good at your job." As soon as she hit the parking lot she realized he was walking her to her car, so she stopped. "Honestly, she's the best hire you've had since I left. Don't you trust me?"

"You know I do."

She nodded once. "Good. Now leave me alone and don't try to talk me into staying any longer than I have to."

He stopped as she continued on. When she opened her door, he shouted, "Love you, too!" in his typical smart aleck Jarod voice.

Smiling, she waved once and took off in her sports car.

One quick change, and half a sandwich later, she was on the road again headed to Blue's. She parked easily in back, noting the early dinner crowd hadn't arrived yet, but Davie and Lance were throwing darts.

"Where's Dusty?" Marguerite asked Trey from behind the bar.

"On his way. He had to deal with a problem at summer camp."

"Shit."

"Exactly."

Trey left her to clear an empty table. Marguerite watched the troublemakers for a moment before she opened her register, and prepped the bar for a busy service. Declan walked in at the same time she emptied a bag of Chex mix into a bowl.

"Thank you."

"For what?" She popped off the top of a long neck from the fridge under the bar and slid it to him.

"Sonja. I got a text. She's having a blast." He tipped the bottle toward her in thanks before taking a pull.

"Jarod's been warned about the feds and promises not to blow a gasket." She raised her eyebrow at him then transferred some Clamato juice into a pour bottle.

"You're the best, Blondie."

"Don't call me that!"

The bastard chuckled before taking another swig. He tipped his chin towards the dart board and the two idiots who weren't supposed to be there. "Do you need me to escort them out?"

"Nah. Dusty'll do it when he gets in. This is their routine. They act up on a busy night, Dusty kicks them out and bans them for a month, they show up a week later during the day to prove they can behave themselves, and Dusty either lets them off the hook or throws them out again."

Declan studied the doofuses a while before turning his attention to the news program playing above the bar. "I'll stick around until Dusty shows in case he needs some backup."

Marguerite rolled her eyes and finished prepping for her shift.

Men.

Chapter Seven

DINNER WITH THE KINGS

Declan rested a forearm on the saddle horn pretending to survey the cattle he and James had just moved into the field below. He shook his head in awe, unable to pull his eyes from the beauty. The horses stood on a small vista giving him, and James, an overview of green pastures bordered by rolling hills covered in sage and pinion pines. Vein-like tributaries from runoff flowed into the river, and above, a vast blue sky held white clouds. Every once in a while a cloud shadow offered the land a small piece of shade for a moment before drifting slowly into infinity.

Heaven.

"How much land do you own?"

"Sixty-five hundred acres, or just about 10 square miles. Takes my breath away every time I get up here."

Not wanting to leave, Declan sat a few more minutes.

Unfortunately, James interrupted his peace. "Are you coming to dinner? Camille will be upset if you don't show. My wife loves having family meals."

Meaning James' sons and their wives and children would

be in attendance. Marguerite would be there, too, since her little sister was married to Josh.

Not one to beat around the bush, Declan stared James in the eye. "You playin' matchmaker again?"

"Wouldn't dream of it." James reigned his horse toward The Estate.

After a thorough brushing, and some feed, they secured the horses in their stalls and sauntered over to the mansion, picking their way around the vehicles crowding the oversized parking area situated between it and the barn. He zeroed in on Marguerite's red sports car and took a steadying breath.

Their relationship seemed to take one step forward and two steps back when they were around each other. He couldn't stop himself from pissing her off in some way, and most times it wasn't on purpose. Something about her drove him nuts.

Most of the time her confidence kicked him in the gut, especially when he knew she faked it. She'd be faking it tonight. Though she'd never admit it, the women intimidated her. He hadn't understood why until Fred Wilkins tipped him off...

Marguerite's a good girl. People 'round here like to talk crap about her, but I know her family. She's good people.

She had a reputation in Timbisha Township, a damaged one. He'd heard little whispers here and there he didn't like and it made him want to set these people straight. Sure, James's family accepted her, but he didn't think Marguerite believed it.

He'd have to figure out how to navigate the prickly situation.

The chaos inside could be heard, Declan guessed, from the road. He prepared himself for the onslaught of noise as James opened the side door which led to the family kitchen and dining area.

Rounds of "Papa! Papa!" began as miniature humans occupying a makeshift corral hailed James, who grinned and laughed, lifting each of his grandchildren in turns to offer kisses and hugs. Declan ignored the pang of *something* burrowing in his chest by clashing glances with Marguerite. With the coolness of a man, she simply lifted her chin in acknowledgment before turning back to the women gathered at the table who were deep in discussion.

A longneck landed in his hand. "Thanks," he grunted at Josh.

"Dinner's gonna be a while. We're playing Mexican train to kill time in the other room while the girls finish up their business."

Once in the den, Josh took a seat on the sofa. The coffee table had been cleared off for the dominoes. Jason, sitting on a fluffy chair, spoke with Jarod seated next to Josh on the sofa. An oversized ottoman had been moved in front of the coffee table opposite the couch and he held his hand toward it. "Hope you don't mind but have a seat." Then Josh dumped a bag of dominoes into the center, spilling tiles into a pile, some sliding to the edge of the table.

"Can I play?" asked seven-year-old Jessica.

A beautiful little girl, Declan pitied Jarod. The man would be fighting off teenaged boys left and right as soon as she hit puberty.

"Of course, Darlin'." She wore an impish grin as she squeezed herself between Jarod and Josh. Jarod rubbed her back once before settling his forearm behind her on the back of the sofa. "How come you're not helping Mommy with the meeting?"

"I don't want to be there when the twins break free."

Jarod and Josh exchanged glances with each other before staring at Jessica. Declan stifled a laugh at Jessica's award-winning talent for wrapping them around her little finger. He didn't know why but he found ornery children amusing. Jessica reminded him of Rosie and Rodney, who were usually up to no good.

This should be entertaining.

He'd seen the giant corral set up in the dining room before entering the den. There'd been four children who'd showered James with affection. He'd also noticed the expressions on their faces, all indicating their dissatisfaction with their accommodation.

"Jessica, they can't get out of the play area. Daddy made sure." Jarod set a tile into place, breaking off a new line of dominoes. Jessica nodded before selecting a tile.

"They figured out the lock an hour after you installed it."

Josh shook his head. "That's impossible."

Jason, the father of the twins, let out a chuckle. "She's messing with us. I checked the latch. It's secure."

A dimple formed on Jessica's cheek as she placed her tile, connecting it with Jarod's.

Declan selected a tile and placed it, chuckling as he did so because James, who'd just entered the den sighed long and loud. "How long do we have, Jessica?"

Josh stood right before a tribal shout echoed down the hallway signaling freedom had been achieved.

Marguerite sauntered into the room grinning ear to ear. She plopped onto the ottoman next to Declan. "The animals have escaped."

Just then four rambunctious preschoolers ran screaming and laughing into the den demanding entertainment from their fathers and uncles.

"No shit, sweetheart."

Instead of cussing him out for the endearment, she laughed. "Well? Did James talk you into staying?"

Declan stared at her for a long moment, pleased she felt comfortable enough to sit so close to him. The urge to put roots down with Marguerite hit hard and he leaned back, not wanting to give too much away at this point.

He glanced at the little girl again. "What grade are you in, honey?"

Jessica turned her piercing blue eyes his way. "Second." She tilted her head, thinking. "Are you Rosie's uncle?"

"I am. You helpin' her get settled in at bible school?"

Jessica grinned and nodded. "I like her. Her brother's kinda gross, though."

Declan let out a laugh before coming to Rodney's defense. "He's not so bad. You hafta get to know him."

At this point, Jarod glared at Declan, making him laugh harder.

"Well?" Marguerite prodded, returning him back to the subject at hand.

Declan glanced around the festive room filled with craziness, and lots of smiles. The gnawing feeling pulled at his chest again when he met Marguerite's inquisitive expression.

"Do you want me to?"

She put her hands up in defense. "It's your life, McKinley. My opinion doesn't matter."

He put his shoulder against hers and lowered his voice, not wanting the others to hear. "What if I said it matters to me?"

When her eyes grew round with surprise the caveman living deep inside nodded his approval, especially when she blushed.

His nostrils flared.

Then, in typical Marguerite fashion, she licked her lips, and relaxed her body. He knew what she was doing—covering up her feelings, and the caveman inside growled in frustration.

"I'd say you have an over-inflated ego?" Then her taunt turned into a frown. "I'm sorry." She touched his knee. "Of course, it would be a good thing if you took the job, McKinley. You could stop tracking bad guys all over the country and focus on the jerks who live in Timbisha Township." She shrugged afterward as if to say *It really is none of my business either way.*

He debated pressing her for more when she said innocently, "And, if you stayed, you'd be closer to your sister and her children now that she's working for Jarod."

The caveman inside beat his chest in triumph.

Marguerite schooled her features. It wouldn't do to have Declan read her mind, knowing deep down she wanted him to stay. Damn it, she grew more and more attracted to him by the minute.

For a moment they sat together watching the family entertain each other before Jason said, "You're move, McKinley."

She surveyed the table and discreetly shook her head when he picked up the wrong tile. Declan rolled his eyes, chose the one she wanted and placed it.

She made sure he saw the smirk on her face and he chuckled.

"Did Dusty talk to you about peewee football?"

At first, she thought Jason was addressing Declan. When he didn't answer she turned to the biggest King. "Who, me? No...why?"

"His assistant coach moved to Henderson. He's in dire straits."

She picked up her cell and tapped out a message. Three seconds later Dusty called.

"Can you help me out?"

Declan's stare burned her skin.

Focusing on Dusty's voice, she turned away from Declan. "What do I have to do?"

"Stand there and look pretty."

"Don't be an ass."

Did Declan just growl? She glanced his way but he was staring at the dominoes.

"You won't have to actually coach. I mostly need your organizational skills with paperwork and equipment, maybe fend off some parents when they get too mouthy."

Why not? It'd give her something to do in the afternoons before her shift. "I'm in."

"Girl, you are the best friend a Soldier could have."

"You're lucky to have me. Remind me of it when I want to punch you for roping me into this. I'm not great with kids, you know."

"They're boys. You can handle yourself."

"Thanks a lot."

He laughed. "I'll text you the schedule. See you tomorrow."

"Bye." She shoved her phone into her pocket and found Declan's eyes on her with a simmering behind those deep brown orbs. "What?"

Geez, she almost felt guilty.

"You let *him* say goodbye."

Oh, for the love of...

"I mean, it's only civilized." This from Josh, who was now holding Violet who smiled around a worn out pacifier.

Ignoring both men, she looked at her niece. "Aren't you too old for that smelly thing?"

Violet's grin widened as she shook her head in the negative before leaning her head on her daddy's shoulder.

Josh frowned. "It helps her sleep. At least she's not sucking on a bottle like some people's kid is still doing."

At that insult, Jarod opened his mouth to defend his son but Jessica interrupted. "Don't rock the boat, Uncle Josh. My brother isn't ready to give it up yet."

Josh poked her in the stomach, provoking a sweet giggle. "Have you been reading your mother's parenting magazine's again?"

"No!" she exclaimed before Josh began tickling her for real.

Marguerite never got enough of watching Josh with the kids. Her sister was lucky to have him and Marguerite couldn't be happier.

She slid her eyes to Declan, who watched the whole scene with a grin on his face. When his eyes collided with hers, unwanted warmth filled her chest. "I better go see if Camille and Julie need help."

Yeah, she was running but it was only to the kitchen. Already she felt better by putting space between herself and Declan. He did funny things to her heart.

"Need an extra pair of hands?"

Camille handed her a platter filled with green beans and almonds. "We're eating in the main dining room, please."

Wow. Marguerite marveled at Camille's skill in all things homemaker. The long dining table was set to hold a King's battalion. Yet, there were extra chairs along the walls on either side indicating there were more extensions if needed. She carefully placed the platter at one end. She'd been followed by

Camille, Julie, and Lauren, and within minutes the feast was ready to be served.

Josh pulled a chair out next to Violet's highchair, and Marguerite promptly took it, making sure to snap the toddler's bib around her neck. Busy, she didn't know who'd taken the seat next to her until Declan said, "Pass the beans, please."

Since Jason, across from them, did the honors Marguerite tried to ignore Declan's proximity but whatever cologne the man used always got to her.

"Sorry I'm late." Missy rushed into the dining room looking worn out.

"We're just glad you made, babe." Josh pulled out the chair on his other side and planted a kiss on her lips. "You look tired."

"Took the calf puller and two ranch hands to deliver twins but they lived!"

Jessica threw her hands in the air in a hurray gesture before tucking into her meal again. She didn't say anything because her mouth was full.

Declan chuckled and leaned into Marguerite. "That girl is a character."

"Between Jessica and my sister, they are the world's biggest animal advocates. Which is saying something since this whole family loves animals."

"Even you?" He took a bite and waited.

"I guess so. I've never had time for pets, other than the animals Missy brought home when we were kids. Why?"

He pressed his lips together, drawing her attention to his mouth. For a moment, all sound in the room dimmed as she fought the urge to kiss the big jerk. He let out a breath. "Just wondering if you'd be interested in a ride one of these days. The land here is beautiful."

The way he said beautiful implied he was talking about her. Goosebumps ran up her arm.

No, he wasn't flirting. She was projecting her own feelings onto the conversation. She picked up her knife to cut into her steak. "Sure, but not on a horse. I like four-wheelers or dirt bikes."

His dimple appeared before he turned back to his plate.

She didn't have time to assess the damage he'd done to her emotions before Jarod got a call. He sighed long and hard then pushed his chair away from the table.

"I'm sorry. Another body's been found."

"NEED SOME EXTRA EYES?"

"My deputies are on scene now, McKinley. I'll call if I need you. Go ahead and finish your meal." The sheriff hurried out of the room and Declan shared a look with James, who rolled his eyes.

Why ask me here and then not want my help?

Marguerite had gone stiff next to Declan. "You all right?"

"Fine. Why wouldn't I be?"

He stared at her a moment, disappointed the call had ruined their good rapport. No one at the table said anything until James cleared his throat.

"While my son handles the ugly business, I'm wondering what you thought about my job offer here, McKinley?"

Now all eyes landed on him. He gently set his silverware on the table and wiped his mouth. "I think we can come to an agreement."

"I'm all ears."

"I'd like to make sure my sister, Sonja, and her children are settled first. Her oldest boy, Ryan, will have the hardest time. He left a good youth football team in Reno, and the twins can be a handful. Can we settle things in say, two weeks? That should give us time to sort ourselves out."

"Then we have a verbal agreement."

"We do."

James stood to shake Declan's hand. He copied the move and accepted, and applause broke out around the table.

Huh. He hadn't known everyone was so onboard with him working for the family. It felt nice to be wanted.

Marguerite bumped her shoulder into his. "Told ya."

When she retreated from his space, Declan felt it viscerally, already missing her touch. Her spicy perfume lingered before he mentally shook himself, needing to pay attention to the conversations going on around him.

"How are the new renters working out, Julie?" Marguerite asked.

"Great. I think Declan knows them."

He jerked his head up. "Sonja rented from you? I hadn't realized."

"Yup! I really like her and her children."

He nodded, started to eat again, but James cut him off. "Unfortunately, the ranch house might not be completed for a while."

"Why'zat?"

"Supply issues, trucking issues. Plagues of the construction business. Our working sites have first priority to incoming product."

Declan did the math in his head on the weekly rent at his motel. "Got an estimated timeframe?"

Jason chimed in. "Four to six weeks if we're lucky. I'm really sorry it won't be earlier."

"Not to worry," Camille spoke up. "I can have a room ready for you by tomorrow."

Declan shook his head. "Thank you, Mrs. King, but I'd rather be closer to town, and my sister, for now. I appreciate the offer though." He ended on a sincere smile when her face fell. Honestly, he didn't want to be under so much scrutiny living at The Estate.

Another silence fell as everyone finished their meals. By the time dessert was served, conversation ebbed and flowed at a normal pace.

Marguerite slid her half-eaten dessert plate away. "I need to get going. Camille, Julie, it was wonderful as always."

"I'll walk you out." Camille set her napkin by her plate and pushed herself away from the table.

Once the matriarch of the family stood, everyone began scooting chairs back, signaling an end to the meal and the beginning of clean-up.

Declan shook James's hand one more time even as the man followed him outside.

He caught Marguerite's taillights speeding down the road on her way back into Timbisha Township.

"You sure you don't want to stay here? We have more than enough room."

"Positive. I need to check on Sonja. I thought I'd take a poke around the sheriff's station to see if Lightfoot has any new information on the case."

"Good idea. Maybe keep my son from losing it with the FBI agent." James looked up at the sky, and rocked back on his heels, hands in his pockets. "You and Marguerite seemed comfortable with each other tonight."

Declan opened the driver-side door and hopped inside his

pickup. "Don't." He started the engine. "I'll call you later if there's something to relate."

He noted James's half-smile before he stepped back in order for Declan to back out. He lifted a hand in farewell before taking the driveway with a purpose toward the main road, and then the motel to freshen up.

As usual, his mind drifted to Marguerite and what she'd wear to work tonight.

God, the way those men gawked at her had his heart pounding with the need to hit something. Never one to think of himself as the jealous type, he didn't like the feeling.

Not.

One.

Bit.

But he wasn't dumb enough not to recognize it for what it was, nor was he immature enough to ignore it.

He wanted her.

The flickering lights of Timbisha Township greeted him as he descended the hill into town, the river running slow and lazy outlining the city limits.

After crossing the bridge, he made a right into the little grove of trees giving the motel its name. A flickering neon sign welcomed him into the parking lot but the flashing yellow lights from utility vehicles didn't, especially the large one specializing in water damage.

"Mr. McKinley, I'm so sorry," the manager said by way of greeting. "The water main broke and your room is completely flooded, several others too." The man wrung his hands together, clearly upset.

"My clothes?" Declan hadn't brought much. He'd hung most of his shirts in the closet, but his boxers and t-shirts he'd stowed in the dresser.

"I took the liberty of moving your things there." He pointed to a spot where his duffel sat on the table they'd moved out of the room, along with most of his gear. Thankfully, he kept his weapon in a holster behind his back, and his extra ammo in the duffel. He perused the items. The manager followed him. "I think your boots will be okay, but those tennis shoes need a good washing. I'm so sorry about this. I've got a refund check for today's stay waiting in the office.

Well hell.

He pulled his cellphone from his pocket and dialed Sonja's number. Excited to hear from him, she told him all about the rental, its small size and how her furniture hadn't arrived yet. He only half listened before saying goodbye and hung up.

Why he dialed Marguerite's number next—and not James's—he wouldn't examine closely but when he explained the situation she didn't hesitate one bit.

"It'll be awkward but, yeah, we have an extra room here. I'm home now. I've got a half hour before I need to leave for Blue's."

His brain screamed *Don't do it!* but the prospect of sleeping under the same roof with Marguerite had his heart pounding like thunder and he couldn't keep his hands and feet from stopping himself from his fate.

"I'll see you in five minutes."

Chapter Eight

PEEWEE FOOTBALL

True to his word, Declan parked his pickup at the curb in front of Marguerite's house a few minutes later. She waited in the doorway while her mother fussed in the background about linens and towels, and wanting their "guest" to be as comfortable as possible before she climbed the stairs.

He carried only a large duffel bag in one hand, and a pair of dirty tennis shoes in the other with a sour expression on his face.

"Do you need help with the rest of your things?"

His mouth quirked to the side. "Naw, this is it." He lifted the tennis shoes a bit higher. "Can I use your washing machine? They're pretty ripe and might need tossing but I thought I'd try to wash them before giving up."

She opened the door wider as he stepped inside her home. "Laundry room is through the kitchen. Go ahead and set them on top of the washer."

"Oh, dear." Her mother had descended the stairs and held her hands out to Declan. "I'll take those. What happened again?"

"Motel flooded. Bad plumbing apparently."

Marguerite didn't miss the disgruntlement in his voice. She couldn't fault him for his bad mood because she'd be pissed too if she lost her home—or at least in his case—a place to lay his head at night.

Declan stopped dead and faced Darla. "I can't thank you enough, Mrs. Theroux. I would've stayed with my sister but her furniture hasn't arrived yet and apparently the house is small."

"It is," Marguerite affirmed. "It's not far from here, actually."

Declan nodded. "Good to know. Thanks again."

When he stood there looking handsome and helpless all at the same time, she grinned. "Come on, I'll show you to your room. It's upstairs."

She led him the short way up to the landing, then down the hall to the room next to hers. She opened the door revealing a feminine space covered in stuffed animals and veterinary textbooks. "You're in Missy's old room."

Her mother returned from the laundry room a little out of breath. "I would've put you in the master, but I'm using it for storage and it's a mess." She wrung her hands as if Declan deserved better and would disapprove of his accommodations. Marguerite rolled her eyes.

"This will be fine, Mrs. Theroux."

"Darla."

"I'm grateful, Darla. Thank you."

"That's better. Now, there's only one bathroom upstairs so you'll have to share with Marguerite. The towels are in that closet there," she pointed to the door in question, "and please help yourself to anything in the kitchen. I'll go put your shoes in the washer, though I think you might need to buy a new pair. They're pretty wet and the soles are curled up."

Marguerite waited until she heard her mother's footsteps on the hardwood downstairs. "I emptied some of Missy's dresser drawers for you and there's plenty of room in the closet to hang your shirts and jacket."

This is going to be awkward as hell.

He met her gaze. "When are you leaving for work?"

"Right now unless you need anything else."

"I'll see you in a while."

Nodding, she spun around on her heel and tried not to run down the stairs. Having him sleeping on the other side of the wall from her was going to be brutal.

Sighing to herself, she grabbed her purse from the hook by the stairs and yelled for her mother. "I'm going to work! Love you!"

A muffled "love you too" issued from the laundry room before the storm door shut behind her.

As she drove to Blue's for her shift she contemplated whether or not she'd made the right decision in allowing Declan to stay at her house. There were a few hotels and motels in the area he could've called.

However, she didn't know his finances. *Because they're none of my business.* He'd called his sister who apparently couldn't accommodate him so Marguerite wasn't his first choice.

She wondered why he hadn't asked Mr. King but then, having spent so much time with Declan on the task force she knew he liked to be private and no one in Timbisha Township could keep their noses in their own business.

Speaking of which, she mentally prepared herself for the shit storm of tongue wagging once the community found out he was staying at her house.

I can't catch a friggin break.

Packed as usual, she maneuvered her car into a compact space at the back of Blue's and took the employee entrance. Frustrated at being late, she threw her purse in her locker and practically ran to the bar to relieve Dusty, who'd been covering for her when she texted to let him know she had a house guest, leaving out the particulars.

He gave her a brief nod when he spotted her then left to check in with the kitchen and then to his office for his mid-shift paperwork. He'd be back out in a hour, depending on what adjustments he had to make to his inventory spreadsheet.

She settled into her routine serving the regulars, and arguing with Cheryl about treating customers with respect and a smile. The shift flew by before she had time to catch her breath. It dawned on her after last call that Declan hadn't shown up.

Dusty flipped up the chairs on the tables closest to the bar.

"You never did tell me what happened at summer camp," Marguerite said as she counted out the till.

He glanced her way. "Chance got into another fight. And it wasn't camp. Chance is doing a stint in summer school to catch up on his grades."

Marguerite continued straightening the bills. "He start it?" She didn't comment on the summer school bit because she knew how hard he'd been working with Chance on his schooling.

"Of course not, but the kid can't stop himself. He thinks he's everyone's savior."

"Huh. Wonder who he gets it from?" Marguerite raised her eyebrow and Dusty laughed. "How did it end? He's not suspended, is he?"

"Naw. Detention all week, which is fine with me because he needs to catch up on his homework. If his grades slip he can't play football."

Marguerite nodded. "Is that rule part of the youth league?"

"It's Uncle Dusty's rule." He wiped his hands on a rag. "You ready to close up? I'm beat."

"Let me get my purse." She'd long stopped insisting he didn't have to walk her to her car. Not wanting to keep him from his charges, Marguerite retrieved her things as fast as possible and met him on the bar's front steps.

"Tomorrow morning's the first game of the season and it's at the new park. Team meeting at nine at the southwest practice field. Do you want me to pick you up?"

Marguerite had forgotten the time. "Yeah, that'd be great since I'm not a morning person lately. You sure you think I can help? As I said, I'm not good with kids."

"You're great with Violet."

"She's my niece."

He chuckled. "You'll be fine and, yes, I need the help. See you tomorrow, Girl."

"Later, Soldier."

Marguerite climbed into her sports car and started the engine. She waited at the parking lot's exit for Dusty before turning onto the main road.

God, she was beat and an early morning meeting at the park didn't sound like fun. Working late and waking early was bound to give her wrinkles. She still had some recipe tweaking to do but decided it could wait until after the game. She'd have time to experiment before heading back to the bar for her shift. Saturday night tips were the best.

Thinking about the new outfit she'd buy with those tips,

she'd almost forgotten about the black pickup parked at the curb in front of her house.

She'd almost forgotten about Declan.

Not in any mood for drama, she pulled the storm door open and cringed at the screech, before gently letting the door close behind her. She locked the front door and surveyed the living room.

Empty.

She listened for conversation.

Nothing.

Shrugging her shoulders, she climbed the creaky stairs, which sounded super loud in the quiet house. Trying not to disturb anyone, she tiptoed down the short hallway but, unfortunately, hit the loose board on the landing. She stopped again and listened. Still she heard nothing from her new roommate. After a moment, she continued on but noticed Missy's door was cracked and she couldn't help herself from looking inside.

A half-naked Declan in jeans and bare feet lounged on her sister's bed with a laptop on his legs—and his gun pointed right at her.

Delicious as he looked, she rolled her eyes anyway as she pushed the door open. "Put that thing away. You knew it was me."

For crying out loud.

"Sorry," Declan growled. "Habit."

"Yeah, I get it." She did. She woke up some nights in a cold sweat and trembling in fear from her nightmares. Shaking it off she nodded towards his laptop. "How's the research going?" She couldn't take her eyes off him. Good gracious, the ceiling fan swirled his manly scent around her sister's room hitting Marguerite straight in the face. She closed her eyes for a brief moment to enjoy it.

Declan didn't appear to notice as he ran both hands over his face. "Dead ends left, right and center."

Because you don't know what you're looking for...but she wasn't going to help. "Well, I'm beat so I'm going to crash. See you in the morning."

Marguerite shut the door and practically ran the few steps to her own room. She was only now figuring out her life, and Declan McKinley was a major distraction.

Marguerite sighed—*just sighed*—before ripping off her clothes, threw on a nightie, and crawled into bed.

She needed sleep but knowing the man who drove her crazy slept on the other side of the wall would keep her from it. Counting to ten, she drew in a deep breath and thought of smoked almonds...chocolate...sea salt...

...then the annoying sound of her alarm had her throwing her arm over in a wide arc onto the nightstand. She fumbled around until she found the off button.

Seven blessed o'clock in the morning!

Grumbling, she stumbled out of her room to the bathroom across the hall where she rammed headfirst into a damp chest.

"What the—"

Arms wrapped around her to keep her on her feet. She glared into tobacco warm eyes and a grin worthy of Alice's Cheshire Cat. "Steady there, Blondie. I'm all finished."

Before she could rip him a new one, he flipped her around by the shoulders, pushed her into the bathroom, and even closed the door for her.

It's too early for this!

She needed the toilet, a shower and then coffee if she was going to verbally spar with McKinley so early in the morning.

As the hot water soothed her muscles and cleared her mind she realized she didn't want to spar with anyone. Declan had found himself in a predicament, asked for her help and she'd given it.

It's not like he gives a crap about my feelings anyway.

She finished up in the bathroom, peeked out the door to make sure the hallway was clear then headed for her bedroom to change. Dusty was due to arrive soon and she wanted to get some coffee and toast into her stomach before the game.

She found McKinley and her mother sitting at the table in the kitchen. Ignoring them, she headed for the coffee pot.

"Good morning, sweetheart."

Once she'd armored herself with her mug of coffee, she turned around and leaned her butt on the counter. "Good morning."

"Why're you up so early?" McKinley asked.

"Chance's game is this morning. Dusty'll be here in a bit to pick me up."

"Who the hell is Chance?" The growl in McKinley's voice was unmistakable.

"None of your business." Marguerite winked, pleased when the action elicited another growl from the man.

No way is he jealous...is he?

Darla harrumphed, throwing Marguerite a frown before explaining the situation. "Chance is Dustin's nephew. He's in peewee football and they need help with coaches, so Marguerite's filling in."

McKinley's eyebrows lowered in thought. "How old is Chance?"

"Eleven."

"Do you think they'd have room for one more on their team?"

"I don't know, why?"

McKinley cleared his throat. "My sister's oldest son, Ryan, is eleven. He was on a team in Reno and I thought maybe..."

Marguerite nodded. "You can ask Dusty. It's his team."

The doorbell rang and she called out, "It's open!" before pouring the rest of her coffee into a travel mug.

"Hey," Dusty said, as he and Chance entered the kitchen. "McKinley, good to see you."

Marguerite noted the friendliness from Dusty and relaxed. "This is my nephew, Chance."

"Where's Tessa?" Darla asked.

"With her cheerleading team. She'll be at the fields soon." He turned to Marguerite. "Are you ready?"

"Let me get my bag." She left the room and heard McKinley ask about open positions on the team but didn't hear Dusty's answer.

Once in Dusty's truck, he asked with a shit-eating grin, "How the hell did he end up staying at your house?"

Cute neighborhood.

Declan skirted the moving truck parked backward in the driveway of his sister's rental. Marguerite had been correct. It was a smaller cookie cutter in an older neighborhood around the corner from her place.

As his feet hit the grass, Rosie hug-tackled him at the knees almost knocking him over.

"I missed you!"

"I missed ya too." He swept her up in his arms. "Did you grow again? I can barely lift you." Then he pretended to be weighed down by her small body.

"Don't drop me," she squealed.

"You know I won't."

Ryan cleared the front porch, followed by Rodney.

"You found a team for me?"

"Maybe."

Sonja stepped around a mover loaded down with a box. "You sure you don't mind taking them?"

"Positive."

"Honestly, I think I can get more done with them out of the way."

"What about our room?" Rosie asked.

"Once the movers have all the big stuff put away, it'll be easier for you to empty your boxes." She hugged Rosie, then looked at Declan. "Get all the forms and stuff if they've got a spot for Ryan and let me know the cost."

He leaned in and hugged his sister. "Don't worry about a thing."

Once all the kids were belted, he started the engine. "Your mom said you spent the day at summer camp at the church. How was it?"

"Okay."

"Great!"

"Stupid."

The last muttered from Rodney.

"Why's it stupid?"

"Kids here are mean."

Rosie shook her head. "You're the mean one."

"Am not!"

"Are too!"

A migraine began to pulse behind Declan's left eye. "Knock it off." He glanced at Ryan. "How is it for you?"

"Okay. I'm the new kid so they're still interested in me."

He shrugged like it was no big deal but Declan knew they'd had to move around more than any children should.

"Maybe you'll know some of the kids on the team." He gave Ryan a sidelong look.

He fidgeted. "Maybe."

"Do you know a kid named Chance?"

"Is his last name Boots?"

Declan nodded.

"I've met him. He's kinda wild."

Great, juuust great.

"I'm friends with a girl named Jessica. She's really nice," said Rosie.

Rodney guffawed. "She's one of the meanest."

He stared at the twins in the rearview mirror; Rosie looking smug, Rodney looking irritated. "I know Jessica's daddy. He's the sheriff so you better be nice to her, Rodney. Wouldn't want to have to bail you out of jail."

Rodney's eyes rounded before he slapped his hands on his thighs and laughed. "Yeah, right, Uncle Declan."

Declan chuckled as he pulled into Timbisha Township Sports Complex, a newly developed park with fields for baseball, soccer and football. Declan wondered if the Kings had helped build it.

He parked as close as he could to Field 6 where Boots said his team would be playing and corralled the twins, Ryan following close behind. Declan kept an eye out for trouble, a habit he couldn't quit if he tried. Full of families, the park held a lot of children donning some sort of youth sports uniform. The clicking of cleats melded with birdsong and the chatter and screams coming from the playground.

Hard to tell who's louder, children, cheerleaders, or parents rooting for their teams.

He spotted Marguerite first; tight jeans, tank top and hair tied in a knot on top of her head. She held a clipboard and a whistle hung from her neck. She stood next to Boots in the middle of a team huddle.

Declan checked the scoreboard. Two minutes to halftime.

"Let's find a spot on the bleachers. We can talk to my friend during half."

Ryan nodded, scoping out the team and picked a spot close enough to hear Boots's voice.

"Etch, you're not covering your man and he gets through every time. Turner, Chance, I need you downfield in case their QB fires a rocket."

"Yes, Coach," all three boys said.

Declan approved of the discipline so far, especially when Rodney said, "He seems nice, Ryan."

Declan squinted at his youngest nephew. "Do you want to see if there's a team you can play on?"

"Sure, Uncle Declan."

Rodney didn't have a quiet voice and at the sound of Declan's name he caught Marguerite glancing their way.

She waved. "Boots will talk to you at the end of half, if that's okay?"

Declan gave her a thumbs up and then the team took the field.

"That's Chance there, number 65." Ryan pointed. "I don't know the other boys."

The last two minutes played out, Chance's team not letting the offense score.

He knew Ryan could throw the ball and since they'd caught the end of the half without seeing Boots's quarterback he wasn't sure how this would go for Ryan.

True to their word, after the half-time team huddle a group

of mothers brought out a cooler on wheels and started handing out waters and fruit snacks. Boots made his way over to Declan, followed by Marguerite.

"Glad to see you could make it. This must be Ryan." Boots stuck his hand out. "Coach Boots. What position do you play?"

Ryan looked at Declan who said, "Tell him."

"Receiver and quarterback, sir."

"You can throw?"

"Yessir."

"Good. As of this morning, I don't have a quarterback. Ours broke his arm riding his bike to the park." To Declan, he said, "His mom works on Saturdays, no dad in the picture. I offered him a ride but he refused."

Then he turned to Marguerite. "Check the equipment bag and see if there's another set of pads and a helmet that'll fit Ryan. I know I've got an extra jersey."

"Uh," Ryan said as Marguerite began rifling through the equipment.

Declan asked, "You wanna put him in now?"

Boots chuckled. "I'm pretty desperate. Chance can throw but he hates it. He likes to tackle. Besides, his aim is terrible. No one else has any experience so I've just been running the ball all game hoping our defense can hold them back but you can see we haven't scored."

"We've got everything but cleats."

Boots shrugged. "What he's wearing will have to do. That is, if you're willing to get in there, kid."

Declan hadn't seen a smile that big on Ryan's face in months.

"Where can I change?"

MARGUERITE STARED HER CHARGES IN THE EYE giving her best stern eyebrows. "If either of you step foot onto the field, or away from the sidelines I'll have you running with the team afterward, got it?"

"Yes, ma'am."

Marguerite noted Rosie's sweet grin and the ornery twinkle in Rodney's eyes before turning back to her coaching task, which was to keep track of who was going in and out of the game. Dusty really did all the work, which was fine.

This is fun.

Declan and Ryan returned from the restroom, Ryan in full uniform, except for his shoes. "You ready?"

The boy took a huge breath. "As I'll ever be," and headed toward the end of the field where Dusty and the team did warmups before the next half began.

Declan followed Ryan without a word to Marguerite and she enjoyed the view.

Damn it.

She looked at the twins. "Come on."

Dusty gave the ball to Ryan, showed him something on one of his laminated cards and blew a short burst of his whistle. The team moved, Ryan stepped back and let the ball fly. It landed perfectly in Chance's hands and the team erupted in cheers.

"My brother's really good at throwing," Rodney said with pride.

"I can see that."

"Guess we'll be seeing you every Saturday then." Rosie grinned.

From behind them a high-pitched voice yelled, "Rosie!"

"Jessica!" and Rosie took off.

For half a second Marguerite panicked until she saw Lauren and Jarod. They waved and then Rosie sprinted back to Declan, almost taking him out at the knees from behind. "Can I go with Jessica and her mommy and daddy to the playground?"

Declan and Jarod shook hands while Lauren sauntered up to Marguerite.

"They really like each other."

At first, Marguerite thought she was talking about Declan and Jarod until she caught Jessica and Rosie giggling. "It appears so. Are you okay taking her?"

"Of course." Then they noticed Rodney sulking. "Should we see if the little guy wants to hang out with us?"

Declan said, "He's gonna stick with me in the stands, aren't you Rodney? There's another team Coach Boots wants us to look at for you."

"Okay, Uncle Declan."

"Can we go?" Jessica said, her hand pulling on Rosie.

"Yes," Lauren said. "I'll see you later, Marguerite."

Whistles blew and Marguerite jogged back to the sidelines where Declan and Rodney had now moved to watch Ryan.

"I had no idea he could throw like that," Declan said with awe as they watched Ryan throw the ball downfield over and over again until the team scored a touchdown.

"By the look on Dusty's face, you just won him over for life. He hates to lose." She began to laugh when Dusty jumped up and down with the boys.

"Guess this means Ryan found a team." Declan nodded towards the celebration. "Games are every Saturday?"

Marguerite pulled a schedule from the drawer beneath the clipboard. "Here you go. You'll need to have Sonja fill these out, and get him some cleats. There's probably a registration fee listed somewhere."

Declan flipped the papers. "Found it." He reached for his wallet and pulled out some bills.

Marguerite held up her hands. "Handling team funds is above my pay grade, McKinley. Hold on to it until after the game."

She didn't miss his dimple as he returned the money to his wallet.

When the offense came off the field, Rodney wandered over to his brother, who patted him on the back.

"That's adorable. Are they close?"

Declan grunted. "Just when I think Rodney hates everyone, he proves me wrong. They've had a rough time."

"It's good they're here, then."

She didn't have time to continue her conversation because the other team fumbled and the offense was back on the field.

In the end, Dusty's team won, Ryan running the ball in for the final touchdown.

"Marguerite?" Sonja called as she came into view from the parking lot. "Where're the kids?"

Marguerite smiled and pointed to the end zone. "Final team meeting. Rosie's with Jarod and Lauren at the playground. Apparently, the girls are best friends."

Ryan ran over. "Mom! We won!"

Sonja grinned with confusion. "You played?"

Marguerite began organizing the sidelines in order for the next team to set up for their game.

"Here, let me get that." Declan moved the water jug while Marguerite collapsed the foldable tables. Dusty finally made it over as Sonja finished filling out Ryan's paperwork.

Marguerite watched the interaction between Sonja and

Dusty, wondering what they were saying while Declan stopped moving altogether.

"What's wrong?"

Declan sighed. "I know that look."

"Who's?" Marguerite didn't see anything unusual until Dusty's dimple appeared. "Oh, thaaat look."

McKinley grimaced.

"For heaven sake, they're two grown adults. Sonja's a beauty and Dusty's a catch. Leave 'em alone, McKinley."

"You don't understand. My sister is a grade-A bum magnet."

Marguerite shook her head. "Do I need to get rough with you? Dusty isn't a bum, he's a great guy and I suspect you already know it or you wouldn't have allowed Ryan to play today."

He gave her a sidelong glance, before dropping his shoulders in defeat. "Fine. I won't interfere—"

"Good."

"—unless I need to."

Marguerite rolled her eyes and began carrying the table to Dusty's truck.

When she returned for another load, McKinley, Sonja and Rodney had left. She turned in a circle looking for them and Dusty said, "I sent them over to the seven-year-olds to talk to Cliff. Rodney wants to play."

"Ah."

"Then they're meeting us at Blue's for the after game lunch."

She squinted at Dusty. "Did you invite McKinley or Sonja?"

Dusty didn't look at her. "Both, I guess."

"Ha! You guess. Well, I can tell you she's a very nice woman but a word of caution. She confided with me men are off her radar for a while because of her recent breakup, and McKinley is a very protective big brother."

When his famous panty-dropping smile crossed his face Marguerite couldn't stop herself from laughing.

"Oh, Soldier. You just don't know how to stay out of trouble, do you?"

Still grinning, he said, "Apparently not, Girl."

Chapter Nine

WHAT'S HE UP TO?

Declan checked his watch as he surveyed the bar patrons. The crowd should be thinner this time of night but it was Saturday, the local band still grinding it out.

A bottled water plopped in front of him and he caught Marguerite's retreating behind as she sailed passed his section of the bar to the other end.

He had to hand it to her, she was organization personified into one beautiful woman who didn't know how to slow down.

"You still here?"

He spun around to find Jarod in full Sheriff's uniform leaning against the bar. "Dusty picked up Marguerite this morning so I thought I'd take her home since we're going to the same house."

"I heard about that. Couldn't get my wife to stop laughing."

Declan ignored the jibe. "What are *you* doing here?"

"I try to stop by Saturday nights. Most folks see me and it reminds them to get a ride. Discourages drunk driving."

The band finished their set and Marguerite rang the bell. "Last call. You don't have to go home but you can't stay here!"

Boots shook his head. "Must you always?"

Marguerite laughed as she began wiping down the bar top and moving dirty glasses into the sink. She'd pretended to ignore Declan while she worked but she hadn't fooled him. She made sure his glass remained full, whether it be with a beer or soda, and now a bottled water. At one point he found a basket of wings sitting in front of him.

"That's my cue," Jarod said, before speaking into the mic on his uniform as he walked out the door.

"He'll sit down the road with his lights flashing. Most might not like it but I sure do appreciate his presence." This from Fred, the barfly.

"How'll you get home?"

Fred held up a cell. "Wife's waitin' outside." He tipped his beer bottle against his lips and set the empty on the bar. "See ya later, Beautiful!"

"Tell your wife hi from me!" Marguerite shouted back while she cleared the other end of the bar.

Fred smiled and nodded to Declan before making his way to the exit.

Declan kept his eyes on everyone as they gathered their things and departed the building, all while keeping Marguerite in his peripheral.

The band took a while to pack up and at one point, Boots helped them carry their things through the back door.

Declan stayed inside not wanting Marguerite left alone. A niggling feeling just beyond his subconscious, the same feeling he'd had when she'd gone missing in Rock Springs, pulsed there and he couldn't shake it.

He searched the bar and restaurant. It was empty except for

Marguerite, two waitresses, one busboy, and now Boots who'd returned from helping the band with their equipment.

"You still here, McKinley?" Marguerite asked from beside him.

He filled his lungs with air and slowly exhaled. "Yup." He turned to face her. "Thought I'd give you a ride home."

Her eyes widened and she glanced at Boots.

Declan felt the green-eyed monster growl inside but Marguerite nodded.

"Sure, if you don't mind waiting a little longer. Still have some things to finish before I can go." She tilted her head. "Are you all right? You have a funny look on your face."

I bet I do. Get it together, dickhead.

"I'm good. Need help with anything?"

She stared at him a heartbeat before drawing out, "Nooo. Dusty and I have the routine down." She raised her eyebrow and Declan braced himself for the smart-ass comment coming. "You'd just get in the way."

There it is.

"I'm sure I would. Take your time. I'm not going anywhere." When he said the last, he knew he meant it in more ways than she would comprehend at the moment.

He felt it, felt *her*, in his guts. She's the reason he'd moved to this town, why he'd come running when the sheriff called him for a consult. Why he'd packed up and moved away from his sister, his nephews and niece.

Maybe it was too soon, or maybe he was plain ol' crazy.

Maybe he wasn't ready to admit it out loud, but...

Marguerite belonged to him. He just had to reach out and take her.

Lord, what am I doing?

Frankly, he needed to formulate a plan to make her understand the facts about their relationship. Hell, HE had to figure it out but in the end they'd be together.

He was tired of fighting it.

MARGUERITE FELT MCKINLEY'S PRESENCE IN THE BAR like an irritating fly that wouldn't leave her alone. Sure, she'd taken care of him like one of her regulars—didn't mean she liked it.

Or him.

Who am I kidding?

Fine, she liked him. She liked his face, his hands, and even his cute butt in those jeans, but it didn't mean she *liked him* liked him. It just meant she felt his pull of attraction.

Chemistry.

Yeah, right.

She sighed while stuffing bills into the money bag.

"You okay?" Dusty asked quietly near her ear. "Do you want me to ask him to leave? I can drive ya home, Girl."

She touched his shoulder. "Stand down, Soldier. I can handle McKinley."

"Ya sure?"

Now she patted him before handing him the bag. "Positive. You drop the money and I'll get my things so we can get out of here."

Without a word she turned on her heel and headed to the lockers to get her purse and tote bag where she'd brought her change of clothes. When she returned, the lights were off and Dusty and McKinley waited for her on the front steps.

"Ready?" McKinley asked.

"More than. I'm beat." As all three walked to the parking

lot she said, "I'm not sure I can keep doing early mornings and late nights on game days."

Dusty chuckled. "It's only for football season. The time will fly by, Girl. I know you're tough."

McKinley grunted. "More than you know."

Dusty stopped and gestured behind them. "I'm parked out back. You got this?"

"Hey, don't talk about me like I'm not here or I'll hafta smack ya one."

Of course, both men ignored her.

"On it. Thanks for what you did for Ryan and Rodney. My sister is relieved and the boys are happy."

They shook hands before McKinley placed his warm palm at the small of her back, sending tingles up her spine, and steered her toward his pickup.

"Thanks for getting her home safe."

Marguerite turned. "What did I tell you, Soldier?"

Dusty grinned. "Love you, Girl"

She huffed out, "Love you back, Soldier."

She felt McKinley's hand flex before he added more pressure to guide her toward his pickup. He escorted her to the passenger side and opened the door for her.

"Thank you."

"You're welcome."

He shut the door hard enough to rock the truck.

She tracked him with narrowed eyes while fastening her seatbelt, until he got behind the wheel.

Prickly bastard.

"You didn't have to wait for me, Grouch. Dusty could've driven me home."

He pushed the ignition button and jerked the gearshift in reverse. "He could've but I wanted to."

"Ooo-kay." She faced forward and settled in for a quiet ride home where her bed beckoned and her brain—for the first time in weeks—wanted nothing more than to sleep.

"I got...that feelin'."

"*That Lovin' Feelin*?" She snickered remembering the argument they'd had over his taste in old music. God, it seemed like a million years ago.

Nope, just two. Don't think about it.

A dimple appeared as he smirked. "No, smart-ass." He put his blinker on to make a left onto her street. He shook his head as if debating whether or not to continue. She opened her mouth to prod him when he admitted, "*That* feeling." He glanced at her a second before turning back to the road. "The one I had when you went missing."

A chill ran up her spine. They'd never discussed what happened in Wyoming and she hoped they never would but, of course, the jerk had to bring it up.

She swallowed. "When exactly? All day, at the park, or tonight at the bar?"

"After you rang the bell." He drummed his thumbs on the steering wheel as they approached her house. He hit the blinker again before he paralleled at her front curb. After he pushed the gearshift into park and turned off the engine, he swiveled in his seat to stare at her. "I hate *that* feeling."

She nodded, all urges to be a brat gone. "Yeah. Me too."

"Good." He got out and came around the truck. As her feet hit the grass he clicked the fob. The lights and beep from the pickup echoed around the quiet neighborhood. Once again he urged her forward with the palm of his hand at the small of her back. Only, this time, she welcomed it. Being reminded of their injuries, the serious nature of their shared past event—the unspoken loss of Uncle Dane—brought it all back full-force.

Being with McKinley right now helped squash the horrible memories.

As usual, the storm door screeched when he pulled it open and she unlocked the front door with her key. One lamp lit the living room, which left the rest of the house dark and silent. Her mother had gone to bed a while ago.

"Should we put out the light?" His hushed voice brought goosebumps to her skin.

"No, I keep forgetting to pick up a nightlight in case Mom gets up in the middle of the night. The living room lamp puts out enough light to keep her from tripping on something."

She climbed the stairs, McKinley behind her. Knowing he stared at her butt made the goosebumps worse so when she hit the landing she hurried to her room.

"Goodnight, McKinley."

He stood still half a moment...then, "G'night, Marguerite."

Not Blondie. Not Brat.

Nor Maggie, nor Magpie.

Marguerite.

Her heart fluttered as she smiled and pushed her bedroom door open. The sleep her brain wanted barely ten minutes before left the building like Elvis, and now she couldn't stop thinking about McKinley.

No. *Declan.*

Could she open up her heart a tiny bit for him?

Should she?

Body exhausted, brain on overdrive, she stripped out of her clothes, threw on a t-shirt and climbed into bed.

It felt like hours as she stared at her sparkly ceiling but before she could blink the sun peeked through her curtains.

DAMN IT, I NEED A PLAN.

Declan's mind raced as he readied himself for bed.

The pleased expression on her face when he'd used her first name made his heart thump but he needed more.

Never one to put much thought into pursuing a woman, Declan wondered if his tracking skills would help.

He made a list of things he knew about her.

First, even though *he* hated it, she liked working the bar. Always a people person, the job provided her with information and it kept her busy.

Second, she hid it well but she was curious about the bodies, which would never do. He had to keep her from all things criminal, all things dangerous, especially with a potential serial killer on the loose. Jarod still hadn't discussed the third body found with him but Declan's gut told him Timbisha Township had a big problem. He wouldn't tolerate Marguerite getting hurt again—or worse.

Third, he'd tasted her chocolate treats. Camille King certainly appreciated them because, damn, they were little pieces of heaven. He'd have to make an effort to tell her how good they were, tell people about them.

As he contemplated more ways to please Marguerite, the late hour caught up to him.

The annoying noise coming from his phone signaled he'd fallen fast asleep and it was now time to get his ass out of bed. He'd set it a little later than usual, as it was Sunday morning and they'd had a late night.

By the time he'd showered and dressed, the sun sparkled midway to noon in the bright Nevada sky. Voices drifted upstairs letting him know he was the last to be up and about. He entered the eat-in kitchen to find Darla staring at Marguerite's back.

"G'mornin'."

Darla put on a wide smile for him. "Good morning, Declan. Sleep well?"

"Like a rock, Mrs. Theroux."

"None of that, now. You know it's 'Darla'." The older woman nodded once before turning to her daughter who was dropping something onto wax paper. "Well? Are you coming to Mass or not?"

"Can't right now, Mom. I'll go to the late morning service," she muttered, concentrating on her task.

Declan wandered over to Marguerite to take a peek at what she was doing. He hadn't seen the metal rack sitting on top of wax paper. Another sheet pan filled with blobs of chocolate sat next to the bowl she worked from, dipping the balls into liquid chocolate, then setting them on the rack to drip dry.

A mix of sweet and spice hit his nostrils, not unlike Marguerite's natural scent, and every muscle in his body tensed. "What are they?"

Marguerite jumped before turning to scowl at him. "Do you mind?"

"I try not to," he said on a shit-eating grin he knew she wouldn't mistake.

After a double-take, she let her shoulders drop before turning back to her project. "Mayan truffles, or at least, my take on them. I added shaved espresso beans for an extra kick."

He surveyed the truffles on the rack and noted some were shinier than others. "Can I try one?"

She tipped her chin in the area of the most shiny. "Those appear dry. Let me know what you think." She continued on with her task without missing a beat.

At first all he tasted was chocolate, followed by a burst of coffee. Then the heat of cayenne flowed over his tongue and he smiled. "I wanna buy 'em all."

Her luscious lips tipped into a pleased smile. "They aren't for sale. They're for Camille King." Then she faced her mother who was on her way out the door, and yelled, "I'm meeting Camille after the eleven-thirty Mass at the grange hall for the fundraiser. Are you sure you won't wait and go with me?"

Darla reappeared on clicking heels. "Why didn't you say so in the first place?" The older woman shook her head. "But I already told Camille I can't go to the event because the ladies auxiliary are meeting later. I'll have to take my own car."

While they settled their schedule, Declan snatched up a mug and poured himself some coffee. He took another chocolate off the rack before sitting his butt in a dining chair.

"Let me fix you something to eat, Declan," Darla said after setting down her purse. "Eggs and toast?"

Declan jumped back to his feet and pulled out the chair next to him. "Oh no, please. Don't fuss over me, ma'am. I've been takin' care of myself for a while now."

From behind him he caught Marguerite's sarcasm. "Yeah, a long while," followed by a snicker.

He stood and looked at her. "Really?"

She stopped her chocolate dipping and eyed him. Lips pressed together—to suppress a smile he had no doubt—she finally said, "Sorry. I'll fix you something." A grin bloomed across her face. "No, I don't want your help. You'd only be in the way."

He shook his head. Mockingly, he retorted, "Thank you, *Marguerite*."

Ah, there was nothing better than surprising his woman.

She licked her lips and started pulling eggs from the fridge. "You're welcome, *Declan*."

They stared at each other a moment and he felt his heartbeat speed up.

Then she cleared her throat. "How about you, Mom?"

"I'm good, honey."

As both women shared a look he couldn't decipher, Declan resumed his seat and engaged in some small talk while Marguerite fluttered around the kitchen.

Damn, he'd made the first breakthrough and something peaceful settled in his chest. Hope maybe but...nah. They were playing a game with each other, one he hoped would pay off.

Marguerite brought his plate to the table before resuming her chocolate dipping.

He wanted to say something but the words got stuck. She'd be busy today and for some reason he didn't want to lose sight of her. He rationalized it came from the niggling feeling he'd had the night before.

"What time did you say Mass was?" He forked some egg onto a slice of toast.

Darla said, "Eleven-thirty. Are you coming with us?"

Declan didn't miss the note of excitement in the woman's voice. He glanced back at Marguerite who stared back at him. He caught her eyes and held them as he nodded.

"Yeah, I think I will."

Chapter Ten

THEROUX-LY OUTRAGEOUS CHOCOLATE

"I didn't know you were Catholic," Marguerite said from Declan's passenger seat. She kept finding herself there. Not wanting to dwell on it, she checked the chocolates to make sure they hadn't melted while they were at Mass.

"All my life. Stopped going for a while but I've been finding myself in unfamiliar pews in random churches lately." He drummed his thumbs on the steering wheel, a habit Marguerite had noticed when they were hunting down the drug mule.

What he said made sense. When you do what Declan did—travel for work is the best way to describe it—and dealt with the worst of the worst, finding your way to church often loses priority over apprehending fugitives and murderers.

"I get it. Been away a while myself."

She felt him look her way before returning his eyes to the road. "I have ears."

Yeah, and the tongues were for sure wagging today, especially with the way Declan kept his hands on her, either on the lower back as they walked to their pew, or the way he leaned in and pecked her cheek at the Sign of Peace.

Tingles still lingered on the site where his lips met her flesh. She sucked in a huge breath and let it out slow.

"What's the fundraiser for?"

"Timbisha Township's back-to-school drive. Camille, Julie, and Lauren have a booth and asked if I'd bring some chocolates."

"The ones from this morning?"

"A few, but they wanted a variety of samples." She tapped the cooler between her legs. Man, she hoped they liked them.

"You selling them today?"

"No. Just leaving them out like I do at Blue's. I think Camille's going to use them to entice future catering customers, which will be offered on the menu. At least, that's the plan."

Declan found a parking spot and escorted her into the building, opening the door for her as they entered.

A *Cafe Armstrong* banner stood out as the premiere booth in the center of the room. The Kings knew how to go big and Marguerite felt giddy about being a part of their business. Or at least, a subcontractor for them—*if* the chocolates did well. Giving them out for free to bar patrons was different than presenting them to prospective event planners and the public.

Marguerite's nerviness made her stumble. Declan turned in question but she ignored him and forged on toward the booth.

Will people like my little treats if they knew I made them?

She straightened her shoulders as she marched into their booth like she belonged. "Hey Julie. Here's the samples."

Julie jumped with an "Oh!" She'd been bent over a box retrieving something, her back toward Marguerite. "Hi! I've been waiting to ask what you think about serving them in this?"

Julie held up a three-tiered dish similar to the one she used at the bar. "It's perfect, as I've brought three flavors." While she and Julie loaded up the layers, Marguerite didn't lose sight of Declan. He'd wandered around the booth tasting other samples of soups, sandwiches, and fruit pies, all items Julie served out of her food truck and for their catering business. Marguerite also didn't miss his watchful eyes.

As he bit into a chili sample, he scanned the area as if he were picking out the next booth to visit. Marguerite, however, knew he studied the people instead of the actual booths. The back of her neck tingled and she suddenly looked around.

Davie leaned against a support post, sipping on a lemon icy from the high school cheerleader booth. His eyes lingered on the teens a little longer than he should before finally spotting Marguerite. Her skin crawled at what she saw on his face.

Lust.

Lance interrupted their stare-down and the two trouble-makers melted into the crowd.

"You alright?" Julie snapped the lid onto an empty container.

It was Marguerite's turn to be startled, this time back to reality, and she nodded. "Yeah, just thought I recognized someone."

Julie laughed. "Well, you are in Timbisha Township. Don't we all know everyone?"

"Unfortunately," Margerite muttered as she placed the final chocolate on the dish. "There. All done."

Julie set the three-tiered dish next to the makeshift register area where Lauren commanded the helm and said, "Oh, yummy!" and took one from the bottom near the post making sure not to disturb the display. She'd grabbed one of the spicy Mayan truffles and Marguerite impatiently waited for the woman's reaction.

And waited.

"These are outrageous."

Marguerite hadn't held a great relationship with Lauren over the years, but now that they were sort of related, Lauren's animosity had withered. However, Marguerite hadn't expected this much enthusiasm.

A customer who'd just paid, stopped and spun around to query about Lauren's excitement, and she immediately went into business mode. "Oh, you need to try one," and handed it to the woman.

Marguerite watched as pleasure graced the customer's face and then she agreed with Lauren. "Thoroughly."

To which Declan stepped up and popped one into his mouth. The rascal already knew they were delicious but he played along. "Yup. *Theroux-ly Outrageous*," as he glanced at Marguerite who squinted in confusion.

Camille, who'd been organizing the menu displays, came over to investigate the fuss. "You're a genius word smith. We have to get to work on branding."

"Wha—?"

"I'm on it." Lauren found her iPad and started tapping.

A crowd now surrounded the booth and within a few minutes the three-tiered display was picked clean. Camille leaned closer to Marguerite. "You're a hit, my dear."

"I am? But..." She let her words trail off not wanting to share her lack of confidence simply because she'd never shared those feelings with anyone but her sister.

Declan's hushed voice got her attention. "You better open the other two boxes before a riot starts, Marguerite."

The sound of her name rolling of his soft lips had her blinking. "Yeah, okay." She turned to face him. "You're staying, right?" For some reason she didn't want him to leave. She needed to tell him about Davie and Lance but Camille, Lauren and Julie began barking orders and suddenly she found herself working the biggest booth of the craft show.

At one point, she caught Declan leaning against the same post Davie had used. He lifted his chin indicating he planned on staying until they closed.

———

DECLAN KEPT WATCH OVER MARGUERITE WHILE SHE worked her chocolate magic on the customers. Speaking of which, the prickly feeling from the other night crept up his neck and he searched the crowd for its source. He saw familiar faces from both Mass and Blue's, mostly staff and some regulars. Cheryl worked a small booth in the corner. The busboy, Trey, hung out near the high school cheerleaders' table selling tickets for TTHS's first home game. The two idiots he'd helped Dusty vacate Blue's meandered in from the back entrance and Declan narrowed his eyes on the pair.

Nothing but trouble.

Declan's spidey sense kicked into high gear. He pulled his phone from his pocket and texted Jarod, who immediately called.

"Why do you want to know about those two clowns," the sheriff asked without preamble.

Declan explained about the other night. "I've got that feeling."

Silence reigned on the other end for a few seconds. "Damn it. I *hate* that feeling. I'll see what I can find out about them. Did Boots say how long they've been in town?"

"I didn't ask. Why? I thought there were local boys."

"They are, but they also pick up shifts at the mines." Jarod sighed long and loud as if he was irritated about the project. "Alright, let me get back to you."

"Thanks."

"How's the booth going? Lauren hasn't checked in for a while."

"Busy. Marguerite delivered on her promise for chocolates and there's been a crowd ever since.

"Good. Mom will ask her to join them in the catering business. Hopefully, Boots will have to find a new bartender."

Declan stared at the phone after Jarod's abrupt disconnect and shook his head before stuffing it back into his pocket. *Why the hell does he care so much whether she works at the bar or not?* Declan rubbed the back of his neck. God, he needed to tamp down his jealousy.

As the crowds began to dwindle, Declan moved closer to the booth. Marguerite and Camille were in deep conversation and he didn't want to disturb a possible job offer.

"You're still here?" Lauren had begun to clean up by removing empty baking trays from the counter.

"Looks like. You guys about finished?"

"We've sold out so we're done. Marguerite's treats are a big hit. Camille booked three weddings, a birthday party for a senior citizen, and a couple of mothers want to hire us for graduations in the spring."

Declan nodded, happy for their success. "Think she'll hop on board?" He lifted his chin in Marguerite's direction.

"Camille's making an offer too good to turn down. We *want* her on board. She's a natural." A teasing glimmer touched her eyes and Declan braced himself. "Does she know how you feel about her?"

"Nothing gets by that woman, Lauren."

"True, but you still need to talk to her. I've known her

forever—didn't like her for most of it—but she's different now. Hides her fragility behind false bravado. Now that she's part of the family we're all looking out for her. Understand?"

Declan chuckled. "Championing her, too, huh? Don't worry about it, Lauren. The last thing I want to do is hurt her again."

Yeah, he'd hurt her when he'd left Salt Lake City without a backward glance but, damn it, he'd needed to finish what they'd started. And he did—the cartel was gone and now he had to move on with his life. He didn't want to do it alone. He wanted to do it with *her*.

Then he tilted his head to the side. "Have *you* told Marguerite how you feel about her?"

Lauren gave a half grin and turned to finish what she was doing.

He clocked Davie and Lance following a couple of cheerleaders out through the main doors. They purposefully blended with the crowd and the prickles goosed him again.

"What is it?" Lauren's forehead crinkled with concern.

"Your husband workin' nearby? I called him earlier but he hasn't gotten back to me yet."

She pulled her cell phone from her pocket and asked—all business, "Who's he looking for?"

Declan gave her the details and Lauren wasted no time relaying the message to the sheriff. "He says he's on it." She nodded once and stuffed her phone back in its place.

Marguerite walked up behind Lauren. "Everything okay?"

"All good here." Lauren met Declan's eyes before turning to Marguerite. "I'll have a mock-up for your brand in a couple of days."

Marguerite shook her head. "Oh, you don't have to do that. You're busy with Jarod and the kids."

Lauren touched her shoulder. "It's on me, gives me something to do when Jarod's busy. I'm happy do to it. See ya later, Declan." Lauren patted Marguerite on the shoulder one last time as she turned to help Julie and Camille clean up.

"Do they need help or are you free to go?"

Marguerite didn't answer, instead smiled at someone behind Declan.

Turned out to be two someones. Jason and James, the latter saying, "We've got it handled. Thanks for hanging around."

"You got it, sir."

"None of that, now." The older King passed by to hug his wife. Jason had given Declan a nod of acknowledgment before making a beeline for Julie.

Declan looked away and collided glances with Marguerite who wore a melancholy look her face as she watched the couple embrace.

Does she have feelings for Jason? Declan cringed at the thought before clearing his throat. "You've got some time before your shift at Blue's. Wanna grab a bite?"

He liked the surprised look in her eyes before she schooled her features. "Sure. Molly's?"

"Sounds great." He placed his hand on the small of her back and let her warmth seep into his palm, as he guided her to his pickup. He opened her door, again surprising her—by the look on her face—and hurried around the front of the truck. He pushed the button and turned on the A/C. Then he pulled out of the parking lot and hit the main road to Molly's Diner.

"What'd Camille have to say?" When she didn't answer right away he glanced at her to find a smile on her lips. "Marguerite?"

"Oh, yeah, she wants me to come on board with their catering business."

"What'd you say?"

She faced him. "I told her I'd think about it."

He raised his eyebrows. "Why? Sounds like a great opportunity." He alternated between watching her expression and the road.

"Oh, it is but I started chocolatier-ing on a whim, as a distraction from...everything." She shook her head as if to dismiss something. The past, he guessed. "Anyway, I'm not sure I want to turn it into a j-o-b if you know what I mean."

He stopped at a red light. "Because people who do what they love for a living end up hating it?"

"Something like that, yeah. Plus, I like working for Dusty. I like the bar."

Declan thought about it. "How often do they cater?"

She shook her head. "I'm honestly not sure. It's something to consider, but just making the chocolate for today stressed me out."

"Too much work?"

"No, it wasn't that." She didn't elaborate and Declan considered what she'd said. Knowing what he did about her, and how the town had treated her all of her life, he had an inkling of the problem.

"Marguerite, you're very talented. Does it have anything to do with proving yourself?"

She glared at him. "I don't have to prove a damn thing, McKinley."

Uh oh. Open mouth, insert foot...dumbass.

He had to fix this and fast. "That's not what I meant, honey."

"Don't call me that."

Shit.

He cut the engine once he'd found a spot at Molly's and looked at her. Her chest rose and fell on angry breaths and Declan had to regain control of the situation before he took too many steps backward. He reached for the hand closest to him, the one resting on her thigh, and held on in case she decided to rip it from his grasp.

He felt her flex and his grip tightened. "I'm sorry, Marguerite. Truly."

He held his breath and counted to ten...

Eleven... Twelve... Thirt—

"Okay, you're forgiven," she said on a huff of breath. She turned her face to him and he flinched at the anguish living there. "I may have overreacted."

A clump of hair had slipped from her clip and he released her hand to smooth it behind her ear. "So...we're good? Cuz I'm starvin'." He added his best grin in hope she'd smile back.

His hope wasn't wasted when her lips turned up.

"Yeah, we're good, Declan. Let's eat before we say too much to each other and start another misunderstanding."

———

MARGUERITE STARED AT THE ALL-TO-FAMILIAR MENU to let her brain—and heart—rest a moment while Declan decided what to eat. Something about him had changed, something *momentous* but she was too afraid to guess what it might be, or how it would affect her heart.

"What can I get you?"

Marguerite closed her menu. "Hey Carmen. Turkey croissant sandwich and a diet Pepsi, please."

"Barbecue burger with an iced tea, please." Declan handed

the waitress their menus. After Carmen—whose belly showed off a baby bump—walked away, Declan folded his hands on the table. "Know her long?"

She stifled a chuckle. "Timbisha is a small township. Everyone has known everybody all their lives, Declan."

"Fair enough."

"What about you? Where'd you grow up?"

He drummed his thumbs on the table. "Rural Texas but moved to Austin when the University offered me a scholarship."

Marguerite narrowed her eyes. "Academic or athletic?"

She had to give him credit. His face didn't change expression until she raised her eyebrows in expectation. Then he half smirked, showing off one of his dimples.

"I played wide receiver two years for the Longhorns." His grin faded and his thumbs drummed the table again.

Marguerite tilted her head. "What happened? Injury or incident?" Something definitely kept him from finishing out with the football team."

"Broken collarbone on a personal foul which set me back a season. By the time I healed up I'd been replaced. It ended up being a blessing because my grades had slipped anyway. Gave me a chance to bring 'em up and get my criminal justice degree, which led me to the marshals service."

"I know you're leaving out a huge chunk but I'm glad you told me."

"Why?"

"Because now you can *help me* help Dusty coach the boys. I have no idea what I'm doing."

Declan leaned his head back and laughed, the kind to make her smile along with him and give her goosebumps at the same time.

She liked making him laugh. It was so much better than having him criticize her for... well, she didn't want to ruin her good humor at the moment.

Over his head she noticed Cheryl, the waitress from Blue's, sitting at the counter with her boyfriend. They looked like they were having a quiet argument. Either that, or it was just Cheryl's resting bitch face.

"Here you go," Carmen said as she placed their plates on the table, distracting Marguerite from Cheryl. "Can I get you anything else?"

Declan grabbed the ketchup already on the table. "No thank you, Carmen."

"Enjoy your meal."

Marguerite took a bite and hummed. "So good."

"The food here is excellent. I'm glad it's still here."

Marguerite wiped her mouth. "Where would it go?"

Declan shrugged and took a bite. She waited, entertained by the bliss on his face as he chewed. "Never know when a business will go belly up."

"True, but not this place. See the newly built hotel in the back?"

"Yeah."

"James and Josh King."

"Figures." Declan slid a fry through some ketchup. "They own the whole damn town, don't they?"

Marguerite knew he didn't mean it in a bad way but she felt the need to defend the family anyway. "Without them I think this town would've floundered. James has lots of connections and with the combination of agriculture and mining, Timbisha Township has a lot to offer. But when a town grows so does the criminal element, which is a shame."

Her mind wondered to the bodies and the reason Declan had come to town in the first place.

"But you're not going to get involved in it again."

She didn't appreciate his commanding tone. Though she had no intention of getting involved, she resented his feelings on the subject.

"Look. I know I screwed up, and I swear I learned my lesson well. I no longer have any interest in being in the field of law enforcement." She took a bite of her croissant.

"But...?"

"But nothing. It's a period. I'm done. My problem, and yes I admit I have one, is my curiosity gets the better of me, which is something I'm working on."

Declan leaned back. "You've been investigating on the sly, haven't you."

It wasn't a question but a verification of his suspicions. She lifted the last bite to her mouth. "Maybe." Then she popped it in and looked out the plateglass windows. The bright Nevada sky and the hint of fall colors never ceased to amaze her.

"Damn it, Marguerite," he mumbled before taking a sip of iced tea. "What have you discovered?"

She leaned back. He wasn't going to like what she had to say. She licked her lips.

"After broadening my search to the I-80 corridor a pattern emerged."

"Shiiiiit."

"Exactly my reaction but I have no proof of anything, only a simplified pattern and I'm not willing to share anything yet so don't say anything to anyone."

"You know Lightfoot's in town, right?"

She choked on her diet Pepsi. "I knew he was on his way. When'd he show up?"

"Right after I did."

"They probably already know then." She shrugged, relieved she didn't have to get involved.

Until Declan speared her with his glare. "You know they don't or they'd already have a task force forming instead of a couple of federal cyber geeks."

God, she hated it when he pointed out facts. "Well, I don't know anything for sure either. I'm just going off what I hear on the news and we all know the media doesn't know their ass from a hole in the ground."

Unless the sheriff's office had a leak, but she hadn't been watching the news lately and didn't know what information was out there for the public to digest. She polished off the rest of her fries and placed her used napkin on the plate. When she reached for her purse he cleared his throat.

"What?"

"I've got it."

"You sure?"

He nodded. "Yup. I like taking you out to eat."

"You think this is a date?"

"The first of more to come."

Marguerite felt a blush coming and covered it by taking a sip. "Fine but I warn you, I can be picky."

"Don't I know it."

Chapter Eleven

THE BRAWL

As soon as Marguerite went upstairs to change for her bartending shift, Declan called Jarod. When he answered, Declan got to the point. "She's been diggin'."

A split second of silence came and went. "She find anything?"

Declan sighed. "Yeah but she isn't willing to say what because she doesn't have any proof. Says she found a pattern along Interstate 80."

"I'll let the team know and maybe one of those idiots will see the same thing she's looking at."

The line went dead.

Typical Jarod.

"Who're you talking to?"

Declan swung around to find Marguerite standing on the bottom tread, wearing painted-on sparkle jeans, Doc Martins, and a black see-though blouse over a fancy, white bra. She had her hip cocked and rested a hand there.

His mouth went dry at her sexy, but accusatory-at-the-same-time pose. He wanted to tell her to go change. He didn't want other men seeing her like this—didn't want *Dusty* seeing her like this—but instead he growled, "None of your business."

He regretted it the moment the words left his mouth because her cocky smile faded into a guarded mask. He waited for her to explode but instead her warm demeanor changed to icy nonchalance.

"See ya later, McKinley."

She was out the door a second later, hips sashaying to her little red convertible.

Damn it.

Declan launched himself out the door and down the three steps, only to reach her as she fired up the engine. "Marguerite, wait a second."

Sunglasses covered her eyes but he knew hurt lived behind them.

She put the car in reverse. "Sorry, I'm going to be late."

He watched helplessly as she backed out of the driveway before speeding down the street.

Now what do I do?

He hadn't meant to snap at her, and truly his annoyance was more at himself than her. He recognized jealousy when he felt it and he hated it, hated the loss of control, especially with his mouth.

God, getta grip, man.

He checked his watch. 4:30...he'd go to The Estate, check in with James before heading to Blue's to try to patch things up with her. He had a plan, damn it, and he knew better than to lose his cool.

He locked up the house before making the trek.

Once on the road, he rolled down the window to soak up the warm Nevada sunshine, letting the dry climate and blue sky clear his head. Yeah, he was out of practice when it came to women but he'd never had trouble getting one to cooperate with him.

Except for Marguerite.

Seeing her hurt expression—again—pissed him off. Geez, she was so tough, and brave, and brazen with everyone, even him. At least, she used to be.

She's a different woman now, stupid. Physical trauma along with personal loss and grief tend to change a person.

As The Estate came into view, he knew he had to keep this visit short, and avoid having a meal with the family. Camille would invite him, he had no doubt. Maybe he'd ask for a to-go box for himself and Marguerite to try to smooth her rough edges.

He immediately dismissed the idea. The bar kept her busy with barely time for a break. No, he'd have to think of some other way to, not only apologize, but show her how much he regretted his behavior.

As the thought left his head, he'd stopped his pickup next to Jarod's cruiser. Maybe they'd had a break in the case. Nothing like a murder investigation to give him new focus.

Camille opened the side door the family used as entry and greeted Declan. "Well, this is a surprise. They're in James's study."

"Thank you, ma'am."

Camille rolled her eyes and Declan corrected himself. "Camille."

"That's better."

He followed her into the kitchen where he found Julie and a corral of toddlers. "Hey, Declan. You staying?"

His stomach perked up at the scent of chili, regretting his

earlier plan to skip the meal. "Depends on what's going on in the other room."

"I'll set a bowl out for you," Jason's wife said, before turning back to her work.

Camille joined her. "They know you're here, just head on back."

"Ladies," Declan said by way of a thank you and followed the sound of male voices.

"Dad, the pattern crosses state lines."

Declan found not only Jarod with James, but Roland leaning against the wall with a foul look on his face. "This doesn't look good."

They turned to face him and Roland muttered, "Thank, God."

He stared at them a moment and sighed. "Who am I looking for?"

James held up his hands. "Agent Lightfoot needs more help on his task force."

"For what?"

Declan shared a look with Roland, who shrugged. "If Marguerite's found something she needs to be on the team."

Declan stared at the agent. "She's still traumatized. What she's given you is enough."

"So you want to wait for another body to show up when Marguerite could have this thing figured out in a couple of days?"

"What the hell does Marguerite have to do with finding a serial killer? I think we all know what happened the last time we brought her into the field. There's no way in hell you're even asking her to do it, Roland."

"Thank you." Jarod let his hand fall to his side in relief. "I appreciate her cyber skills but she's not ready to go after this kind of a predator."

"I'm not saying she needs to be in the field again, I'm just saying she should work the cyber side of the damn task force." Roland sighed in disgust. "The men I brought are fresh out of Quantico, and none have Marguerite's talent for sniffing out a pattern. She's an asset."

"No." Declan and Jarod said in unison. They nodded at each other.

A heartbeat of silence ticked by. Then Declan admitted, "Look, let's agree she's tenacious. The fact she was peckin' around her keyboard, sticking her nose where it doesn't belong and found something is one thing. Bringing her on in an official capacity would only encourage her to keep goin' and we all know that scenario only leads to danger for her and those around her." Declan purposely looked at Dane's picture sitting on James's desk.

"That wasn't her fault." Roland stepped forward to look Declan in the eye, empathy written there which Declan didn't appreciate in the least. "You know it, McKinley. You have to stop blaming her."

"I've never blamed her." Declan argued. "It was *my* fault. I let her walk off alone. One of us should've gone with her. We relaxed. I won't risk her again." He turned away from Roland, dismissing him. "James, I'm ready to discuss what you'd like me to do for you on The Estate."

Which was true. He'd been looking up feed costs and found James had been overpaying.

Thankfully, Jarod turned to Roland. "Come with me, Agent Lightfoot. I think this meeting's over for us."

MARGUERITE WIPED THE COUNTER AFTER A customer paid. There weren't many patrons but the game hadn't started yet. Finished with the counter she checked the guide to make sure all the TVs showed the game, or the alternate affiliate games.

"You okay, Girl?"

"Why wouldn't I be?"

"Cuz ya been frowning and quiet since you got here. I think you hurt old Fred's feelings."

Marguerite looked at the long time barfly and sighed. "I'll give him one on the house."

"That's not what I meant. Hey." He touched her shoulder encouraging her to look at him. When she met his eyes it was all she could do not to burst into tears. She didn't know why. McKinley's behavior wasn't unexpected, or unusual. She knew where she stood with him, and everyone else, so why the way he spoke bothered her, she didn't understand.

"Do I need to smack him around some?"

The thought of Dusty going a few rounds with Declan made her chuckle. "No. I'm fine, now. Thank you."

"You're welcome. But I'm serious. I know what it's like to have your heart stomped on—"

"Stop." She held up her hand, palm up. "My heart is just fine. I promise."

"Don't make promises you can't keep." He rubbed her shoulder before heading back into the kitchen.

She rolled the ache out of it before turning around to find Declan glaring at her from the opposite end of the bar.

God, what now?

Instead of waiting on him, she asked Cheryl to do it.

Serves him right.

As she refilled one of the mixer bottles, Cheryl tapped her

on the shoulder, hitting the sore spot. "He wants you and only you. His words, not mine."

"Thanks for trying." Marguerite didn't bother hiding the fact she was pissed at him. He wanted to be snappy? Fine, she'd show him exactly how unpleasant she could be.

"What do you want?"

The mean expression disappeared from his face and his shoulders slumped. "To apologize. I didn't mean to shut you out."

Marguerite studied him for a moment, thinking she'd never heard him apologize like this before. "I accept. Now, what will you have?" She ignored his slow grin, knew what was on the end of his tongue and she shook her head at his expression. "To drink, smart-ass. Geez."

He chuckled. "I'll take a beer but I brought you dinner. Julie insisted." He placed a paper sack on the counter.

"Julie?" She quickly opened the bag and smiled. "Her chili? Fantastic!"

"I wasn't sure if you'd have time to eat it."

"Puh-lease, I'll make time." She looked at him to confirm how good the stuff was and his smile confirmed he'd tried it.

"Best chili this side of Texas."

As she took a spoonful, the doors opened to a few men, all truckers she'd seen before, and she raised her hand. "I'll be right with you."

She noticed Declan searching the men with his eyes. "You blabbed to Jarod what I told you, right?"

"Yup."

She shook her head while placing the lid back on her chili. "And?"

He turned to her. "He relayed your information to Agent Lightfoot and his team confirmed what you found. He," and she didn't miss the angry tension in his voice, "wants you on his task force." Declan's brown eyes bored into hers. "I don't like it, Marguerite. I know I don't have any right, but I'm beggin' you not to join up."

She crossed her arms around herself. "I told you already I didn't want any part of it. But..." She closed her eyes.

"But what?" His menacing voice was back.

She snapped her eyes to his. "Sometimes I can't help myself. What if someone else gets hurt?"

"What if YOU get hurt?" He stood up and pushed his hands through his hair. She'd never seen him this rattled. "This is a different kind of animal, Marguerite."

She straightened and loosened her arms. "I know." And she did. Her plans hadn't changed. Caped crusaders fighting criminals wasn't her game anymore.

"I need to get back to work now. Are you staying or are you going to brood all night?"

He squinted at her. "Both."

"Fine."

"Fine," he said back, defiantly.

"*Fine*," she growled and spun around to finish refilling the mixer bottles before taking more orders. The bar began to hum with patrons and football fans. Trey didn't work Sundays as he had school the next day so it was just Cheryl and Marguerite working the floor, with Dusty filling in when he could. The dayshift waitress was only part-time.

As her shift wore on, Declan remained planted at his barstool taking everything in. She wondered if he'd end up following her home. It wasn't an unpleasant thought, and honestly she liked having someone watching over her, even though she was loathe to admit it, even to herself.

When Lance and Davie came in, she knew the evening

wouldn't end on a good note. It never did when those two showed up. They weren't alone, either. They had an entourage of miners with them, most she recognized but there were a couple she'd never seen before. She caught Declan's eye as he sent a text out, she assumed to Jarod. If he hadn't called then Dusty would, but he was busy with the eight-top table near the big screen on the other end of the bar.

A few people started a game of shuffleboard during half-time, but when the second half started, Lance and Davie took over with a couple of the guys they'd walked in with.

In Cheryl's section.

"Don't worry," Dusty murmured in her ear. "I moved Cheryl to the big screen side, and McKinley said he called it in. Jarod's on his way."

Marguerite nodded and moved back behind the bar. Declan never took his eyes off the group. It's a good thing too, because as Jarod walked in, the fight broke out over the shuffleboard, of all the stupid things.

Cheryl screamed. The eight-top emptied to mix into the melee and somewhere between the broken glasses and the overturned tables, Cheryl disappeared.

———

"HER CAR'S STILL PARKED OUT BACK," DUSTY SAID.

"I checked Cheryl's locker and it hasn't been opened. Her things are still here." Marguerite returned from the hallway which led to the restrooms and Dusty's office.

Declan had a hard time containing his anger. Once again, Marguerite was in the middle of something she shouldn't be, and he'd been right there the whole time, and hadn't seen it coming.

"Well, I've got Lance in the cruiser, and my deputies have several more waiting to be booked. Where the hell did Cheryl go? There's no sign of Davie. Think she's with him?" Jarod said.

"Security footage?" Declan asked Dusty.

"I checked. It stopped working in the second quarter of the game. Don't know why."

Jarod cursed foully, expressing pretty much what was on the tip of Declan's tongue.

"I'll call her." Marguerite whipped out her cell phone. "Her phone should be in her apron. God knows I've yelled at her enough times to put the damn thing away," she said as she dialed the phone.

All their heads turned as Cardi B's obnoxious voice walked through the front doors in Agent Lightfoot's hands. "This our missing person's phone?"

"Yeah, where was it?" Jarod asked.

"Right out front."

"Damn." Marguerite put her hands to her cheeks.

Declan went to her. "It's not your fault, we'll find her."

"I know, but how? If she's not with Davie, we don't know where to look!" Her eyes shone bright with fear and frustration and he wanted to punch something.

Jarod answered a call on his shoulder mic, then addressed Declan. "We need to take care of business, get the suspects booked. I'll let you know if they say anything pertinent. I doubt they will, though." He muttered the last before taking his leave.

Marguerite looked at Agent Lightfoot. "Aren't you going with him?"

Declan wasn't surprised at her aggressive tone.

"No. Thought I'd take a look around, maybe look at the security footage. That okay with you, Mr. Boots?"

Dusty raised his eyebrows, glanced at Marguerite as if asking if it was okay, but then said, "Knock yourself out, Agent. But as I just told everyone, it stopped working earlier."

Roland shrugged and Declan waited for the man to disappear down the hall before he sat Marguerite on a barstool in front of himself and Dusty. "All right, we were all here. Hell, it feels like even I could recognize the regulars. I wanna know if either of you *didn't* recognize someone."

Marguerite nodded while Dusty concentrated on the floor, hands on his hips. When he looked up, frustration lived in his expression. "Hell, it got so busy, and once Beavis and Butthead showed up, all my attention was on them." He glanced at Marguerite. "Did Cheryl stay in your line of site?"

"Dusty, I was busy at the bar, you know how it is when the orders are flying. Shit, let me think." She tapped her fingers on the bar, her eyeballs rolling around and Declan understood she was playing the evening out in her mind. "Okay, after you took over with Dumb and Dumber, Cheryl was irritated because she thought she'd lose her tips. I told her to shut it and get to work, and then I brought Tyler another drink, both Fred and Frank flirted with me, then with a couple of women at that table..." she pointed to it... "Cheryl put in at least four orders before the fight broke out."

Her eyes welled before she put her hands to her face again, and Declan pulled her into his chest, thankful she didn't resist. "Don't. I didn't see much more than that myself."

He released her only so far as to look into her face but almost growled when Dusty reached over to rub one of her shoulders. Fortunately, Declan kept his green monster in check, especially after Dusty admitted, "You noticed way more than I did, Girl. You've got good recall."

Declan chuckled because he'd thought the same thing, however Marguerite misunderstood his humor.

"Don't patronize me." Then she punched him when he laughed harder. "It's not funny, damn it."

"No, ma'am, it's not."

"Don't call me that." It came out more pitiful than demanding.

Agent Lightfoot reappeared from Dusty's office. "You're right, not much to see—"

The door opened, revealing a disgruntled Cheryl. "Anyone find an iPhone with a pink cover? Mine fell out of my apron."

"Where the hell have you been?" Dusty yelled at the same time he jumped the bar and pulled Cheryl into a hug.

Her eyes widened over his shoulder and she looked at everyone in the room like Dusty was crazy.

"Frank left his wallet on the bar. I had to walk a mile to catch up with him. Geez, that old fart moves fast."

"His wife didn't pick him up?"

Cheryl grinned when Dusty released her. "They had a fight and she told him he had to walk his drunk ass home tonight."

Declan's adrenaline-rush crashed and burned. He shared a look with Marguerite right before her ire at him laser-focused onto Cheryl.

"Didn't you see the flashing lights?"

"Well, yeah," Cheryl answered with a touch of aggression, "but I thought they were for the fight Davie and Lance caused. Sheesh. What's crawled up your butt?"

Declan pinched his lips closed to prevent another laugh when the young woman huffed down the hallway to where he presumed she'd retrieve her things, but not before she snatched her phone off the bar.

Marguerite mumbled under her breath and Boots looked at the ceiling as if in conversation with a higher power.

"This has been interesting." Roland leaned on the bar next to Declan. "You heading out?"

Declan sighed. "As soon as they do." He hadn't taken his eyes off Marguerite.

"Gotcha. Be seeing you, McKinley."

As Roland left the building, Boots looked at Marguerite. "Come on, Girl. I got a babysitter I need to relieve, and you and Declan need to get on home."

"I can't believe that idiot woman left on foot."

Declan recognized the look on her face, the one where her sharp mind wouldn't leave well enough alone.

"Doesn't matter now, Marguerite. Let's get home before your mom starts to worry. I'm sure news has made the rounds by now."

Her eyes bulged as she fumbled for her phone. "Crap. Mom's texted me a dozen times. You're right. Let's go."

Pleased she'd forgotten about their earlier spat, he placed his hand on her lower back and escorted her to her car. She didn't say much as she typed out a message for Darla, no doubt letting her know she was all right and that they were on their way home.

She hit her fob and Declan opened the door for her. As she sank into the driver's seat, he couldn't help repeat, "I'm sorry about today, about snappin' at ya. I'm just worried. After tonight I think you understand why, right?"

She nodded once before pushing the ignition switch, firing up her engine. "You're forgiven."

Chapter Twelve

ANOTHER BODY

Marguerite blinked a few times collecting her thoughts after accepting Declan's apology. As usual, his headlights kept a safe watch over her as she drove home. Having a protector felt sort of... nice.

Once home, she waited for Declan to catch up to the front porch before going inside and trudging up the stairs to their rooms. He put his hand on his doorknob and stopped. "What are your plans tomorrow?"

"I honestly don't know." Falling into bed face first sounded so good right now. "I don't plan on waking up until noon."

A dimple appeared in one of his cheeks. "Got it. Rest well, Marguerite."

"You too, Declan." She pushed her door open, closed it and did exactly what her body wanted to do.

Too tired to change into pajamas, she wriggled out of her tight jeans, blouse and bra, snuggled into the covers and closed her eyes. Apparently, she'd been too tired to dream because daylight filled her bedroom in what felt like minutes. A glance at the clock read 11:23 am.

Marguerite rolled over and stretched like a cat. She listened for the tell-tell signs of human inhabitants in the house and heard nothing. Sighing in happiness that she wouldn't have to speak to anyone first thing after waking up, she donned a robe and headed to the bathroom.

After making sure she'd used up all the hot water in a luxurious shower, she took her time drying her hair, applied some eyeliner and mascara, put the robe back on and returned to her bedroom to get dressed.

Declan's bedroom door stood open and she heard the clickety-clack of computer keys.

Damn. She'd hoped to have at least a couple of hours to herself. While in the shower her thoughts turned to chocolate and she wanted to mess around in the kitchen without distractions.

Declan was definitely a distraction.

Dang it! Now I'm thinking about him.

What was he working on in his bedroom?

The fact he *was* in a bedroom with no desk meant he was sitting on the bed using his lap.

Now her brain thought of him *on* a bed. Was he in boxers, shirtless, or jeans and shirtless like last time, or was he in a t-shirt and sweats... nothing at all?

Stop it! Do not go there.

Of course he's dressed, the door's open.

As she stood there running her mind over different scenarios of Declan's state of attire, Declan called out, "Wanna get some lunch?" which startled her so hard back into reality a squeak issued from her throat.

There he stood in a nanosecond. "What's wrong?"

"Nothing," she said too quickly as his eyes roamed over her body and she recognized the heat.

Thinking she'd been alone she hadn't tied the robe securely and he was getting an eyeful of cleavage.

His gravelly voice saying her name was the only warning she got before he pressed her up against the wall and ravaged her mouth.

It took her brain a moment to realize the situation.

First shock, then outrage, then...

Oh-my-God-the-man-can-kiss.

He tasted so good, warm and masculine. He must've brushed his teeth after a cup of coffee because both lingered on his tongue but not in a bad way.

She hummed a little and he pressed himself against her body as she smoothed her arms around him to hold on, pressed him a little closer, enjoying the feel of muscles under her hands.

When he came up for air he didn't go far. "I want you."

Yeah, baby, I can tell... but one of them had to be reasonable. She'd never had sex in her mother's house and she never would. Smiling, she pushed him back. "We can't."

He rested his forehead against hers. "I know."

The moment had passed and now she just felt humor. "I take it you want to have sex today." She used her most teasing voice, the one she used to lighten a mood when a suitor wanted too much. "I'm sorry, but I think I have other plans."

Instead of getting mad, or calling her a prick tease, Declan laughed.

A hearty full-of-humor laugh and not at all at her expense.

She pushed him completely away so she could get past him. "Let me get dressed and I'll meet you downstairs."

She didn't wait for his answer but closed her bedroom door in his face and found some comfortable jeans and a light knit top. Once appropriately clothed, she grabbed a hair clip and twisted her hair into a messy bun while descending the stairs. She found Declan in the kitchen holding a note.

"Darla says she's at The Estate. Camille needs to see you and James wants a meeting with me, too, when you finally get up. Apparently, they knew you'd be a lazy slug today."

He was teasing, of course, but there was something underneath. "What is it?"

She'd seen his face go blank before. A total tell he wasn't aware he had, probably because no one had ever called him on it. She raised an eyebrow and motioned with her hand for him to spill it.

"Jarod just texted. They found another body last night."

"Where?"

"Two miles from Blue's."

"Oh no. Is that what you were working on upstairs?"

He chuckled. "No, I was looking up beef prices. Seein' if I could find a better deal than James for his livestock."

She leaned a hip against the counter. "I know it was just a handshake but you really plan to stay, don't you. In Timbisha Township. You're not going to leave after they solve the case?"

"Depends."

"On what?"

"You."

Declan reached for her again, incapable of stopping himself. He'd tasted her once and now he never wanted to stop.

Upstairs he'd expected a slap or a knee to the balls, which would be Marguerite's style. Instead, he'd found something he'd never felt before—a little piece of Heaven. Sure, he'd had no complaints from women over his adult life, but this woman…

Swear to God, Marguerite was made for him.

When their lips touched she reciprocated his kiss, this time tender, sweet, and his knees wanted to buckle.

"If you think you can stop kissing me for a while, maybe we can head out to hear the news in person?"

God he loved her teasing.

He couldn't wait to tease her back.

Oh, there would definitely be teasing, but even more than that—satisfaction. "You're no fun."

"I'm totally fun!" She leaned away as if she'd been insulted.

A laugh escaped him. Her lips were plump from his kiss and he smoothed a thumb over her bottom lip. "Of course you are, honey." He kissed her once again, quickly to stop her from complaining about the endearment. "Grab what you need. I'll drive."

"Be right back." His eyes dropped to her ass as she climbed the stairs and he took in a breath.

Damn.

Shaking his head like a cartoon dog to clear his mind, he touched his pockets to make sure he had everything, grabbed his folder because, yes, he still liked paper, and opened the front door as Marguerite descended.

"Ready." She sailed outside, and didn't stop until she reached his pickup parked at the curb. When he hit the fob, she opened the door and climbed in before he could reach the truck.

Once they were out of Timbisha Township, she rolled down the window. "I love fall. The weather is usually perfect, the air isn't a blast furnace anymore, and the leaves are so vibrant. You can really feel it coming on today."

"Change is good." He drummed his thumbs to the beat of the song playing, something she'd picked which, to his surprise, wasn't obnoxious. He relaxed a bit and his mind wandered from Marguerite to the bodies. He didn't tell her it'd been Fred's wife who'd discovered the victim while walking their dog, an excuse she'd used to wait for Fred himself to walk home from the bar. At least that's what she'd told the deputy who'd been first on the scene.

When they turned into the King's long driveway Jarod's cruiser appeared in the rearview mirror, and the unmistakable silhouette of Roland Lightfoot sat in the passenger seat.

Declan's blood began to boil.

The thuds of their four car doors had James opening the side door. He threw his thumb over this shoulder. "The study, gentlemen. Camille's ready for you in the dining room, Marguerite."

Declan glanced back at Roland and met his stony eyes before they switched to Marguerite's who nodded at the agent, resigned.

Son of a bitch.

"Hey, guys," Julie said as they passed through the kitchen. She pulled out a chair. "Got your spot right here, Marguerite. Lauren will be down in a minute and Camille had to take another call. We just booked a wedding and they're asking for those Mayan chocolates. We need to go over the details, too. Are you ready?"

"No, she's needed in the study," said Agent Lightfoot, which surprised the hell out of everyone.

"Sorry Julie. Can it wait until after?" Marguerite's voice was dull as she indicated the men in front of her.

Declan felt her unhappy resolve, and not only because he was touching her as he guided her through the house.

It reached his soul.

The last time he lost his control came to mind. He flexed his hand and Marguerite leaned into him before they crossed the threshold into James's study.

Declan didn't like the way Lightfoot had taken over. By the way Jarod's shoulders stiffened, he knew the sheriff didn't either. Declan's mood continued to sour.

James sat behind his desk. "What's going on?" He turned puzzled eyes to Declan and then stood to reach out a hand. "Agent Lightfoot. Back so soon?"

"Hello, Mr. King. Sorry to barge in but I have some things I need to discuss with your employee, and since Jarod said everyone would be convening here, I asked if I could tag along."

"What's going on, Roland?" Declan's voice held no emotion—because he needed to keep his temper in check.

Lightfoot met Declan's eyes. "I need you two back on the task force, ASAP."

Foul words inappropriate for any gathering flew through Declan's mind. He flexed his fist, itching to punch something.

"No."

Declan turned to Marguerite—who glared at Lightfoot—and he sighed with relief.

"Miss Theroux, I don't think you understand. I'm not asking."

Marguerite shook her head. "No, you don't understand. I'm not cut out for whatever you need me to do. I've moved on. You have your pattern. Run with it. You don't need me." She folded her arms over her chest and cocked a hip, and Declan grinned.

"You don't need me either, Roland. Hell, you're the one who insisted I retire. I'm done." He put his arm around

Marguerite's waist and she didn't pull away. In fact, she kept her glare squarely on Lightfoot. They were a united front and Declan's chest swelled with emotion he couldn't afford to show.

Finally, he turned to James. "Here," he said as he handed him the folder outlining different auction houses and beef companies, prices, and reliability of transport. "I also found information on selling ranch to table."

"Thank you." James took the folder never taking his eyes off Agent Lightfoot—or Jarod.

Silence reigned for a moment. Then Roland finally relented, and broke the stalemate. "Marguerite. You know we have to find this guy before another woman is killed. You have to join up."

Oh, hell no. "It's not Marguerite's fault these women are dying," Declan growled through clenched teeth, but then sucked in a shuddering breath.

Do not lose control.

"I know." She quickly swiped a hand under her eye and Declan shook his head.

"This is bullshit." He took her by the shoulders. "Honey, you don't hafta do this."

A quiet sniffle escaped her lips that only he could hear. She looked at him with the saddest eyes he'd ever seen. "Yeah, I do. Uncle Dane would want me to do whatever I can to save these women. I'm sorry, Declan. I have to break my promise."

DECLAN'S GRIP TIGHTENED AND MARGUERITE JERKED out of his hold. "Stop it. You know as well as I do we have to help. Who else is gonna track down this monster, huh? I mean, he's killing in my friggin' backyard, Declan. I've been fooling myself."

Jarod spoke before Declan could. "As much as I've wanted you back, I would never put you in harm's way. If you do this, you will stay in the station at all times. You are not to be in the field." He then turned to Agent Lightfoot. "Is that understood?"

Agent Lightfoot pulled his stare from Marguerite and narrowed it on Jarod. "She'll go where I tell her to go."

Jarod stepped up to the FBI man but Marguerite forced herself between them. The last thing they needed was a King brother brawl to break out, for goodness sake. "I've got this, Jarod." Then she turned to Lightfoot. "No I won't unless you want to cuff me right now." She held her wrists out to him and, surprisingly, he chuckled.

"I want your help, not to put you in custody."

"Then knock it off. I do this *my* way. I have a life now and I've got a lot on my plate. Speaking of which, I have another meeting to get to in the kitchen. So, if I do this, it's on my terms." She turned to Jarod. "I'm not working at the station house either. I can't spend every waking hour fiddling around on a computer within the confines of those walls." She turned back to Lightfoot. "Give me back my clearance on the FBI's networks and I'll get started on it as soon as I can, from *home*. Your team can update me and send me an email. No texts. No DMs. I'll give you a report when I know more."

She stormed out of the den, leaving poor Declan behind to deal with her fallout. She was actually surprised the FBI agent hadn't followed to give her another guilt trip.

Her skills were in computer forensics and analysis and she'd stick to it. Zero field work. She'd leave all of that to the professionals. Besides, she knew the pattern she'd found was correct, but incomplete. All she had to do was work backwards from the most recent body. She didn't need the grizzly details of how the woman died, just who she was and where she was from.

She entered the kitchen and walked straight into utter chaos. Children, food, women and plans for her to grow her business.

"How'd it go?" her mother asked.

"About what you'd expect."

Julie cringed. "Are they making you work for them again?"

"They tried but we came to an understanding."

Camille frowned. "Oh, please tell me you can still make those chocolates."

Marguerite grinned. "Pftt. Of course. I'm not letting those jerks reel me in again. This is my life and I want to move forward, not back."

"Good for you." Julie then produced an ornery smile on her face. "Now, tell us all about Declan and when you two are hooking up."

Marguerite had taken a sip of iced tea and choked on it. Darla patted her back while Lauren, who'd just come in from picking up Jessica, laughed. "Come on, Marguerite. We've all been there before. Don't deny it. He's a hunk."

She'd finally cleared the liquid out of her lungs. "Yeah, he is. But I don't kiss and tell." Then she looked up and gave the ladies a full wattage grin that had them all saying, "oooohhhh!" including her own mother.

"What are you guys clucking about?" Jarod asked, walking in to first kiss his wife and catch Jessica as she leapt up for a hug from her daddy.

She said, "They think Declan's cute."

"They do, do they? Whatta 'bout you, Darlin'?"

"He's not as handsome as you, Daddy."

Jarod kissed her cheek. "That's my girl." He placed her back on the ground and Jessica skipped over to the kiddie corral to play with her brother and cousins.

"So wrapped around her finger," Lauren murmured. "You know, if she's already noticing how boys look, what's she going to be like when she's a teenager?"

"I have a gun, Sassy." He kissed Lauren one more time. "I gotta get back. Tell Lightfoot he can ride back with McKinley... If he'll allow it."

"Well," Camille sighed. "That must've been quite a meeting." She turned to Marguerite for verification.

"Jarod and Declan have been trying—and failing— to discourage me from investigating the murders." She shrugged. "I can't stop myself from poking around online, especially if I can't sleep. Unfortunately, I found something and Declan had to tell them. Now they're suddenly desperate for my return. Jarod wants to keep me safe at the station but I don't want that anymore." She met Lauren's eyes, who nodded.

"I get it. Once you're out of the office you don't want to go back. Believe me, I don't miss it. Of course, a lot of my problems stemmed from you and Brad Anderson."

At the mention of the dead deputy's name, both Lauren and Marguerite shuddered. "You know it was just an act, right?"

Lauren took a breath and pinched her lips closed, as if thinking of something nice to say. Marguerite knew she'd been an asshole back then but it was just a ruse.

Lauren blinked few times, then finally broke the tense silence. "I've come to understand it now. And I want us to be friends, especially because we're pretty much family."

For the first time, Marguerite actually felt like she was with family, other than her mother sitting next to her. These women would have her back if she needed them.

Maybe.

Declan poked his head around the corner and Marguerite realized she did need them. Especially if she was going to have to deal with this man who she knew had the hots for her.

A man whom she had the hots for in return.

This man I love.

The thought hit her as she met his eyes. He signaled her to meet him in the hallway, undoubtedly to update her on what Agent Lightfoot wanted to do.

"Excuse me, ladies. I'll be right back." She ignored the sly grin Julie had on her face and caught up with Declan. "What's going on, now?"

He tilted his head and had the same intense expression on his face before he kissed her that morning. She took a tiny step back. "Don't."

He stepped into her space. "Don't what?" He was teasing her because his dimple made an appearance.

"Declan," she warned, not wanting to cause a scene here, in this household with this family looking on. "There are children present."

"I see." He cleared his throat to cover a laugh, the bastard, and poked his head around the corner again and grinned. When he returned his attention to her he was all business. "First, you annoyed Lightfoot but he's got no choice. If he wants us both to do our thing, he has to deal with it because neither of us work for the government anymore."

This she already knew. Lightfoot's posturing was only a bluff. "What about Jarod. He didn't say much when he left."

"He's pissed at the situation."

"Also normal. What else?"

He touched her face and then dropped his hand away. "I told Roland to back off. He didn't like it. We've never had any big disagreements. But on this, I'm not going to budge. I want to protect you, Marguerite. I need you safe."

She felt tears well up before she could stop them and swiped them away in anger. Normally, with this much emotion she'd say something snarky and stomp off but she needed to stop doing that. She swallowed the lump in her throat. "I want us both to be safe."

He grinned and goosebumps flared up on her arms when he said, "Us. I like the sound of that."

Chapter Thirteen

CONFESSIONS

Instead of hitching a ride with Declan into town, Roland had to call one of his men to pick him up.

Declan went over his ideas about the ranching operation with James while Marguerite's meeting went long with the catering business. She didn't expound on anything other than a need to make more of those amazing spicy chocolates he loved.

Fine by him. Hell, he'd help her if she needed some.

As he watched her busy herself with the other women preparing the evening meal, he noted how much she'd changed since the first time he met her. She wore little makeup now but it didn't take away from her beauty. Instead, it enhanced it. She'd let the bleach blonde color grow out leaving her hair healthier, a little darker, and oh so soft. He'd touched it a few times already and all he wanted was to see it spread over his pillow at night.

Or maybe on his chest as she slept while he held her.

"Whatcha thinkin' about?" Josh startled him out of his wool gathering.

"How you got to be so ornery."

James chuckled from where he sat at the head of the table. "I tried to beat it out of him but he was born that way."

"You never beat me once," Josh said with disgust. Then he pointed at Jarod, who'd just returned from the station house. "*He* tried but I got him back in the end."

"You keep saying it and I'm wondering if you're trying to convince us or yourself," Jarod replied, not missing a beat as he sauntered out of the kitchen and—presumably—to find his family. Lauren had taken the kids to wash up.

Josh shook his head. "He's never learned the art of hello or goodbye."

Declan laughed. "I thought he only did that on the phone."

"He likes to get to the point, is all," said James. "Speaking of which, we got a head start on the manager's house. Supplies came in."

"Dinner is served." Camille placed the last platter of food on the table.

Marguerite took the empty seat next to Declan. "I bet you're ready to have your own place."

Declan shrugged. "Honestly, I've moved around so much I'm not sure what I'd do with a place of my own."

"But you are going to take it, aren't you McKinley?" James wore a panicked expression.

"Mr. King, I'm honored you've asked me to work for you, and I really do want to settle down." He peeked at Marguerite. "However, with the task force, I don't want to leave you in a pickle. I've agreed to work with the FBI on limited duty but if things heat up I might have to go out of town and I don't want to leave you, or the herd, without help."

"We've been managing for this long. I'll consider you a *yes* until you say otherwise. We're about a month out on the house, sooner if possible. Darla, can he stay with you until then?"

Marguerite's mother grinned. "I didn't know he was staying with me now. We hardly ever see him, cleans up after himself, and only eats breakfast with us." She winked at Declan making him smile with fondness for the older woman.

"Thank you, Mrs. Theroux." When she narrowed her eyes at him, he corrected, "Darla."

"That's better. Don't worry about a thing. As long as you keep an eye on Marguerite you can stay as long as you want."

"Mom," Marguerite whined and it was the cutest thing he'd ever heard her do.

Everyone at the table laughed and by the time the meal was over and the men did the dishes, it was time for them to head out.

Once on the road to Timbisha Township, Marguerite leaned against the window watching the scenery go by.

"She used to hate me, you know."

"Who?"

"Lauren."

He nodded. He'd heard the stories from Jarod, and Lauren had admitted as much at the craft fair. "It's good you two have become friends."

She grunted. "I wouldn't call us friends, more of a tolerated in-law relationship. But..." she trailed off and Declan waited.

He didn't want to push her because he felt she was about to impart something big, some insight into her wonderful mind. When she suddenly scrunched her eyebrows, he caved.

"But what, honey?"

"Don't call me that," she murmured, almost out of habit. Before he could apologize she forged on. "The only real friends I had growing up were Missy and Uncle Dane."

Growing up in this small town must've been torture for her. "Why?"

She smiled at a long ago memory. "Missy was constantly in trouble. Not the delinquent kind but misunderstood. She's truly the most awkward human on the planet. If it wasn't for Josh bringing out her true self I think she'd be in real trouble. She's an amazing vet and that's because she has an uncanny way with animals. Humans? Not so much. Anyway, I spent most of my childhood keeping her out of awkward situations which sometimes meant drawing the focus away from her and onto myself."

Declan could imagine what Marguerite was like then...a young girl afraid her baby sister would be hurt by the cruelty of bullies. "Did you ever confide in your mom?"

"Mom was mourning the death of our father. Uncle Dane was a great help when he showed up but he had no experience with children, especially girls. When he discovered my problem he took me under his wing and taught me what to look for in human behaviors. I was able to circumvent any problems Missy might get into with her peers. She had a terrible habit of blurting out information she shouldn't, not understanding she was hurting people's feelings. As she got older, she shut down completely."

Declan honed in on Bainbridge's part. "How did you feel about Bainbridge teaching you to be aware of your surroundings?" Because Declan had no doubt that's exactly what Dane had done. You can't solve a problem if you don't know one exists.

"Flattered. He was proud of me. I'd already discovered people liked to talk to me. They didn't want to hang out but if they wanted to gossip it ended up coming at me, or for me. When I left for college and returned to take the position at the sheriff's office, that's when we found out I was good at developing relationships to gain information. Which is what I did with Brad Anderson."

"The man killed when he kidnapped Jarod's wife and daughter." He didn't form it as a question because he knew the basic tale. "How close did you have to get with the bastard?" Declan grew angry at how her uncle had put her in danger.

She looked him straight in the eye. "Close enough."

"Marguerite," Declan whispered, reaching out to stroke her hair.

She summoned a nonchalant air. "Don't sweat it, Declan. He's dead, Lauren and Jessica are with Jarod, and they all lived happily ever after."

"Did you?"

She squinted at him. "Did I what?"

"Live happily...after."

Had she been happy? Yes, she was excited to move forward in her career, go on the hunt of a drug mule with Uncle Dane and catch some more bad guys.

"Well, I met you, didn't I?"

He shook his head in disgust. "Can't say it turned out good for either of us, did it?"

"You are the most confusing man. Are you saying you're sorry we ever met?" Declan McKinley had her in knots.

"No, no, no, that's not what I'm sayin' at all." He shook his head back and forth as if she was the problem.

"Then what?" She crossed her arms over her chest ready to do battle. Or pout—she wasn't sure which.

"I'm glad we met. Hell, even if you hadn't tagged along

on that epically failed adventure, I probably still would've ended up right back in Timbisha Township just to harass you."

He liked her? Even then? "You were terrible to me. And what do you mean by 'tag along?' I didn't tag along, I was recommended—and hired—by you!"

"You weren't so nice to me either, as I recall." He completely ignored the last part of her point, aggravating her further.

He was correct, though. The first time they'd met he was an absolute misogynistic jerk-face but, damn was he a good looking one. She'd flushed from her hair to her toes and hadn't known why. She shook her head at him. "Damn biological chemistry."

"You felt it too?"

"Of course I did, stupid."

"Stupid?" He squished his face in mock confusion. Marguerite felt herself crack a grin when he added, "If I called you that you'd punch me in the face."

Yeah, she would. "Sorry, it slipped out and I'm only teasing." She touched his arm, giving herself goosebumps. "Truly, Declan. I'm only joking with you."

"Honey, you can joke with me all you want."

My goodness. He could turn the mildest of comments into something...else.

Declan parked at the curb in front of her house and noted her mother had beat them home.

"We need to discuss how this is going to work." He was all business now, talking about the investigation, not their mutual attraction.

"I'm sure Agent Lightfoot will have some suggestions—"

"More like arguments."

"—but honestly I'm going to follow my instincts." She said the last a little louder to cover his interruption.

Declan grabbed her hand. The warmth and steadiness of his grip had her looking at him again. "How's this; you do any and all research from home while I'm with you. That way if you discover something, even the smallest clue, you tell me right away so we can work it out together."

"You don't trust me."

"Wrong, Marguerite. I trust *you*. I don't trust anyone else when it comes to this case."

She didn't understand. "For heaven's sake, why not? You can trust Jarod with anything, he's the most honest law enforcer I've ever met. And, even though he's a pain in the butt, Agent Lightfoot is a good guy. What makes this case so different?"

She studied him while he glared at her, a myriad of expressions floating across his handsome face. When concern finally made its appearance he said, "Please say you'll keep me in the loop on what you find out. I can liaison with Jarod and Lightfoot. Right now, I'm not real happy with the feds."

His intensity burned her. She was used to her Uncle's determination but with Declan it felt like more.

"I promise to run things by you. I don't want to actually be there when they catch this creep and neither do you. Do you?"

"Nope." With that, he opened his door to climb out of the truck and she followed suit. They walked to the front door together and found her mother waiting for them in the living room.

Darla didn't waste any time. "I almost lost you last time, Marguerite. Please tell me you're not going back to work for the FBI."

The fear on her mother's face nearly broke Marguerite.

"It's not like the last time, Mom. I promise. I'm not going out in the field. Only working on computers, that's it. And the furthest I'll go to do any research is the station house. Jarod will be there along with the FBI team, and Declan."

Marguerite reached for her mother's wringing hands and held them. Her mother had fought cancer and won, but her health wasn't perfect and stress wasn't good for anyone. "Mom, I promise it's not going to be like the last time. I don't want to be where the action is. I still have my job at Blue's, and I have to help Camille, Julie, and Lauren with their catering. I'm not leaving, I promise."

Darla took a deep breath and nodded.

Marguerite glanced at Declan, before leaning into her mother, and hugging her tight. "Love you. I'm going to bed."

Her legs felt heavy as she trudged up the stairs, but her heart felt heavier. She'd promised herself she'd left all this behind her, even when she pecked around on her computer to scratch the itch of solving the puzzle of the murders.

She never should've admitted to Declan what she'd found.

No, she wouldn't blame him. He had the same itches to scratch and catching killers was a skill he had and needed to fulfill. It's why she liked him so much, even if he drove her nuts.

Sighing deeply, she grabbed her MacBook from her night-stand and placed it on her lap. Agent Lightfoot had sent the information needed to access the government's bigger search engines.

Time to get to work. Once she found this maniac she could get on with her life.

As she clicked away, visions of Declan on horseback with her following along on a four-wheeler clouded her vision and made for a peaceful backdrop while she tracked a killer through cyberspace.

———

"PLEASE DON'T WORRY ABOUT HER," DECLAN SAID quietly to Darla as they watched Marguerite ascend the stairs. "I'm going to do everything in my power to keep her safe."

"I know." She turned and invited him into the kitchen with a wave of her hand.

Declan nodded his thanks when Darla put a beer in his hand, turned back to the old fridge to get an iced tea for herself. She slammed the door closed, startling Declan. Bottles and jars jingled inside at the abuse. He'd never seen the woman angry before.

"My brother encouraged her to put herself in harm's way. Did you know that?"

Declan took a seat across from the woman at the old dinette set. "I figured it out while we were on the road together."

Darla pinched her lips together, then took a sip of her drink. "He told me it's what she's good at, Declan, but I don't think that's true. You wouldn't understand. I want her to be happy, to feel useful. I know she's overqualified to be a bartender, but I don't want her hurt again. I can't lose her." She sniffed and rubbed the back of her hand against her nose.

Declan studied Marguerite's mother. Age and illness hadn't been kind since the shooting. Though her hair was white, it was thick and she tied it up in an elegant twist. Worry clouded her hazel eyes, the same color as Marguerite's.

"Hell, I wish she didn't work there either." He pointed the

end of his long neck at Darla. "But those chocolates she makes are damn tasty...pardon my french."

She shook her head. "It's her therapy, a hobby. I hope it works out with *Cafe Armstrong*."

"Why wouldn't it work out? The ladies seem mighty pleased with her concoctions." He took a pull, waiting to see if Darla understood Marguerite's lack of self-esteem regarding her treats. She didn't disappoint.

"Marguerite is good at self-sabotage, Declan. I've talked to Camille, and I understand my daughter hurt her family while my brother had her undercover. I think Marguerite and Lauren came to an understanding tonight, but...sometimes I think Dane's ghost is riding on her shoulder." She leaned back and sighed long and loud.

Declan shook his head in disgust because he'd thought the same thing.

"She thought the world of Dane, and in his way I've no doubt he loved her, too, but he wasn't a father. It's times like these I miss my husband so much." Suddenly, she stood and took her empty glass to the sink. "You're the best thing that's happened to my daughter in a long time, Declan. Please don't give up on her." With that, Darla Theroux went to bed.

Declan chucked his bottle in the trash and headed upstairs. He needed to check on her more than ever after that conversation. He'd use the excuse of wanting to know if she found anything. He didn't doubt she'd already started on a hard search around the internet. Then he'd hit the hay. It'd been a long day.

The tapping of keys stopped when he knocked.

"Come in." Her eyes never left the screen when he pushed the door open. "Haven't found anything significant yet." She shrugged.

He never asked her before but he was interested in her process. "What are you looking for?"

She kept clicking away. "Running a search on truck drivers who most often take I-80 with their loads."

He sat on the edge of her bed. "There must be tens of thousands."

She shook her head. "Not with criminal records. When I narrowed down dates and times of bodies found, assault and battery crimes, animal cruelty, and cross referenced them with independent drivers and weight discrepancies at the scales, the list is under 50."

"No way."

Finally, her eyes met his. "It's not foolproof. None of them could be the killer. This guy's smart, Declan. He may have no record at all. He might not even be working when he's killing, or pulling a trailer, therefore not weighing in. There are many factors. This is just a starting point."

He smiled. "You really are amazing, you know that?"

"Pfft. Of course I do." She returned her eyes to the screen, but he didn't miss the slight flush coloring her cheeks. He reached over and touched her fingers.

"What?" she asked, a hint of annoyance in her voice.

"Just this." He leaned in and touched his lips to hers. He'd meant it as a kiss goodnight, one to say he liked who she was, but once his lips touched hers he couldn't get enough.

Apparently, she felt the same because she pushed her MacBook aside in order to put her arms around his neck and pulled him closer.

Instant combustion. Before he knew what was happening he had her beneath him, pressing her to the mattress. One of her legs had wrapped around his hips and he groaned.

Or was that her?

Hell, he didn't know, nor did he care. He didn't want it to end.

"Did you close the door?" she asked out of breath and still holding him tight.

Had he? "I don't know."

She pushed up and he immediately let go, but she only looked over his shoulder, then sighed and flopped back to the pillow. "Move."

Stronger than he estimated, she shoved him to the side, not off the bed but the other way, and padded barefoot to her bedroom door.

"I'd better go ba—"

He shut his mouth when she closed the door and turned the lock. "Guess I'm going to break my vow."

Then she pulled her shirt off. His eyes devoured every inch of her naked flesh. He hadn't paid attention when he'd arrived, but Marguerite had undressed for bed.

Under the t-shirt she wore panties and nothing else.

A vixen's smile touched her lips as she sauntered back, and climbed on top of him. "Now, where were we?"

Heaven. Absolute friggin heaven.

Chapter Fourteen

AIN'T LETTIN' GO

Sunlight filled Marguerite's bedroom and her eyes slowly adjusted to the light. The familiar sense of dread coiled in her chest, the same guilt-ridden self-loathing she had after a night in bed with a man who would never love her.

Is it possible for Declan to love me?

She took stock of how she felt physically—because mentally she knew she was all over the place—still tired but a little more relaxed than before. Declan's magical scent filled the room and, for whatever reason, the usual revulsion of her own behavior never came. She had feelings for him. Hell, who was she kidding, she loved him, which only pissed her off.

Sighing, she stretched and rolled to her back. A strong arm wrapped itself around her middle before warm, masculine breath fanned her ear. "Good morning, beautiful."

Holy crap, she'd thought he'd left. It was on the tip of her tongue to tell him not to call her that but then his lips grazed her earlobe and his hand began to wander.

"Good morning, *McKinley*," she said to get a reaction.

He didn't disappoint her, as he wasted no time pressing her to the mattress with his body, resting his forehead against hers.

"I think after last night you should call me by my first name all the time. I suggest using something along the lines of 'honey' or 'sweetheart' if the moment grabs you."

Marguerite laughed as she put her arms around him to stroke her fingernails down his back. He wanted her to act on her feelings? On what she wanted in the moment? Fine, she could do that—with her tongue.

She put it to work licking the side of his neck up to his earlobe and sucked.

"Yeah," he groaned out like a lion starting to purr. "I wasn't hungry for breakfast either."

***

"Good morning." A sweet, but knowing voice came from behind Marguerite as she poured herself a much needed cup of coffee.

"Morning, Mother." She didn't turn around, not truly ready to face anyone yet. She took a sip of coffee and hummed, needing the dark elixir for strength.

Declan was still upstairs taking a shower. While she really wanted to join him, they'd decided to get cleaned up separately, not wanting to push the privacy issue in the house. She honestly thought she'd feel a little more guilty about what she'd done with Declan in her mother's home but the feeling never came. Instead, she felt lighthearted. Still, she clung to her mug...just in case the insidious feelings made an appearance. Yet, the impending doom hadn't quite hit her. After all, her track record with men wasn't great.

"Have a good night?"

She spun around and leaned her butt against the counter.

"I did." Sip. "How about yourself?"

"Tossed and turned. Couldn't get comfortable." There was a teasing tilt to her mother's mouth, like she was hiding her smile.

She stared at her over her mug as she took another revitalizing sip. "That's too bad."

"When are you heading to the station house?"

Declan appeared in the archway between the eat-in kitchen and living room. "After we eat. Do you need anything before we go?"

Marguerite couldn't take her eyes off him as he nonchalantly strolled toward her and kissed her right in front of her mom, making her heart skip a beat.

Guess we aren't hiding this.

Darla, however, didn't skip a beat at his use of PDA. "No, I need to run some errands today, though. Nothing you can help with but thank you for the offer."

Declan hadn't moved, just stood in front of her, caging her in between his arms and the counter, with a shit eating grin on his face. "Mornin'."

She nipped his chin. "Want some coffee?"

"Please." Still he didn't move so she turned in his arms and filled a mug for him. When she handed it over he looked into it and asked, "Do you have any of those spicy chocolates?"

Her eyebrows raised in surprise? "You really did like those, didn't you?"

"Mmhmm."

She reached for a small container sitting on the counter and opened the lid before offering them.

He set his mug down in order to choose a treat without removing his arm from around her waist. He drew out two, dropped one in his coffee mug and popped the other in his mouth, which made him groan.

"Damn, woman. These are so good." He let the chocolate melt in his mouth and leaned in. "Just like you."

Darla stood and pushed in her chair. "And that's my cue to give you some privacy. I need to get going anyway. Oh, I'm so glad things have worked out between you two."

"Mom, you don't have to rush out!" but her mother had already closed the front door behind her.

Marguerite tilted her head to the side to study Declan. Did he mean it or was this just afterglow? Was he playing with her? She didn't think so, she wasn't undercover or trying to get information out of him, but was he trying to find out something from her? If so, he only need ask—she'd tell him anything he wanted to know.

With Lightfoot and the search going on, would Declan leave her like he had in Salt Lake City?

"Hey." Concern etched onto his face. "Where'd you go?"

His question startled her and she met his eyes, denying she'd been anywhere other than right there, in her kitchen with Declan sharing chocolate, coffee and a peaceful morning after. Going on tip toes, she pecked his lips.

"I'm right here." She pasted on a smile before bending to duck under his arm to escape the space between him and the counter. "Let me get my purse so we can go."

Was she a coward? Maybe but she wasn't going to talk to him about her feelings or anything else until she was sure he felt something more for her than sex. Call it self-preservation but she didn't really trust men. They tended to be fickle beasts. At least, she understood they processed feelings differently than women, and their priorities were definitely different.

Declan had come to Timbisha Township to apply for a job

with the Kings, but then been thrown into an investigation. Would he decide to stay when all was said and done or would he move on because as far as she knew he hadn't signed any agreements with James King.

Only time would tell.

DECLAN TOOK A DRINK OF COFFEE WHILE TRACKING Marguerite's retreat from the kitchen. He hadn't figured her for a coward, never seen her back down from a challenge, but he hadn't thought he'd challenged her. Their night together had been nothing short of miraculous, at least from his point of view. There'd be no going backward for him.

He'd never been in love before but love was the only explanation for what he felt for Marguerite—a madness which grew into an all-encompassing need to have her forever. No ifs, ands, or buts about it. He never wanted to be without her. Hell, just her walking away now left him with a loneliness he'd never experienced before, which is saying something because he'd spent most of his life alone, and she'd only escaped him to get her things.

This is ridiculous.

He rinsed out their mugs before placing them in the dishwasher.

He found Marguerite at the base of the stairs reading something on her phone. "Everything all right?" Her eyebrows were pinched in a V.

She looked up as if she hadn't heard his approach. "Yes, sorry. Missy wants to go to lunch but I told her I didn't know what my schedule was going to be like from now on."

"Tell her you can make it, Marguerite. You need to see your

sister. I don't know about you, but I don't want this to be like the last time."

Her shoulders had been hunched but now she straightened and looked him in the eyes. "You're right. Thanks." She typed something out while walking to the front door.

He opened it for her and by the time they'd climbed into his pickup she'd finished the conversation with her sister. She tossed her phone into her bag and ran her fingers through her hair, displacing a few strands which had been hanging in her eyes. "She's picking me up at one this afternoon from the station, barring any animal emergencies on her end. She's been super busy lately."

His fingers itched to run through her soft tresses again. The image of her leaning over him as she unbuttoned his shirt had him squirming in the driver seat.

He drummed his thumbs on the steering wheel.

They stared at each other a moment before she chuckled. "What are you thinking about."

"Last night." His voice may have been a little gravelly but he wasn't going to shy away from her.

It pleased him when her eyebrows crawled up her forehead and the most tender blush filled her cheeks.

She cleared her throat. "Uh. What about it?"

He reached for her hand and raised it to his mouth where he placed a kiss. "I like you in my bed."

"You were in mine."

"Doesn't matter. I'll sleep anywhere with you, honey."

She pulled her hand from his. "Would you, now?"

"What's wrong?" He didn't understand her guarded reaction. Unless...

"Marguerite, last night is not a one-time thing, at least not for me. Tell me now if I've got this wrong so we can move past it. I don't play games."

He swore her lip quivered before she pressed her mouth into a hard line. "No, I know you don't."

They were almost to the station where they couldn't have this conversation. He needed to know if they were on the same page or not, but he didn't want to push her either.

Damn. It.

"It's okay, Declan. I think my mind is on the case, the deal I'm making with Camille, Blue's, you…everything. I'm sorry. Last night was wonderful. Of course I don't want it to be a one-time deal."

Well, okay then.

At least he had a baseline of her feelings. She had a lot going on. He understood the situation. Maybe he should back off a bit. He was known for his patience. He could wait for her. It was fine.

As long as he didn't have to sleep alone anymore.

Chapter Fifteen

SISTERS

Lightfoot's black SUV shone out of place in the station parking lot. Not because it was the only SUV. The whole parking lot was full of them. It was the matching diesel pickup with the custom black fifth-wheel attached to the back, complete with mini satellite dishes and other antennae on the roof which made it stick out like a sore thumb.

"So much for inconspicuous." Marguerite opened her door to climb out of the pickup. "Think we should knock?"

God, he loved her smart mouth. "No, just try the knob. If they don't want us in it'll be locked but he's expecting us."

He followed her across the warm asphalt and noted she was scanning the area. "Wonder where Jarod is?" She pointed in the direction of his cruiser. "He's here somewhere."

"I'm behind you."

The three of them stormed the back of the trailer without knocking, Jarod the first to enter making Declan chuckle. The sheriff's territorial personality tickled him sometimes. Other times he wanted to facepalm himself.

Once all three stepped inside the trailer, even Declan was

impressed with its size. Lightfoot stood next to a state of the art terminal.

"How big is this place?" Marguerite asked.

Lightfoot had the decency to sigh. "It's over forty feet long and a pain in the ass to pull."

"Which is why it was delivered here on a flat-bed," Jarod said with disgust.

Marguerite laughed out loud. "That must've been some spectacle."

"They came undercover of night," Lightfoot said. "It doesn't matter. It's here now and we might as well put it to good use. At least there's enough room for the whole team so we won't be crowding you out of your station, Sheriff. The government thanks you for your cooperation in this matter."

Jarod scowled. "I guess that's my cue." He put his arm around Marguerite's shoulders and it was all Declan could do to keep from ripping the man's arms out of their sockets.

Damn green-eyed monster.

"If you need me I'm right inside or a phone call away. You hear me?"

Declan looked away when she squeezed the sheriff in a return hug. "Thank you, Jarod."

On his way out of the trailer, he pulled Declan to the side. "I'm serious. I'm here if you need me. Don't let them rope her into something stupid. You either."

Declan took a deep breath because he knew Jarod meant well and wasn't trying to insult him. "Appreciate it."

"Now that's all out of the way, tell me what you found last night. I know you accessed the database." Lightfoot directed Marguerite to a desk built into a sidewall of the trailer.

Declan sat back and listened to Marguerite brief Roland Lightfoot, a major reversal from the last time they worked together as a team. She discussed timeframes, cross referenced body dumps and went over any and all digital footprints indicating to everyone in the trailer that the killer had to be someone moving from season to season, across the country. She'd found at least ten other body dumps the FBI hadn't related to the case, all of which had been found relatively in the same condition, CODs being strangulation after sexual assault.

At one o'clock Marguerite's phone dinged. "Sorry, fellas, but I gotta go. My sister's here. I'll be back in an hour." She stood and made for the back door.

"Wait, what are you talking about? We need to get on this." Lightfoot tried to follow her out but Declan stopped the agent at the door.

"She's given you and the team plenty to work on so I suggest everyone get started. This isn't like before, Roland. I'm not screwing around. She has a lunch date with her sister and she's keeping it. Understand?"

Roland blew out a breath. "Fine. Be back in an hour."

When Declan glared, Roland added, "Please."

To his surprise, Marguerite leaned in and kissed Declan's cheek. "Thank you. You want me to bring you back a burger?"

He touched her chin between thumb and forefinger and kissed her lips. "Sounds great. You know what I like," he said, making sure she blushed before she headed out the door. He didn't want her to think she could just leave him here with these dopes while she was off with her sister. But damn, it felt good she'd thought to bring him back something to eat and not offer anything to the other agents. Those bastards could fend for themselves. Speaking of which he turned back to the room at large.

"What else did you find?"

One agent had set up a glass board and now stuck pictures

of victims in rows to one side. After Marguerite's presentation, there were twenty-four so far spanning back a decade. Across from each were the victims' demographics and the logistics of where they'd been found.

Declan interpreted Lightfoot's expression as shocked, then pissed before settling on frustrated. "How the hell did we miss this?"

"You're sure all the vics were found in the same condition?"

A young agent nodded. "Mostly...all strangled for sure. Some have more injuries than others, but it'll take time to determine if they were killed in the order they'd been found. Even though they were all wrapped in plastic, their rate of decomp's all over the place. We'll need an entomologist and a forensic anthropologist to determine the age of each victim and how long they've been sitting out in the elements."

The crime scene photos were pretty graphic. A third of the victims had already been autopsied by local coroners. They had a lot to weed through. A few had been identified, found in locations far from where they lived.

"What's churning in your head, McKinley?"

He turned to Agent Lightfoot. "Nothing except how much I hate chasing down serial killers."

"I FEEL LIKE I HAVEN'T SEEN YOU IN A MONTH," Marguerite said the minute she climbed into Missy's SUV.

"That's because you haven't." Missy didn't get angry very often but ever since she'd married Josh, became a mother and a partner at the Timbisha Township Veterinary Clinic, she'd definitely found her voice. "I'm worried about you. Why's the

FBI literally parked at the sheriff's station and why are you working for them again?"

"You've seen the news about the bodies found in Timbisha Township, right?"

Missy glanced at Marguerite before returning her eyes to the road. "Please don't tell me you're involved with the case, Marguerite."

She sat there contemplating what to say. She couldn't give away anything to civilians on an ongoing federal investigation but this was her sister. "Well, I'm not the murderer if that's what you're thinking."

Missy pulled into Molly's Diner and shut off the engine. "Seriously? Joking isn't going to make me any happier, you know. Are you back with the FBI? I thought you were going to work for Camille."

Marguerite pushed open the door and got out, Missy following her inside the diner. They found two stools at the counter and ordered. Once the waitress moved on, she leaned into her sister for a little privacy. "I'm helping. I'm like a private contractor. Declan, too. Neither of us wants to get sucked into it again but," here she trailed off knowing Missy was going to throw a fit. "I couldn't help myself. I found a pattern on my own and made the mistake of telling Declan, who then told Jarod who'd been compelled to tell Agent Lightfoot because the bodies here are connected to twenty-four others from all over the US."

Missy shook her head in disbelief. "Twenty-four?"

They both stared at each other for a moment. "I know. It's awful. Besides, even if I hadn't capitulated, Agent Lightfoot would've pressed me into service. He's determined to have me back. Sometimes I think Uncle Dane is manipulating things from above."

"Don't say that." Missy grabbed her hand. "He only wanted what was best for you, even if Mom and I didn't agree."

"You didn't?"

Missy's eyes widened. "Of course not!"

"He wanted what he thought was best for me. He'd never approve of me working at Blue's. Speaking of which, Dusty is going to be pissed when I tell him."

"Are you quitting the bar?"

"Hell no." Their food arrived and Marguerite took a healthy bite of her turkey croissant.

"You called him Declan, not McKinley." She tried to hide a smirk behind chewing but Marguerite knew better.

"So?"

"You slept with him."

"Missy," Marguerite hissed.

With wide innocent eyes, her sister faced her. "I've never known you to shy away from the subject." She continued to bore her beautiful violet eyes into Marguerite who began to squirm.

"Okay, okay. I slept with him. What of it?" She felt defensive. She didn't want to talk about her love life with her sister. Missy was too happy in this stage of her life and Marguerite...

...wasn't.

Missy shrugged her shoulders before taking a sip of ice water. They ate in silence for a moment before Missy decided to have another go.

"How long has it been since you were in love?"

Marguerite set her sandwich down and leaned back. The vinyl squeaked in protest.

Must've just been cleaned, she thought, distracting herself from this painful topic.

It took about three seconds to realize she'd never truly been in love with anyone.

Oh, she'd had plenty of crushes, three of them she now called family. Jarod, Jason, and Josh held legendary reputations from as far back as high school so of course she'd been smitten at some point with each of them.

But love? No, never.

Marguerite dated in college, been *in like* with a couple of those frat boys but in the end she realized they couldn't give her what she needed. Which is crazy because she didn't really know what she needed.

She licked her lips. "I've never been in love, Missy." She shook her head. "I'm not even sure I'm capable of it."

Marguerite picked up her iced tea for a drink but promptly set it back down on a painful... "Ouch! Why the hell did you hit me?"

"Because you're being an idiot. Of course you're capable of love. Everything you do, every time you put yourself on the chopping block in the name of justice, to get answers—every time you protected me from bullies—you did it out of love and caring for the people around you."

"Yeah? Then why do people hate me so much?" No, it didn't bother her that she had to prove herself over and over again...or did it?

"Because we are surrounded by ignorant people, of whom you are not, so stop trying to convince yourself you aren't worthy."

"You think that's what I'm doing?"

"Frankly, yes." Missy turned in her seat to face Marguerite head on. She was still getting used to her little sister being confident. "Uncle Dane's death was not your fault."

"Missy..." Marguerite warned. Now she was just picking at the wound.

"It's not. No one blames you."

"Declan does. Agent Lightfoot does."

Missy shook her head. "Declan absolutely *does not* blame you. He blames himself. It isn't anyone's fault except that horrible man who's now in prison for the crime. As for Agent Lightfoot, I have no clue, nor do I care, what he thinks. However, with him bringing you in on this new case I seriously doubt he blames you either. So stop blaming *yourself*."

A damn tear slipped from Marguerite's eye and she killed it with her napkin.

"Marguerite, you're in love with Declan McKinley. I suspect he loves you back, which is why he's here in the first place. I don't take him for someone who'd try to hurt you."

"Oh Missy. I'm so out of my element. I don't know how to do this." Honestly, real relationships weren't in her wheelhouse.

"Yes, you do. Just be *you*. Everyone loves the *real you*, not the person who's always undercover."

Marguerite wrinkled her eyebrows at her sister. "But I'm always me when I go undercover."

Missy raised one eyebrow.

"Okay, okay. You're right."

She tossed the last bite of her sandwich into her mouth. "I'm always right."

Once they'd finished lunch and were on the way back to the station, Missy asked, "What are you doing tonight for dinner?"

"Not sure, why?"

"Josh and I want you and Declan to come over, just the two of you. He's grilling and your niece misses you."

"I saw her yesterday."

"See? Everyone loves you. So be done with your investigating by six."

"What about Mom?"

"She's a given. I think she's already at my house watching Violet while Josh is working in the home office."

Missy was right. They hadn't spent much time together, and a quiet dinner with just her sister and brother-in-law sounded like the break she needed.

"I'll do my best to be there on time."

"SHE LOVES YOU."

Declan's eyebrows dropped over his eyes. "She'll get over it soon enough."

"How can you say such a thing?" Missy was insulted on her daughter's behalf.

"Because eventually they all get tired of me." He sighed as Violet kicked her little feet in the universal sign of all toddlers to be let down.

They watched the little girl climb into Marguerite's arms and fling her little hand around her aunt's neck. "I think she's found who she wants to hang out with for a while." Declan winked at Missy and joined Marguerite on the patio with Josh who was babying some steaks on the grill.

"Tell him the potatoes are almost done."

"Ten-four." He admired the deck of Josh's newly built home and informed the man he needed to speed it up on the meat.

Josh nodded and Declan took in his surroundings. Their home was a classic modern ranch sprawled out on a vista overlooking the King's property. "You've got a great view of the valley from up here."

"Thanks. Initially, I'd never planned to build on my lot but it's a prime location when Missy's on call. She doesn't have to head back to the clinic for emergencies. It saves her about twenty minutes each time she's needed at one of the ranches." He grabbed a wooden cutting board and moved the steaks from the grill, then yelled into the house. "Steaks are resting!"

Missy'd already set the patio table and Marguerite put Violet in her highchair and scooted her up between Josh's chair on the end, and herself. Declan sat on the other side of Marguerite.

"Do you need any help?" Marguerite called into the kitchen as she buckled Violet into her chair.

"Nope." Missy pulled the screen door closed with one hand then set a platter of baked potatoes on the table next to the broccoli salad Darla brought, who was now seated next to Declan at the end opposite Josh. Missy took the chair across from Marguerite.

Declan's mouth watered.

Josh turned from his steaks holding a barbecue fork in his hand. "All right, pass me your plates."

In turn, they handed over their plates where he set a perfect t-bone on each before taking his seat. "Who wants to start?"

"I'll go." Declan felt a strong urge to thank God for sending him to this family, this small community and, especially for his woman. "Bless us oh lord, and these thy gifts..."

As he recited the prayer everyone joined in and at the end Violet yelled *A-men*!

"Good job, sweetheart." Josh scooped some of his baked potato and some small bites of steak onto his daughter's plate.

"I hear the house is almost finished so you two can shack up soon."

Declan's eyes did a long blink, not quite believing what had just come out of the ornery man's mouth.

"Oh, for heaven's sake, Josh King." This from his wife.

Darla laughed.

Marguerite slugged her brother-in-law.

Declan shared a look with her and grinned when she turned pink. "Yeah, James said the house is ahead of schedule. Only a month left or something. Hopefully we can get this case solved before then. I'm actually lookin' forward to settling down."

"Really?" Josh, Missy and Darla asked at the same time.

Marguerite focused on her salad.

"I'm not gettin' any younger."

Darla shrugged. "None of us are."

"I'm pregnant."

Everyone swung their eyes to Missy before the congratulations started.

Josh, however, scowled at his wife. "I thought you wanted to wait to tell everyone?"

Missy shrugged her shoulders. "Apparently, it's the night to spill the beans."

Declan didn't miss the look she shared with Marguerite. Missy made her announcement to cover Marguerite's embarrassment. The sisters were really close and he loved she had that kind of relationship with her sibling. He wondered what Missy thought about the pressure Dane had put on Marguerite, then decided it wasn't his business. The man was dead, and if it weren't for Dane he'd never have met the most amazing woman in the world...at least she was amazing to him.

"Well, I for one am excited to be a grandmother again."

Darla raised her glass to her children. "Thank you for this wonderful news. I think we all needed some tonight."

"Okay." Josh was gearing up to say something else to piss off Declan, he was sure. "Tell us all about why the Feds wanted you back, Magpie."

"Will you stop calling me that?"

Violet singsonged *Magpie* and Marguerite slugged him again, making Declan cover his laugh with his napkin.

"Well?" he persisted while dodging his sister-in-law's fist. When he wasn't fast enough, he muttered, "Geez, you're a violent thing."

"They appreciate Marguerite's computer analysis expertise," Declan said to hopefully stop a full-on family brawl. "Apparently, they aren't getting the best and brightest out of Quantico anymore." He cut a piece of steak and forked it into his mouth.

Delicious.

Marguerite shook her head. "I would've thought Missy had told you already. I found the pattern and now they want me to do more research to find the killer." She leaned closer to the table as if there were other people listening. "It's a serial."

Josh squinted. "There's four bodies. Of course it's a serial killer. Isn't three the classifying number?"

Missy piped up. "Marguerite found a lot more from across the country which is why they want her, Josh. My sister is *that* good."

"Of course she is, sweetheart." He waggled his eyebrows at Declan, who scowled.

"Anyway..." he said to keep himself from asking his host to step off the deck for a discussion, "...Marguerite and I are working strictly in a consultative capacity."

"Whether Agent Lightfoot likes it or not." Marguerite looked at Missy. "When?"

"Am I due?" She grabbed Josh's hand. "Spring."

"You'd better be careful, Marguerite. I think there's something in the water around here."

Darla gasped. "You don't mean..."

"Josh, you aren't supposed to tell until they're ready." Missy turned scolding eyes to her husband.

"It's just us and they're going to find out sooner or later."

Declan glanced at Marguerite in question, who chuckled. "Apparently there are other pregnancies in the family."

"Oh." Declan looked into his glass. Does that mean she wants kids too?

Am I too old for her?

"You okay?"

He cleared his throat. "Of course." He caught Josh's eye, who grinned from ear to ear but thankfully didn't say anything.

Chapter Sixteen

GOOD MAN

Marguerite couldn't keep the amusement out of her voice. "Don't worry, Declan. It's not something you can catch." Although the situation was funny, a little pang landed in her chest. Her sister was on baby number two. It made her happy but...

It's not the right time for you, Marguerite. Knock it off.

Violet patted her arm and Marguerite gave her some more bread. God, she loved her niece, and she was sure she'd be just as in love with the next baby. It was enough.

For now.

Declan, on the other hand, looked like he swallowed something rotten.

"Seriously, are you all right?"

"Yup."

Josh laughed and clapped his hands together. "Okay, my work here is done. Speaking of finished, if you guys are ready for dessert I can't wait to try Marguerite's treat." When he pushed his chair back, it signaled everyone into action. Marguerite wiped Violet's face, Missy stacked the two empty platters on her forearms and Darla escaped with a few empty dinner plates to the kitchen where Josh pulled a serving knife from the drawer.

"What'dya make?"

"You'll see." She wanted everyone's honest reaction. She'd added bourbon to the ganache, and made sure to make a separate cupcake for Violet without the booze. She glanced into the kitchen to see Josh holding it up and pointing to his daughter. At Marguerite's nod he placed it on a child's plate and set it aside until they were ready.

"How do you make the chocolate shiny?"

"It's called tempering. It's not hard, just time consuming. It's a balance of melting chocolate and humidity control. We don't have high humidity here, thank goodness, but I bought a dehumidifier online anyway for when I temper in the kitchen. It's best to not cook other foods while the chocolate's doing its thing. Plus our house doesn't have a traditional air conditioner, but a swamp cooler, which adds humidity to the air."

She returned his smile at her basic information. There was more to it in order to get the chocolate to set right but most people didn't need a chemistry lesson to understand the basics. It'd taken her a solid year to perfect her method. A year to take her mind off the horrible grief swallowing her whole. They say *time heals all wounds*, but she'd found it only knitted your soul enough not to bleed every time she thought of her uncle.

Grief leaves nasty scars.

"I cannot wait to cut into this sucker." Josh's eyes remained focused on the three-layer chocolate cake, which he now carried to the table. She'd drizzled tempered chocolate over it, and stuck the bourbon ganache leaves on top.

"I love those." Missy pointed at the leaves as she set Violet's cupcake in front of her, before taking her seat. "Are they for the Harvest Festival?"

Darla passed around dessert plates and forks. "I don't think the church would appreciate the whiskey."

"Bourbon," Marguerite corrected.

"Whatever."

"I like grown-up cake," Missy said. "But I don't think I should try these."

Marguerite laughed. "Well, you shoulda said something before, and I would've made you a cupcake too." Violet had chocolate all over her mouth and made yummy sounds. "It's okay, Missy. Only the leaf decorations have booze in them.

Declan took a bite and hummed like Violet. "I've died and gone to heaven."

Josh nodded, the same reverence on his face. "Death by chocolate. The second-best way to go." He waggled his eyebrows at his wife.

When Declan began to choke on his cake, Marguerite patted his back. "Are you all right?"

"Y—," cough, "Yes. Josh you're terrible talking like that in front of the ladies."

"We're used to it," all three said at once.

"Well, since the consensus here is positive, I'm going to make these for the Halloween Festivities at the King Estate, but in cupcake form and nonalcoholic. I hope Camille will approve of them."

"Are you kidding? Mom is going to love this cake. You should definitely offer it for the catering business." Josh shoved another forkful into his mouth.

Missy agreed with her husband. "They're very excited to see what else you can do with your chocolate, Marguerite."

"Of course they are," Darla said.

"My question is," Josh took another bite and swallowed, "when do you have time to figure out who Timbisha Township's killer is? And, if it's a serial killer who's been dropping bodies all over the country, when will the feds take you away with them on the hunt?" He grabbed Marguerite's hand and she felt Declan stiffen next to her. "Tell them to take a flying leap, Mags. I'm serious. And, if you need me to come take care of business for you, I'm there."

She felt her eyes well up, but rules were rules. "Don't call me that." When his dimple showed with his grin, she squeezed his hand in return. "I'm not leaving home again. Plus, I do my research in the evening." She glanced at her phone for the time. "Speaking of which, I need to get going. I have some to do tonight so I can present my findings to Agent Lightfoot tomorrow afternoon before my shift at Blue's. I'm beat."

After hugging her sister and brother-in-law, giving Violet an extra squeeze, and kissing Darla's cheek—who was staying a bit longer since Marguerite had hogged Violet's attention all evening—they headed for Declan's pickup.

"That was interesting." Declan started the engine.

"You're not used to Josh's big mouth, are you?"

"Eh. I guess not." He sighed. "How much work do you have to do?" He took her hand.

"As much as it takes, why?" He had *that* look in his eye, the one that made her body tingle.

He didn't answer as he put the truck in drive and sped down the road towards Timbisha Township.

They didn't say much but Marguerite didn't feel like a conversation. Some things didn't need to be said, and he proved it to her when they got home. He didn't even bother pretending to go to his room. He followed her into hers and spent the better part of an hour taking her mind off of all the things weighing her down at the moment.

In the afterglow, he held her until his breaths evened out and his hand relaxed on her hip. They were spooning so it was easy to maneuver herself into a sitting position. He didn't stir when she slipped on a t-shirt, grabbed her MacBook and started the necessary research to get Agent Lightfoot and the FBI out of her life once and for all.

DECLAN REACHED FOR MARGUERITE BUT THE BED was empty. He sat up and noted her computer wasn't on the nightstand. She'd been up most of the night clicking away on something. He'd tried to take her mind off whatever plagued her mad researching but she'd said, "Go back to sleep, baby. I'm on to something..."

He didn't think she realized her endearment and it was enough to satisfy him she wasn't going anywhere but, damn it, she was gone when he woke.

Pissed, he threw the covers from his body, used the facilities and put on some clothes. The sun was already beating down on the earth but the clock read 7:45, too early for either of them to be up for a nightshift at Blue's. Between the bar, football, Lightfoot's demands and her chocolate making she was running herself ragged.

He found her at the dinette in the kitchen, clicking away on the keyboard but he noted she had the files Lightfoot let her leave with next to her. He knew they contained a few autopsy reports.

"Do you want some coffee, honey?" When she jumped, he really began to worry about her.

"Oh, you scared the shit out of me, Declan." She turned her red eyes to him. "Yeah, I think a mug would be good, especially when I tell you what I've discovered and the theory it's led me to."

He started the coffee maker and braced himself for whatever news she had...

...And boy, was it a doozy. At least they wouldn't need to leave the area to find their killer. When finished with her conclusion, and by god it was a damn good one, he leaned back to process all of the information. He took in her crumpled pajamas, messy hair and bloodshot eyes.

"Go upstairs and take a nap. We don't need to be at the station until later and you need the rest." He leaned forward and pressed a kiss onto her forehead, then helped her out of the chair. "Damn, your brain turns me on."

She smiled, barefaced and looking utterly exhausted. "Does it?"

"Most definitely. Come on. We don't need to wake your mom with all this gruesome crap."

He gathered her notes and the files, and she tucked her MacBook under her arm before leading her upstairs. Once there, he coaxed her into the shower with him, letting the warm water sink into her muscles. Tenderly, he washed the stink of autopsies, serial killers and murder scenes from of her body and, hopefully, her mind. Afterward he took her back to bed where he occupied her time until she fell into a deep sleep.

Satisfied she was out for the count, he stepped out of the room and called Jarod.

"She figure it out?"

"Don't you ever say hello?"

"Why waste time like you're doing now?"

Declan rolled his eyes heavenward as he took the last step

off the staircase. Darla was in the kitchen frying bacon. He nodded to her with his chin and said into his cell phone, "Yeah, she did and it's big. I want you in the meeting when she briefs the team."

"I'll tell Lightfoot..." and Jarod was gone.

Declan stared at his phone then shoved it into his back pocket.

Darla took the skillet from the burner and set it aside. "Are you hungry?"

"Yes, Ma'a—Darla. Thank you."

She filled a plate with scrambled eggs and bacon while he helped himself to some orange juice from the fridge.

"Did she solve the case?"

"Sort of. At the very least she can point the FBI in the right direction, and maybe get Lightfoot to pack his bags and leave Timbisha Township."

"Really?"

He nodded as he took a drink. "You've got one helluva daughter, Darla. I hope you don't mind me sayin' so."

She studied him a moment before she took a sip from her mug of coffee. "I don't. But I need to warn you. If you hurt her, I'll shoot you."

He choked on his juice, the citrus burning his throat, but when he saw the corner of her mouth twitch he smiled. "It's good to know these things ahead of time. With your blessing, Darla, I plan on keeping her if she'll have me."

Darla's eyes widened in surprise before she gave him a motherly hug. "Praise the Lord and, of course, you have my blessing. If she doesn't say yes, I'll have to set her straight. You're a good man, Declan McKinley."

MARGUERITE STOOD IN FRONT OF THE LARGE GLASS board where the serial killer's murder victims were mapped out by date and location. The team had done well adding the information she'd gathered for them yesterday. Unfortunately, they only had sporadic IDs on the victims, all women, all ranging in age between late teens to under 30. She shared a look with Declan who threw her a wink.

"All right, Ms. Theroux. Tell us what you've discovered." Agent Lightfoot stood with his arms crossed, his dark eyes daring her to blow his mind.

Inside, she smirked to herself because what she'd discovered still surprised herself.

Ignoring the agent, Marguerite pointed at a section of photos before stepping forward. "All of these victims are connected—including the first victim found outside of Timbisha Township—to your serial killer. My guess he's a long hauler." She moved the first Timbisha Township murder victim's autopsy photo to the group of twenty-four serial killings from across the country, bodies dumped along interstates.

"But these two," she grouped the second and fourth victims' pictures to the side next to each other on top of the board to the right, "are not from your serial killer." She raised a hand to tell Agent Lightfoot to wait when she heard his intake of breath. "The labs on the third body came in. The fact that she was found in her car and not outside wrapped in plastic indicates she doesn't belong. The coroner said she committed suicide." Marguerite took down those photos and handed them to Jarod.

Agent Lightfoot looked over the board, then indicated to the two murder victims she'd separated. "A copycat?"

"Yes. Well, sort of."

"What do you mean?" Jarod asked not unkindly. He'd stepped forward as well to study the board's new configuration. "How are these two different?

"Well." She touched the pictures of the crime scenes. "Victim number two," she stopped to consult her tablet, "identified as Mary Jo Costa, was found partially buried way up this hill, right? The other bodies were found dumped encased in plastic along the side of interstate 80 like trash. No attempt at concealing them had been made."

Roland nodded. "Okay, but the latest body was dumped off the side of the road like the others, just not off the highway. Only Timbisha's second victim is different."

"Yes, but our copycat would've figured out that detail after our news leak got reported." She eyed Jarod who scowled. He still hadn't figured out who'd squealed the details to the press.

Declan leaned his butt against a desk. "Damn, woman. You've got one sexy brain."

She ignored the man even though her heart sped up enough to make her blush, and Jarod chuckled quietly. When Declan said things like that her heart just...melted.

"Anyway, I think we need to take a closer look at victim twenty-six," here she grabbed a sharpie and crossed out the number, "who I'm renaming Vic 1, to indicate this one belongs to Timbisha county and unrelated to the serials."

"Why?"

She turned around and faced the group of men, some staring openly at her, others looking intrigued. "Because why the hell did a beautiful 23-year-old woman transplant herself to Timbisha Township? We know she took a job at Walmart as a checker." She lifted the file Agent Lightfoot had left on her front porch the night before. "Not a supervisory, or managerial position. The only people who transplant themselves to this part of Nevada on purpose are retirees, or people who wanted to be close to family, or for work. At her age, they come here for a job, and not for minimum wage." She turned back to the board and stared at Mary Jo, the first of the copycat's victims. "She was either running away from something or toward someone."

"You can't possibly know that," said Agent Lightfoot.

"Sir, at twenty-three I could've found trouble in Los Angels, Miami, or New York City. I wanted out of here pretty bad and when I got to college I seriously questioned coming back to this small community of busybodies. Why the hell would I have come back to Timbisha Township if not for my family?"

Here she looked at Declan wondering for the first time why he'd really come back.

Jarod touched her shoulder and stepped back with the rest of the men, but his expression said he understood her. "All we know about Mary Jo Costa is she rented a small apartment near the Walmart, and had been in Timbisha Township two weeks."

"I'm telling you, investigate her life or, if you want, I can do it. My money's on a boyfriend as the reason for her relocating here." Marguerite shrugged. "I think Mary Jo's killer hated her. Her body was brutalized viciously. Victim 2's damage was limited to strangulation. Plus, she was much older—almost like a random kill. And neither Mary Jo, nor Mrs. Lanford, were sexually assaulted according to the report. All the others were."

No one said anything for a while absorbing what she said. She opened the autopsy file and looked up. "The coroner's report says Mary Jo had been dead at least three weeks, meaning she'd been killed before the first body here was found. They also found soil in the wounds and her cause of death was exsanguination, not strangulation. It's like she was buried, then dug up and wrapped in plastic, after the serial killer's body was found."

"You think our copycat heard the news, dug up Mary Jo to add the plastic and then killed another person to cover his tracks?"

Declan cleared his throat. "It's my theory as well, Lightfoot. Look at the amount of damage on Mary Jo compared to the other victims. Someone killed Mrs. Lanford to make Mary Jo's murder look like part of the series of deaths."

"It's only a theory." Marguerite moved toward Declan, done with looking at decomposed bodies and discussing how killers think. "You guys are the professionals. You figure it out. I have an event to plan, and a shift to work at Blue's tonight. I'm outta here."

With that she walked to the door, Declan chuckling as he and Jarod followed her outside.

Once they were far enough away, Jarod said, "Lightfoot and his team will have to pull out of Timbisha Township to look for the serial killer. Mary Jo and Mrs. Lanford fall under my jurisdiction."

"We have to prove Marguerite's theory because the team's still trying to identify the other victims. They need a starting point to catch the long-hauler, or whoever the hell is committing those murders." Declan's voice dripped in disgust.

"God, if Agent Lightfoot asks me to help them with the serial I'm going to tell him to stick it where the sun doesn't shine and I don't care what he does to me if I do." She was finished with this kind of work. But she still had to peruse all of Mary Jo's social media accounts because she didn't have a clue why the woman came here. "Jarod." She stopped in the middle of the parking lot. "Can you ask Sonja to run a report on Mary

Jo's cell phone? Maybe we can find out who she's been talking to while I poke around her Instagram account."

"I'll let you know what she finds. In the meantime, don't worry about Lightfoot."

Declan asked, "Why'zat?"

"Because if he tries to steal Marguerite I'm going to tell him I need her."

"Jarod—"

"—It's just for show." Jarod held up his hand a moment before he walked into the station without a backward glance.

"He even does it in person."

Marguerite needed the laugh as she climbed into Declan's pickup and sighed. When he got in and started the engine she grabbed his hand. "Thank you for backing me up in there."

He raised her hand to his lips and kissed the back of it. "You're welcome. I wouldn't have missed it. Just seeing the look on Roland's face was worth it."

"Why? You know he's going to try to recruit me again."

"Yeah, but he knows there's no way in hell you'd ever work for him again. Right?"

She chuckled at his panicked question. "You know I won't. I'm happy here in my little gossipy town. Speaking of which, it's time for my shift. Are you staying at the bar all night or do I need my car?"

"I'm retired. I go where you go, honey."

Chapter Seventeen

SIGHING

I go where you go, honey

Declan's words still floated through her mind as she handed the man his chicken wings. Even though the jukebox blared and Blue's patrons seemed to be at their loudest, all she could think about was him. Concentration on her work—whether it be at Blue's, making chocolate, or researching cyberspace for clues as to why Mary Jo Costa had moved to Timbisha Township—was often broken by how much Declan McKinley dominated her thoughts.

It'd been a few days since walking out of Agent Lightfoot's trailer. Jarod had a relaxed air about him since the FBI's exit from Timbisha Township. The hunt for a serial killer who liked to leave a trail of bodies along Interstate 80 was now the bureau's problem. Jarod's killer was here, a local living among them, and between him and Declan, Marguerite was sure they'd figure it out soon—without her help.

At least, that's what she told herself when her fingers itched to do some research late at night.

"I swear I'm gonna get Davie and Lance one of these days," Cheryl grumbled as she punched in a drink order.

"What'd they do now?" Dusty had just come from the kitchen. Marguerite was curious because the two troublemakers had been conspicuously on their best behavior all evening.

Cheryl set her tray on the counter and fisted her hands on her hips. "They're disgusting pigs is all. I can't stand guys who treat woman like dog crap."

Since Marguerite didn't think either of the two had girlfriends she assumed they must've been trash talking and Cheryl overheard their conversation. "Ignore them with a smile on your face. Even those two will tip better if you do. They aren't worth your anger, Cheryl."

The waitress speared Marguerite with a dirty look, which she ignored.

Trey walked by carrying a bin full of dirty dishes. "They're messing with you on purpose. Don't fall for it. Besides, Kelvin's laying into them now." He didn't stop but pushed through the swinging door to the kitchen.

Marguerite filled Cheryl's order ticket and set the drinks on her tray. "Who's Kelvin?"

"My boyfriend," she snapped and the waitress carried the drinks to her table to serve.

Declan had rotated his body around to watch the crowd and Marguerite didn't miss his gaze zeroing in on the troublemakers.

"What is it?" Marguerite didn't like the look on Declan's face, the one he often wore while on the hunt.

He turned deep brown eyes to her. "The feeling's back."

Marguerite glanced at Davie and Lance throwing darts while yucking it up with a few familiar faces, and some not so familiar. They weren't doing anything unusual; laughing a bit too loud, cat-calling at Cheryl or any other woman walking by, and challenging men who'd had a little too much to drink to a game of darts. A few of their friends from the mines sat around joining in.

"You think it's both of them?" She knew Declan understood what she meant.

His chest swelled as he inhaled a breath through his nose and let it out slow, thinking... "Maybe." He nodded once then turned back around to finish his wings.

Marguerite set a beer in front of him knowing it'd be his last for the night. Fred flagged her down for another round, who sat on the other side of the bar with his buddy Frank.

"How's your wife?" She poured two more pints.

"Won't stop having nightmares about finding..." he stopped. "They were friends, her and Denise."

"Mrs. Lanford? I'm sorry, I didn't know that."

"Same grade in school, neither of them left Timbisha Township—joined the same bible and bunco groups. Can't imagine who'd want to hurt the poor woman." Frank nodded his thanks when she handed him his beer before he took a sip.

"Damn shame." Fred lifted his pint into the air. "To Denise Lanford."

Marguerite caught Cheryl's dirty look at the two barflies as she breezed behind them on her way to the kitchen to drop off an order.

From the corner of her eye she saw a woman wrap her arms around Declan and Marguerite saw red...until she realized Sonja and her children had arrived.

"Want me to find you a table?" Declan asked Sonja as Marguerite stepped closer to say hello.

"Nah, we can find one. You look comfortable here." Sonja

smiled at Marguerite. "Hi. Thank you again for helping my boys find teams."

"Oh, you should be thanking Dusty. It was all his doing."

At the mention of his name, Dusty came out of his office. "Hey boys... Sonja. Good to see you again."

Marguerite didn't miss the blush on Sonja's face. Apparently, neither did her brother because Declan immediately stood from his barstool. "I see a table over by the pinball machines." He corralled Ryan, Rodney and Rosie—who'd immediately taken her uncle's hand into hers—and moved them across the busy restaurant.

Dusty looked at Marguerite. "Their ticket's on the house. Anything they want."

Marguerite nodded while Sonja began to argue.

Dusty immediately raised both hands. "No buts. It's on me, I insist." Then he turned and walked back into his office and closed the door.

"Marguerite, please, I can pay for our meal."

She laughed. "Once Soldier gives me an order I can't refuse it." At Sonja's confused expression, she explained the situation between herself and Dusty. "It's what I call Dusty because he's a veteran. Please, relax and enjoy yourself. Declan's got the kids settled and there are menus on the table. Let him know what you want and I'll make sure to put in your order."

"O-okay." Sonja caught up with her family and Marguerite got back to work.

Declan remained at his sister's table until they finished with their meal. Meanwhile, Marguerite caught tidbits of different conversations, most of them talking about Cheryl's mood. The waitress had been snapping at most of the customers and Marguerite shook her head in disgust.

If she doesn't want good tips it's no skin off my nose.

But one conversation made by a couple of guys who were just barely able to drink—she'd carded them and they were both twenty-one—caught her attention:

"She completely flipped out on him."

"What'd she do this time? Slit his tires?"

"No, ripped up his clothes and threw 'em into the yard. Kelvin didn't know what to do because she came at him with the scissors."

"Dude, he needs to cut that bitch loose before she kills him in his sleep."

Marguerite watched the waitress snarl and snap at the customers, most of them clearing out of Blue's.

"Hey, Marguerite? Can I talk to Dusty?"

"Sure, Carmen. He's in his office, let me get him for you." Marguerite hustled her butt down the hall and knocked.

"Come in."

"I think Cheryl's on a rampage again. Carmen wants to talk to you."

"Damn it." Dusty followed Marguerite down the hall. Cheryl and Carmen weren't friends and the other woman complained about Dusty's rude waitress all the time.

"Carmen, honey, why do you sit in her section?"

As the woman began her tirade, Marguerite returned to the bar in time to say goodbye to Sonja and Ryan, the twins smacking each other as they headed for the front doors.

"Do they always fight like that?" Marguerite asked once Declan reclaimed his barstool.

He grunted with a shake of his head. "You've got no idea."

Declan's phone buzzed with a text from Agent Lightfoot. *Does this man look familiar?*

The grainy photo Lightfoot sent showed a man in a baseball cap, face in shadow.

Even if he did, I can't see his face. Got anything better?

We found this guy in a few security films from three different truck stops. What's Marguerite think?

As if conjuring her, Marguerite stood in front of him with an iced tea. Declan held up his phone. "Is he from around here?"

She took the phone, squinted for five seconds, then handed it back. "Can't see his face, but no. I don't recognize him. Why?"

"Lightfoot sent it. Apparently, he's been seen around the other dumpsites."

He tapped out a text to Lightfoot. *She doesn't recognize him. Not from Timbisha Township.* If Marguerite didn't recognize the man, Declan was confident he wasn't from around here. The FBI needed to search elsewhere.

Meanwhile, he couldn't shake his feeling. He spun on his barstool and searched out Davie and Lance. They still played darts. One of their friends was having a discussion with the waitress, who looked a little less sour-faced. She turned her cheek and the man kissed her before she stopped at a table with three women well on their way to a hangover.

"Who's the guy lovin' up on Cheryl?" he asked Marguerite the next time she passed by.

"What guy?"

"Over with Tweedledum and Tweedledee." He lifted his chin toward the group hanging around Davie and Lance.

"Must be Kelvin, her boyfriend. Never met him but I remember him from the diner. I think he's new at one of the mines." She turned to put money in the register and came back. "There's something familiar other than that, though..."

When she didn't explain he faced her. "What is it, honey."

She looked at him and grinned. "Don't call me that..." She sent him an air kiss to soften her rebuke "...while I'm at work."

He surveyed the whole of Blue's Whiskey Bar.

Barflies and regulars sat at the mahogany topped bar...

Families and sports fans seated in the restaurant area watching games and enjoying what the kitchen had to offer—and scowling at their grumpy waitress...

Rowdies playing darts or shuffleboard...

Dance floor empty but piped in music filtered through the building's speaker system...

...and somewhere a killer lurked.

He felt it in his bones.

"If you keep glaring at my customers I'm going to have to ask you to leave."

Declan turned to Dusty. "I'm surveyin'. There's a difference."

"Clever. Find anything interesting?"

"What do you know about Cheryl's boyfriend?"

He watched Dusty's eyebrows lower over his eyes. "Some new guy from the lithium mine. Kelvin something."

"Did he grow up here or come from out of state?"

Dusty turned to face Declan, and lowered his voice. "You think he's the killer?"

Declan took a long drink of his iced tea. "Hell if I know." He could barely keep the disgust from lacing his voice. "What can you tell me about him?"

"Nothing other than he started dating Cheryl a few months back. She misses him when he's on shift. Hell, she's so grouchy lately I thought they'd broken up."

Marguerite rang the bell signaling last call. Declan hadn't realized the time. Dusty clapped him on the back. "Gotta close up."

Declan lifted his glass to finish his iced tea only to notice there was nothing left but melting ice. He placed it on the bar and stood, keeping his eyes on the man he needed to research. Other than some lone stragglers, last call was smooth and the next thing he knew Marguerite was climbing into his pickup.

"Where've you been?"

"With you." He put the truck in drive.

"No, you haven't. Something's buzzing around in your head."

He drummed his thumbs on the steering wheel a moment before he jerked the wheel in the opposite direction from Timbisha Township.

"Where're we going?"

"I need to see where they found Mrs. Lanford's body. Do you know where Fred and his wife live?"

It was dark but he could still see her eyes widen. "Yeah, about a mile and half up here on the left."

He passed the entrance to Blue's Whisky Bar and watched his odometer.

"Right there." Marguerite pointed at a double-wide trailer.

"All righty." He slowed down, then stopped in the middle of the road, thinking. "She walked her dog up this way opposite Blue's and found the body..." His words trailed off as he lifted his foot from the brake and let the truck creep down the empty road until he found the police tape. "So, this is a half mile from Fred's driveway, and two miles from Blue's almost exactly."

"What are you thinking."

"Wonderin' how long it'd take a person to dump a body from Blue's on a busy night."

Marguerite puffed up her cheeks before blowing out air. "Damn. You think the killer planned to leave the body here? That it wasn't a random dump?"

"Convenient, is more like it...maybe." Declan drummed his thumbs again. "Hell, honey, I don't know. It's only a guess but somethin's buggin' me about the night of the fight and I can't put my finger on it."

She reached for his hand to stop his right thumb. "Hey."

He faced her and got lost in her eyes.

"Let's go home, rest, and then tackle it together, okay? Two heads are better than one. Honestly, I didn't think researching with another person would be helpful, but it is. Besides," and here she kissed the back of his hand shooting lightning up his arm. "I'm beat and I wanna go to bed." She waggled her eyebrows up and down.

"Hell, woman. Why didn't ya say?"

He wasted no time jerking the wheel around for the second time and broke the speed limit back to her house.

IN THE WEE HOURS OF THE MORNING, MARGUERITE sat in bed with the MacBook on her lap. Declan's soft snores soothed her racing mind as she tapped away on the keys. He rolled toward her and wrapped his arm around her waist, almost dislodging the computer.

She paused a moment waiting to see if he would wake, but he settled down again as her fingers continued their search for Mary Jo Costa's boyfriend.

When Declan had pointed out the man Cheryl was dating,

Marguerite knew she'd never been introduced—yet he looked familiar...

...but not from Blue's, or Timbisha Township.

And certainly not in connection with Cheryl.

Agent Lightfoot hadn't rescinded her research clearance so she accessed the database she needed to look through Mary Jo's video reels—and there it was—the picture Marguerite had seen in her original search; Mary Jo Costa posing with Kelvin.

She clicked on the picture to capture the screen shot and then read the caption. "Me with my love-Arches National Park."

She ran some facial recognition on the man to verify his name, which was taking its sweet time.

Declan's hand moved up and down her thigh now, letting her know he was, indeed, awake.

"Did you find him?" he mumbled into her hip.

She chuckled. "How'd you know who I was looking for?"

"You make a little sigh when you're satisfied."

Marguerite closed her MacBook and set it on the nightstand. "Oh, I think I'm louder than that, surely."

His soulful brown eyes tilted toward her face. In a move she didn't see coming he had her pinned beneath him. He kissed her like his life depended on it before coming up for air. "No, honey. I'm talking about after you make all that other noise, then you sigh."

"Maybe you should show me what you're talking about?"

"Yeah, maybe I should."

DECLAN HAD BEEN CORRECT—MARGUERITE DID, indeed, sigh when she was satisfied.

She chuckled to herself as she poured tempered chocolate over her perfect little ganache witches and ghosts for Camille to try. If all went well, even if the woman wanted changes in the design, there would be plenty of time to tweak them before the Harvest Dinner St. Anthony's put on in the fall.

Strong arms wrapped around her middle and the heavenly scent of freshly showered man floated around her.

Declan nipped her earlobe. "Got any of those spicy ones left?"

"Over there." She indicated to a container next to the refrigerator.

He kissed her neck and squeezed her one last time before reaching for the container. Feeling bereft without his touch she continued her task, not wanting to think about how he made her feel.

Which is what, Marguerite? He's just a man having a good time with you.

Wishing he wasn't like every other man in her life who'd leave her after deciding he'd had enough, she poured chocolate onto the second batch. So what if he'd already taken the job with James King. It didn't mean he'd want her around once he started on with the family full time.

God, the thought was depressing.

"Did you call Jarod to let him know what you found?" He took two chocolates from the container and poured himself a cup of coffee, plopping one chocolate into his mug, and the other one into his mouth.

"Did you make headway on the case?" Her mother, donned in a chenille robe, opened the refrigerator and took out some eggs.

"A little. Good morning, Mom." She leaned in for a hug. "I planned to call Jarod when I've finished with these. Mary Jo hadn't documented the guy's name in her posts, so I'm waiting for a couple of the FBI sources to get back to me."

It bugged Marguerite that Cheryl hadn't spoken much about her new boyfriend. She liked to complain about men but apparently not the ones in her own life. *Maybe she's happy?* Marguerite immediately dismissed the idea. Cheryl only complained. Marguerite had never known her to be content and that probably explained why she hadn't talked about the boyfriend.

"What are your plans today?" Darla asked Declan.

"Meeting up with James. Then Marguerite has to be at the park to help Dusty with the football team. What are you doing today, Darla?" He took a sip of coffee.

She opened the egg carton and cracked a few in a frying pan. "The church committee is working on plans for the upcoming holiday events, starting with the Harvest Dinner."

"So soon? The dinner isn't for a few weeks."

Darla turned to Marguerite. "We have to start early so everything will be ready. It's the reason why Camille is so good at event planning. Did you tell Dusty you'll need the night off?"

"Yes. I'm glad you'll be there too. I really need you to be my eyes and ears for me. Let me know what everyone thinks of these babies." She referred to her autumn themed chocolates.

"Everyone is going to love them, darling."

"I certainly love them," Declan murmured.

At his mention of the L-word, Marguerite's heart beat faster than it should.

Stop it. He's got a sweet tooth, that's all.

Darla finished making breakfast and the three of them ate in companionable silence for a few moments. When Declan took a drink, Darla raised her eyebrows. "How's the coffee?"

"Fantastic." He took another slurp before returning to his eggs.

"You know," Darla said, "I've heard of coffee 'bombs' before. I bet if you made salted caramel, or maybe peppermint, they'd really take off, Marguerite."

She grinned when she locked eyes with Declan. "I'm already on it, Mom."

"HEY, JAROD. IT'S MARGUERITE..."

Declan listened to her one-sided conversation with the Timbisha county sheriff as she explained what she'd found out about Cheryl's boyfriend. Kelvin Robles had taken the job with the new lithium mine four months ago and been dating Cheryl for three. He moved from Salt Lake City, Utah where he lived with Mary Jo Costa. The details were still sketchy but Marguerite thought Kelvin tried to break it off with Mary Jo but she followed him to Timbisha Township.

Declan liked the theory but there had to be some major hate between the two because Mary Jo's body had been viciously attacked.

"That's all I know for now, Jarod. I can keep digging in her socials and cell records but Declan and I both think you should bring Kelvin in for questioning...all right, talk to you later. Bye."

She put her phone in her purse and sat back.

"He bringing in Kelvin."

"Yes."

"But?"

"I don't know. Everything I've found on Mary Jo doesn't

make her out to be crazy." She used her fingers to put quotes around the c-word.

Declan shrugged. "You know how people are, Marguerite. Anything can set a person off and a woman scorned is no laughing matter."

She nodded. "This is true."

She didn't even hesitate and it made him wonder...

"You aren't the crazy type, are you?"

She laughed. "Worried I'll suffocate you in your sleep?"

"Should I be?"

"Only if you decide to piss me off."

"I would never."

"You would and you have and you know it."

"That was before, honey." He reached for her hand and held on. Her skin was so soft and warm it made him relax. God, his need for her was getting out of hand. He didn't want to lose her but he wasn't sure how fast or slow he should go before he declared himself.

He'd never wanted 'long-term' before he met Marguerite.

Would she rebuke him or return his affection?

We're certainly compatible in the sack. He shifted in his seat just thinking about how good they were together.

But how did she *feel* about him? She'd never said and it bothered him something fierce.

"Are you dropping me at the park before you head out to The Estate?"

"Logistically it makes sense." Lord knows he didn't want to, though. He needed to be with her but their schedules were working against them. "Yeah, heading there now."

"Good," she said quietly.

He looked at her before directing his attention back to the road. "If I make it quick with James, I can be back to the park for the last hour of practice. I'd like to check on my nephews and talk to Sonja."

She offered him a stale smile, one she used to use while working with him and he didn't like it. "Of course. Logistically it makes sense."

They'd pulled into the parking lot in front of the fields. Dusty and Chance were unloading his pickup and all Declan wanted to do was call James and cancel the meeting but Marguerite hopped out of the truck. "See ya later, Declan." She closed the door in his face and turned away from him.

"Damn it," Declan murmured.

He put the truck in gear a little too hard and headed out to the King Estate.

God, I wish I knew what I was doing.

He used the drive alone to figure out how to proceed with Marguerite. He needed her, damn it, and didn't want to be without her.

He wanted her to live with him in the new house.

Maybe I should approach it that way.

He met James in his office to go over what needed to be done with the herd, whether or not to move it into a different pasture and when, ever-rising feed costs, irrigation issues, and when to start introducing the bull to the cows. When they'd finished going over all the livestock, including the horses and a few goats they'd purchased for Jessica, James stood and grabbed his keys.

Declan followed suit assuming their meeting was over and couldn't wait to get back into town to see Marguerite.

James opened the side door and led him to his truck. "We got lucky and Jason's had a crew working nonstop on the manager's house. Let's go take a look."

"Sounds good." Declan nodded but on the inside he

cringed. Touring the new house would take time away from getting back to his woman.

James drove a quarter of a mile down the road, then pulled into a newly graded dirt driveway leading to a rather large sprawling ranch with a four car garage and a double front door. Declan hadn't known what to expect but he was more than pleased with what he saw.

It was a simple layout with four bedrooms and an office, but the kitchen was the showstopper, fancier than Declan would ever need. Then a thought occurred to him.

Would Marguerite be happy here?

"James, do you know anything about tempering chocolate?"

James didn't bother hiding his grin. "No, but—don't be angry—Josh thought it best to incorporate a small room off the kitchen with a dehumidifier just in case things worked out between you and Marguerite."

Declan threw his head back and laughed. "Your family is tenacious when it comes to matchmaking but I appreciate the forethought." He had to hand it to Josh. The area he'd appropriated for Marguerite's chocolate business was basically a secondary kitchen—with more counter space than in Darla's kitchen.

"It wasn't all Josh," James said, interrupting Declan's thoughts. "Camille's got a stake in Marguerite's talents now that they're working together. "

Declan reached out to shake James's hand. "Thank you for all you've done here."

Once he was back on the road he pressed the gas pedal a little harder than necessary in his haste to get back to *his* Marguerite.

He found her immediately but Rosie nearly took him out at the knees. "Hi Uncle Declan!"

He lifted his niece in the air once and pretended to drop her before setting her back on the ground. "Hey there sweetheart. Where's your mama?"

"At Rodney's practice. We got lucky. Both my brothers' teams practice at the same time."

"That's quite a mouthful." Yeah, and they were lucky. He couldn't be happier things were working out for his sister. She deserved to have an easy time in her life for once. "How come you didn't go with her to Rodney's practice?"

"Because I get sick of his face."

"Rosie," Declan scolded.

"I know, I know." She ran over to the swings where some other girls were playing. Declan surveyed the park, torn on whether he should stick with his niece or go to Marguerite.

He'd been trying to make up his mind for about ten minutes when Sonja showed up.

"Where'd you come from?" She gave him a brief hug.

"The Estate. Just got back and found your wayward daughter." He nodded toward the playground. "How's Rodney doing?"

"Great. I like his coaches. They were impressed with how aggressive Rodney is and put him on defense."

Declan laughed. "He's definitely got the temperament for it." He turned toward the sidelines where Marguerite stood with her back to him, clipboard in hand. "The house is almost built."

"Now you can move into your own place."

Declan threw his arm around his sister's shoulders. "I know what you're doing."

She laughed. "Yeah, but do you know what *you're* going to do?"

His eyes landed on Marguerite. "Sure do."

Chapter Eighteen

PART OF THE FAMILY

"The house should be ready for you to move into by next week. " Josh eyeballed Declan before scooping a spoonful of stew into his mouth.

Darla had started the meal in the crockpot before she left for church. When Marguerite and Declan got home she'd found a note from her mother saying Josh and Missy were coming over for dinner.

Missy cut the meat, potatoes, and carrots into smaller pieces for Violet, who gobbled it up like the growing toddler she was. "I'm sure you're ready to settle into something more permanent."

Marguerite didn't miss the sly look on her sister's face as she put more meat onto Violet's kiddie plate.

Declan nodded while he chewed. "You designed a great house, Josh. Your father showed it to me today."

"Oh?" Marguerite felt like the end was near. Once he moved out, would he still want to be with her? "What's it like?"

Declan let out a chuckle as a smile formed on his handsome face. "It looks like something the Kings would produce."

Josh sat back. "What the hell is that supposed to mean?"

"Gentleman," Darla warned. "Violet doesn't need to learn new words of that nature."

"Sorry," Josh said automatically, kissed his daughter's cheek, then looked at Declan. "What's wrong with it? I even put in a space for Marguerite."

"What?" She dropped her spoon and stared at Josh who waved her off.

"It's for your chocolates, Magpie."

She took a drink, closed her eyes and counted to three. "Don't call me that and what do you mean it's for my chocolates?"

Darla cleared her throat. "Camille and I were discussing things and, well, we thought it best for you to have a facility to make your concoctions close to The Estate for events, since it's where they do their staging."

She looked at Declan, who said nothing but wore a weird frowny expression—a cross between determination and trepidation.

"Darla," he began, but Marguerite held up a hand.

"Did you guys even bother thinking to ask where the best place would be for me to work? Mom, you know how specific I am. And...what if Declan doesn't want me making a mess in his home?"

"What if I do?" She barely heard his muttered words under his breath, but her eyes shot to his face. He focused on his spoon searching through his bowl of stew for the perfect bite.

"You want me to make my chocolates at your new house?"

"I want *you* at my new house." He cleared his throat,

nodded once, then tucked back into his stew like he hadn't just dropped the biggest bomb she'd ever felt on her heart.

She swallowed the lump in her throat, about to lay into him for saying something like that in front of her family—

A loud knock on the door startled everyone before Marguerite scooted her chair back a little too forcefully making a loud screech on the linoleum. When she reached the storm door, Jarod stood there in full uniform with a scowl on his face to match her own.

"What?"

Her tone raised his eyebrows so far they disappeared under his hat. "Sorry to bother you, Miss Theroux."

She opened the door wider inviting him inside. "Knock it off. What's happened?" She stomped back into the kitchen. "Grab a bowl. There's stew in the crockpot."

All eyes remained on Jarod as he helped himself then turned and leaned his butt on the counter and took a bite. "This is really good. Did you make this, Mrs. Theroux?"

Darla turned to stare at Jarod. "I did but if this isn't a social call you'd better put it down and tell us what's happened. I don't like being in suspense, *Sheriff King*."

Marguerite stifled her grin at her mother's annoyed tone, glad she wasn't the only one ticked off at the moment.

"Sorry, *Darla*." Jarod took another bite, humming his enjoyment then set the bowl on the counter. "I'm actually here to ask Missy where she was the night we found Mrs. Lanford's body. Apparently, you're a suspect's alibi."

"She's what?" Josh yelled. "Who were you with, Melissa?"

Melissa's face turned red, then she lowered her eyebrows at her husband before turning them to her brother-in-law, making Marguerite laugh. "Oh, you've gone and done it now, Jarod."

"Davie called," Missy explained. "His dog needed help birthing her puppies."

"Why'd you bring in Davie?" Declan asked. "I thought Marguerite had cleared him."

Marguerite melted a little at Declan's faith in her theories regarding suspects. Too bad she also wanted to smack him.

"How long were you with him?" Jarod ignored everyone in the room except her sister.

"A couple of hours. He smelled like a brewery. Apparently, his dog started labor while he was out at Blue's. His sister called him in a panic, then he called the clinic's emergency line. I told him to meet me there. I was with him a few hours, probably until two or three. I was the only one on call and needed his help to encourage the puppies to breathe. He was really sweet about it. He really loves his dog, Jarod. I doubt he's your killer."

Jarod sighed, picked up his bowl and resumed eating. "You're right, he isn't the killer but I needed to verify his whereabouts."

"Well, why the hell didn't you just call?" Josh asked his brother while Marguerite grinned.

"Because he has to see the looks on peoples' faces when they tell their story to determine whether or not they're speaking the truth."

Jarod threw her a wink, scooped the last bite of stew into his mouth before rinsing out his bowl and putting it in the dishwasher.

"That was wonderful, Darla." He hugged her mother while she was still seated, then looked at Marguerite. "I'll let you know what I find out about Lance's whereabouts that night before we picked him up after the fight." The front door closed behind him and everyone stared at one another.

Finally, Josh broke the silence. "He's such an ass."

Violet said, "Ass," then pushed a carrot into her mouth.

Declan got up for more stew. "What do you say, Marguerite?"

"Yes, Jarod is indeed…" she looked at Violet, "…a horses rear end."

Missy and Darla laughed.

Declan turned and faced her again, his eyebrow raised and that damned look of determination on his face. "Do you think making chocolates at my house would work out for you?"

All eyes were on her now and she felt like the question he was asking wasn't only about making chocolate.

"Maybe."

Missy nodded at her like Marguerite had done something special. It wasn't so long ago she was giving her little sister pointers on the opposite sex. Oh, how life had changed.

"Well, I for one think you should take him up on his offer. I'd like to use the swamp cooler in the summer again."

Marguerite rolled her eyes. "Fine, Mom. I didn't realize you hated the chocolates so much."

"Oh, dear. I don't hate them. I just think moving your operation to Declan's is the better option."

Josh nodded with excitement. "Can't wait to show you all the stuff I put in for you, Magpie. Mom went to town on state-of-the-art equipment too. You're gonna love it."

Violet singsonged "Magpie" in her sweet little voice.

Marguerite gave him the most evil eye she could muster but didn't bother wasting her breath on her brother-in-law's teasing. *Don't. Call. Me. That.*

Of course, Josh's grin widened before he shoved another spoonful of stew into his mouth.

"THE REPORTS CAME BACK. THEY CONFIRMED THE man on Mary Jo's socials is Kelvin Robles."

Declan didn't bother sleeping in the other room anymore and Marguerite hadn't complained. He stripped down to his boxer briefs and was about to slide between the sheets when she made her announcement.

Declan nodded. "Jarod sent a text. He cleared Lance and Kelvin. They never left Blue's before the fight, and both had alibis afterward; Lance went to the emergency room because he'd cracked some ribs in the brawl, and Kelvin checked in late for his shift at the mine."

Marguerite's shoulders sagged. "So. Back to square one."

"Not necessarily. We couldn't find Cheryl."

He watched Marguerite blink long and hard. "Shit," she muttered as she picked up her MacBook and started clicking away.

"What are you looking for, honey?"

"Cheryl's socials. GPS on her phone won't work because she left it at Blue's..." He watched her face as she studied the screen with the intensity of a mad scientist on the brink of discovery.

"Oh." She clicked some more. Then she stared at him.

"What is it?"

"We have to call Jarod."

"At this hour?"

"Yes."

She picked up the cell phone, tapped the screen and Declan could hear it ringing as she put it on speaker.

"This better be life and death."

"What are you, eighty? It's barely eleven o'clock."

"Marguerite?" Declan heard the man growl, and she laughed.

"Of course it's me. Listen Jarod—Cheryl killed Mary Jo Costa and most likely Mrs. Lanford to cover her tracks."

There was a long sigh, and Lauren's grumble. Jarod murmured, "sorry" on his end before the background noise went silent. "Let's hear it, Marguerite."

She shared a look with Declan but continued on. "I missed it before but Mary Jo had blocked Cheryl from her accounts as she'd been making threats to her over Kelvin. Apparently, the jerk was two-timing both girls."

"Doesn't mean she killed Mary Jo."

"No, but—"

Then Declan said for her, "—Hell hath no fury—"

"—like a woman scorned," Jarod finished the cliche.

"Exactly." Marguerite continued, "and Cheryl isn't pleasant on her good days. I can't imagine what she's like in a relationship, or seriously wronged."

Declan remembered the conversation Marguerite overheard at the bar. "I can. Apparently, she's been abusing Kelvin. Did he cop to anything? Abuse? Crazy girlfriend?"

"No." Jarod sighed. "Look, I need a little more than a hunch."

"She doesn't have any posts around the time of Mary Jo's murder, and she posts pretty regularly, even at work."

"No other bodies have been discovered since the feds left, Jarod," Declan added. "And the other night, I took a dry run from Blue's to the body dump. She had plenty of time if the body was in her car."

"The lab report said they'd found foreign DNA under Mary Jo's fingernails, but there was nothing definitive. She fought her attacker, but," here he sighed long and loud, "I'll call them in the morning."

"Then you'll bring in Cheryl?" Marguerite met Declan's gaze.

"First, we check the labs again. If, and that's a biggie, there's evidence to get a search warrant for her car, I'll call it in."

The line went dead but Declan wasn't surprised. "He does get to the point, doesn't he?"

Marguerite laughed. "Jarod's not one for small talk. I think it's the reason why Timbisha Township likes him as their sheriff."

"I forgot it's an election year." Declan hadn't seen any campaign signs around.

"He's unopposed." Her voice had been muffled as she pulled her shirt off. He watched with hunger as she revealed herself. She was so beautiful; mind, body and soul. Lately it'd been hard for him to reconcile his feelings but it was getting easier. He'd recognized the jealousy. Now he understood why. He was in love with her.

When her face came free of the shirt she sent him a sultry smile. All thoughts of Jarod's reelection flew from him mind. "Come 'ere."

She climbed into his open arms and he kissed her with everything he felt in the moment. When he finally came up for air, she was beneath him staring into his eyes. He had to keep himself from getting lost in the moment. "I meant what I said."

Her eyebrows came down in confusion. "You mean about moving in with you? What you said at dinner."

When he didn't explain she let out a breath and moved to her side of the bed. He didn't let her go far; instead, he pulled her close and spooned against her back, rubbing her belly with his hand, and his nose on her neck. When she remained quiet he let out a frustrated sigh. "Do you feel nothing for me?"

His question must've surprised her because she flipped back over and glared into his face. "Do you feel something for me? I know you like this." With her hand she gestured between his chest and hers—and what a chest it was—"because you've never said otherwise."

He rolled over onto his back and stared at the ceiling. "Marguerite, I'm old, maybe too old for you. I've never had to explain things to a woman because I've never needed to." He rolled onto his side again and touched the backs of his fingers to her soft, soft cheek. "I've never wanted permanent before I met you."

He watched her swallow and her bottom lip quivered before she took his hand from her cheek. "You didn't like me when you met me."

"I liked you well enough." He couldn't prevent cracking a grin only to stifle it when she scowled.

"You thought I was a dumb blonde."

"I misunderstood your position." He leaned in and kissed the tip of her nose. She swatted him away without force and he grabbed her again to pin her beneath him.

She didn't fight. On the contrary, she lifted her mouth to his and all his need for declarations ended with satisfying a different kind of need.

If he'd been asked in his younger days what his perfect woman was, he'd have conjured Marguerite Theroux. Yes, she could be brusque on the outside but, damn it, she was brilliant, beautiful, caring, and had a vulnerability which called to him like a siren.

Later, when they held each other in the afterglow he

breathed in her scent, letting it imprint on his mind, on his heart...and the words fell out of his mouth.

"I love you, Marguerite."

———

THERE WASN'T ENOUGH AIR IN HER BEDROOM. No one other than family had ever uttered those three words to her.

Ever.

When she felt the tears well in her eyes, she kissed Declan's handsomely rugged face, ran her fingers along his whiskered jaw and leaned her forehead against his, breathing in the awesome scent of...

My man.

God, could she let herself believe him? He'd never lied to her but he had walked out of her life without a backward glance. The pain the image conjured had her jerking back to stare into his eyes. "You hurt me."

"I know," he whispered, as he ran his fingertips over her shoulder, then down her torso to the scar just above her hipbone. "I hurt myself...but I had to make sure that monster was put away for good. You were never far from my mind, honey. In fact, it was you who kept me going until Monti was behind bars. After the bureau let me go, I didn't know how to get you back until the Kings called. But I swear to God, Marguerite, even if he hadn't called I would've come for you." He sat up and leaned against the headboard. She copied the move and he took her hand in his. "The thing is, I don't know how you feel about me. I know we're good here," he indicated the bed, "as you said, but do you want to be with me? Can you see yourself as a ranch manager's wife, making chocolate treats for the community? Do you love me, Marguerite?"

Do I?

She looked around her old bedroom which held so many memories—good, bad, and difficult. Dealing with her community after pretending to be a drug-running murderer's whore, and what she'd had to do to get the information they needed to find Brad, what she'd had to endure during that time, the humiliation, losing grace within her hometown, with her church, her...soul.

"The thing is, I do love you."

"I hear a but in there." He kissed her hand again.

"Can you live with a woman whose reputation is so tattered there's going to be gossip everywhere you turn? I know you've heard what people say about me. You were there when Facebook blew up in my face." She referred to the set-up from her sister's stalker before she'd gone on the task force with Declan and her uncle.

God, what would Uncle Dane think about her being with Declan? Somehow, she pictured him smiling from Heaven, or at least growling out his approval.

Declan grinned, his whiskered dimple appearing in all its salt and pepper glory. "Do I look like a man who gives two shits about what other people think, especially those who don't have all the information or might have a grievance we don't know about? Besides, once they get a taste of those spicy chocolates you'll have 'em crawling on their hands and knees for a batch." He pulled her onto his lap. "Will you say it again, this time without the caveat?"

She snickered and hugged him, then kissed his forehead. "I." She kissed his nose. "Love." And now she went for his sweet lips, the ones which turned her insides into mush. "You."

"Thank God above." He groaned as he kissed her mouth and proceeded to show her again exactly how much he loved her.

———

Four days had gone by without a word from Jarod, and Cheryl still bitched and moaned her way through her shifts at Blue's.

Marguerite hadn't revealed to Dusty her theory about the waitress, and there was a part of Marguerite which prayed she'd been wrong. However, her hunches about people usually turned out to be correct.

Declan had spent the day with James going over *ranch stuff*, as she liked to refer to his new position. Jarod hadn't needed him for anything and, if James had any other investigative requests of her, dare she say, boyfriend, Declan wasn't saying.

Since Dusty owned a very popular post-football game hangout for players and coaches of Timbisha Township's popular peewee football league, and he was friends with most of them, they'd decided to hold a fundraiser for the sport, along with the cheerleader squads, at Blue's Whiskey Bar. Because it was basically a family event, Camille had summoned her team of volunteers to help with the cause. The party wasn't until later, but many of the regulars were still on the premises. Marguerite wondered if Dusty would kick everyone out.

Davie and Lance played a game of darts with each other, keeping unusually quiet for once. Frank and Fred took up their usual barstools, mulling over the week, their wives, and discussed local politics, including the election in November. So far, no one at the bar was unhappy about keeping on Sheriff King for another term.

She'd only been on shift for an hour when the front doors opened to reveal Camille, Lauren, Julie, and Darla. They were followed by another group from their church carrying boxes of decorations.

"Hi, Mom. Ladies." Marguerite came out from behind the bar to greet them. "The cook is ready for Julie. He's been prepping all afternoon. Let me get Dust—"

Just then, Dusty came from his office and clapped his hands. "All right, let's get started. Hey! Dumb and Dumber! Get your asses over here and help put this stuff up." He referred to Davie and Lance, who flipped off Dusty but then sauntered over to the group.

"Name's Davie, Ma'am." He stuck out his hand to Camille. "Me an' Lance here are happy to help."

"Pleasure to meet you. If you could start with the streamers and garland..." Camille directed the two misfits and, to Marguerite's surprise, they behaved like perfect gentleman.

She caught Dusty's eye. "How'd you manage that?"

Dusty winked at her. "I have my ways, Girl." He took a tote from Julie and escorted her into the kitchen where she'd be making a buffet dinner for parents, players, coaches and donors. When she saw Lauren climbing a step stool, Marguerite called out, "Are you supposed to be doing that in your condition?"

Lauren's eyes grew wide. "Who told you?"

Marguerite tapped her nose.

Lauren shook her head in disgust. "Josh is worse than an old gossiping hen clique."

Marguerite laughed and refilled Fred and Frank's beers.

The swinging door caught everyone's attention when

Dusty *encouraged* Cheryl from the kitchen, where she'd been no doubt texting, and escorted her into the dining room. "I'm sure being a part of a decorating committee isn't in my job description."

Lance laughed. "Why'd you get your car towed this morning?"

Cheryl growled. "It's none of your business." Then she turned to Dusty. "Listen, I have to go deal with that. Can I get outta here early? There's no customers here anyway."

"Cheryl, the party is starting in two hours. You'll get plenty of tips," he told the girl as he took over for Lauren on the step stool to hang a banner boasting the league's logo.

"You know," Davie said, "I heard they took in Kelvin for questioning about those murders. You wouldn't know anything about that, would you, Cheryl?"

"No!" She snapped a plastic tablecloth over the tables Darla and Camille had pushed together.

"Yeah, I guess Kelvin knew one of the victims," Davie said to Lance as if they were the only two having a conversation. "Where do you suppose Kelvin was that night?"

"Shut up, you two morons know he was here." Cheryl flew past them to get another tablecloth from the bin.

"Well?" Lance asked. "Did you two do something you shouldn't have or not?"

"Remember our deal, boys," Dusty warned as he climbed off the stepladder. "Pissing off my grouchy waitress is against the rules."

"You never let us have any fun."

Marguerite watched Cheryl like a hawk. She looked on the verge of tears, barely keeping her bottom lip from quivering by pinching her mouth closed. Her cheeks were flushed and her movements were so jerky she was afraid the woman would tear the plastic sheet in her hands.

Camille and her mother didn't seem to notice anything as they'd been directing the other volunteers on where to place tables for the buffet, lining it with chafing dishes and serving utensils, but Lauren had taken a barstool in order to put together some table ornaments. "What's with that girl?"

Surprised Jarod hadn't shared anything with his wife, who'd also been his former personal assistant, Marguerite merely shrugged. "Period?"

At Lauren's chuckle, she murmured, "The one good thing about being pregnant."

Marguerite didn't buy it. "Surely there's more good things about it than skipping your cycle."

Lauren's expression lit up the bar. "It's only a figure of speech. We couldn't be happier." Then Lauren's happy grin turned ornery. "You know, you'd better hurry up. You're lagging behind in the baby department."

Marguerite half laughed, half scoffed. "Right. All my reputation needs is an unwed pregnancy to top it off."

"Oh, come on, Marguerite. You know none of us were married when we got pregnant with our firsts, including Camille."

"Shut up! How do you know?"

Lauren shrugged, knowingly. "She told me."

They both started giggling. "Jarod's an accident? How did he take the news?"

"Oh, no..." Lauren shook her head and leaned in conspiratorially. "Apparently, Camille got pregnant on purpose because James was dragging his feet. *Jason*, is the accident."

Marguerite's laughter must've carried farther than she

thought because Darla and Camille turned their heads from across the room. "Thanks, Lauren. I needed that."

"You're welcome. By the way, I saw the new kitchen. It's really amazing."

Marguerite focused on another table decoration while standing behind the bar. "At the ranch house, you mean?"

Lauren nodded as she finished her own ornament and looked at Marguerite. "Declan is a good man. And I know he cares for you."

Marguerite set a bottled water in front of Lauren. "He says he loves me."

"Do you love him too?"

"Yes."

Lauren threw her arms up. "Then what's the problem?"

Marguerite licked her lips and looked around. Some of the women from her mother's church group were listening and whispered amongst themselves. Marguerite looked back at Lauren who said, "Oh. Well, you know Camille would make sure to ostracize anyone who criticized someone in her family."

"I'm not in her family. Missy is."

"Oh, Marguerite. Of course you're part of this family. You, Missy and Darla have been so since before Josh married Missy —because of Dane." She reached out a hand. "You deserve to be happy."

Chapter Nineteen
CASE CLOSED

She loves me.

Declan felt like a lovesick puppy, only he sported gray in his whiskers and a few at his temples. He tried to concentrate on the meeting with James King, who was now his official boss, as he signed the contract presented to him.

His life was about to take a drastic turn, one he used to avoid thinking about but now he couldn't wait for it to begin... settling down would be a fantastic adventure. When he'd sat on the vista overlooking the cattle below, he knew he'd found *home.*

All he could think about was building a new life with Marguerite. He'd never met another woman like her. She was unique and she was his...

"Excuse me." James pulled out his cell phone which must've been on vibrate.

Declan looked around the massive home office, impressed with the self-made man who'd built it. Bainbridge had once told him working for the Kings was both interesting, easy, and worth the life change.

"Yeah, they left a while ago...Are you meeting us there?...Oh?...Really, great news...Yes, he's here." James handed Declan his cell phone. "It's Jarod. Needs to speak to you."

Puzzled, Declan nodded his thanks before taking it. "What's happened?"

When Jarod told him the news Declan let out a puff of air. "Where is she?"

James looked at him quizzically.

"You're damn right I want to be there." Declan clicked off and handed the phone back to James. "I need to go. Jarod's about to make an arrest."

James thumped his desk. "Bout time. I'll see you at Blue's for the fundraiser."

Declan shook James's hand once more and left. He didn't run into anyone on his way out of the mansion and was relieved to get into his pickup. He was even more impressed with Jarod and what he'd done with the information Marguerite had given him.

His thumbs drummed an even beat over the steering wheel as he drove to Blue's Whisky Bar. It was early yet but the people inside were about to get a major surprise; an in-person example of the sheriff's work.

He parked in front of the building and waved to Darla who directed some folks on where to hang a sign announcing the night's festivities.

"What are you doing here so early?"

He hugged the woman who would one-day be his mother-in-law. "Surprise." He winked at her and headed inside. He found *his* woman behind the bar as usual, talking to Lauren seated on a barstool. All of the sudden, Marguerite leaned over the bar as far as she could to hug the other woman. To Declan it appeared the two had been having a heart-to-heart.

"Ladies." He tipped a mock hat at them.

"Well, speak of the devil." Lauren swiveled on the stool to face him. "Your meeting with James all finished?"

"Mostly, but we got interrupted. Your husband's on his way over."

"Really? It's a little early for him to be off duty." Lauren wore a puzzled frown.

Declan shared a look with Marguerite. "It's not what you think."

"Oh?" Lauren paused for a moment before her eyes widened. "Ooh." She looked around. "Who is it?"

Declan shook his head. "You'll see soon enough. I was invited for the grand reveal."

He stepped up to the bar and leaned in to give a kiss to Marguerite. He noticed some onlookers, people he'd seen in the pews at church with disapproving expressions on their faces. He glared back to let them know he didn't appreciate their judgement. He was only moderately satisfied when they went back to their own business of decorating.

He took his usual stool, which happened to be next to Lauren, and Marguerite handed him an iced tea. "Can you tell me if I was right?"

"Honey, you're always right. But this time, there's a bonus prize."

"Huh," she said, stumped as he'd been, because before Jarod spilled the beans, he hadn't put it all together either.

He surveyed the room and found Davie and Lance helping Camille rearrange the tables around the dance floor, Cheryl passed by with the usual scowl on her face; Dusty moved about helping people who must've been on the decorating committee because Declan didn't recognize them as regulars at the bar.

Speaking of regulars, Frank and Fred sat together supervising the whole production. When the kitchen door swung open to reveal Trey the busboy, Declan almost turned away until Kelvin followed the boy into the dining room pushing a cart containing platters of hors d'oeuvres.

Darla came in from the front porch area. She looked around for a moment before approaching Declan and Marguerite, who'd come out from behind the bar. "Jarod's arrived with quite a few deputies. What's going on?"

"Darla, could you do me a favor and stay here with Marguerite?" He offered his barstool but didn't wait for an answer, and approached Dusty. "I need you to lock all the doors except for the front and have everyone come out of the kitchen and the back rooms."

Dusty nodded once, and was off. Glad he didn't have to explain himself, he kept his eyes glued to Cheryl, Kelvin, Davie and Lance.

"I told them the bar was officially closed to the public and they needed to help out here," Dusty said once he'd returned from his task. "What's going on?"

Jarod, Deputy Eli Wallace, and a few others Declan was only acquainted with came through the front doors.

Declan said to Dusty, "You're about to find out. You might want to update your job listings."

Dusty did a double-take and groaned. "Damn it, I knew that girl was trouble the moment I hired her."

Jarod didn't have to announce his presence to have Davie and Lance turn and start looking for the exits. "We didn't do it!" they said in unison.

Kelvin locked eyes with Cheryl, who began to cry. "You stupid bitch. What'd you leave behind?"

"Blood and hair in the back of her vehicle." Jarod said. "Cheryl, you're under arrest for the illegal disposal of a body."

"Turn around, Kelvin." Eli didn't wait for Kelvin to comply. He simply took him by the shoulders, spun him around and put the cuffs on his wrists. "You're under arrest for the murders of Mary Jo Costa and Denise Lanford. You have the right to remain silent—"

"You got no proof. It was all Cheryl. She's crazy, man! Violent! Jealous. I didn't do nuthin'."

"Aw, Kelvin," Lance shook his head with disgust, "I told you not to get involved with her!"

As Jarod and Eli escorted the two suspects out of the building, everyone applauded.

Darla turned to Declan. "Okay, we saw the show. Now tell us what's going on."

———

MARGUERITE SCRUNCHED HER EYEBROWS. *Huh, both of them were in on it.*

Declan grinned at her mother. "You should ask your daughter. She put two and two together.

Marguerite shook her head. "No, I only presented the facts as I knew them. I didn't figure on Kelvin being involved."

Dusty had his hands on his hips looking at the floor. "Well, that was interesting. Not that I'm sorry to see her go but what the hell am I going to do tonight? Jarod's left me short-handed."

"Look around," this from Lauren, "there's plenty of volunteers here. I'm sure Camille will be happy to supply you with the support you need."

"I am." The woman in question approached the group and Marguerite squelched a grin, especially when Darla went back to her original point.

"Well? Who killed those women?"

Marguerite looked to Declan who only smiled. "Go ahead, honey. Tell them."

She took a breath. "I found out Cheryl had been harassing Mary Jo online. Kelvin moved here to work for the mine. By following their online trails of break ups and new relationships, my guess is Mary Jo wasn't about to give up on Kelvin so she followed him here. By the amount of damage done to Mary Jo's body, one or both of them, stabbed her to death and dumped her body up the old dirt bike trail. I think that place was Cheryl's idea because Kelvin's only been in Timbisha Township for a few months."

Declan nodded. "The labs finally came in. They did find DNA under her fingernails but it was too degraded to get a full analysis other than to say it belonged to a male."

"Then how do they know it was Kelvin?" Darla asked.

"Because my son is thorough. He'd sent other forensic evidence to an expert on the east coast and they found something, didn't they?"

Again, Declan nodded. "They got a positive match in one of the stab wounds. Kevin Robles left his DNA in epithelial cells around her neck when he faked her strangulation."

"But it was Cheryl who dumped Mrs. Lanford's body the night of the fight," Marguerite said, tilting her head in thought. "I bet they purposely started the fight to get her out of the building, right? They had alibis and they hoped no one would notice Cheryl was gone. But who killed Mrs. Lanford?"

Declan looped his arm around Marguerite's shoulders. She looked into his handsome face before he leaned down and pecked her lips. "God, your brain is sexy."

"Stop that and spill it."

He sighed while the other ladies in their group giggled.

Yeah, he was definitely a man worth giggling over. "When the news reported about the other murders, they dug up Mary Jo and wrapped her in plastic, then Kelvin saw Mrs. Lanford in the Walmart parking lot, nabbed her, strangled her and put her in Cheryl's car. We'll know more after they interview both of them. I have a feeling Cheryl is going to fess up in order to stay out of prison for the rest of her life."

"Well, good riddance to them. Now, " Camille surveyed the room. "This place isn't going to get prepared with all this dilly-dallying." She moved off to finish her work.

Marguerite leaned into Declan and wrapped both her arms around his waist not giving a fig who saw them. "How did your meeting with James go?"

"Good. I'm officially on the King family payroll."

She kissed his chin. "I'm glad. Are you staying until everyone gets here or do you need to run errands before the fundraiser begins?"

"I'm stayin'." The way he said it let her know he wasn't talking about only tonight.

She kissed him one more time before getting back behind the bar to begin prepping bottles for the fundraiser. Dusty was offering an open bar to encourage folks to donate more to the cause. The kids needed new equipment and some teams were in need of sponsors. The town had grown so much that new teams would need to be established next season to accommodate all the kids wanting to play the sport. Even the cheerleading squads were growing, as evidenced when Rosie came in with Sonja sporting a little cheer outfit, followed by a group of little girls all wearing uniforms including Jessica King, and Tessa, Dusty's niece.

Lauren fussed over Jessica's hair while Rosie chatted away.

Sonja grabbed a table near the buffet and Declan went to sit with his family.

Marguerite felt a little pang when he lifted Rosie up for a hug and kiss before sending her off with her new friends but remained at the table with Rodney and Ryan. Both boys wore their team jerseys and soon the establishment was filled to the brim with kids and parents, coaches and donors to the cause.

Camille came through with the volunteers to help out and soon Dusty and the league had raised enough money to cover the costs of expansion.

Marguerite remained behind the bar most of the evening, slinging drinks of both the alcohol and nonalcoholic variety. At one point, a group of boys in jerseys sat on barstools next to Frank and Fred, requesting her best chocolate sodas. The two older men were more than happy to entertain the youngsters and had Marguerite laughing at their storytelling.

It was one of the funnest shifts she'd spent at Blue's in a long time.

"You have a new fan club." Declan leaned on the bar sucking on a chocolate soda himself.

"I sure do. One of them tipped me with tickets to their first game."

Declan leaned his head back and laughed. "Was it Rodney?"

"Of course." She moved to the other side of the bar to fill an order of drinks then hustled back to Declan who leaned his elbows on the mahogany. "How's your sister?"

"She says she couldn't be happier. Also couldn't take her eyes off your boss."

"Well, Dusty's a looker."

Declan narrowed his eyes at her, and she laughed. "Easy there, cowboy. You've got nothing to be jealous of."

He set his empty glass down but instead of taking his seat he lifted the partition and stepped behind the bar.

"What're you doing? There are children present, Declan McKinley."

He pinned her against the bar and curled her toes with a heart-racing kiss. "But I am a jealous man, Marguerite. I never knew it until I met you." He kissed her again. "Say you'll always love me and maybe I can get the beast back in its cave where it belongs."

She raised an eyebrow at him. "Maybe I like him out of his cave."

He growled and kissed her again, this time ending with the words, "God, I love you, Marguerite."

THREE WEEKS AFTER THE FUNDRAISER, JASON declared the house finished and ready for its new occupants. Declan insisted she take a ride out to the house with him. He didn't have any furniture so his move would be pretty easy for him.

But not for her.

She didn't want him to go and he hadn't mentioned her moving in with him since they first brought it up at dinner with Josh and Missy. Still, she was more than happy to spend the day with Declan. The ride out into rural Timbisha county was quick but still the air was crisper now that August had left and late-September began to turn the tips of tree leaves vibrant yellow, orange and red.

Declan had been drumming his thumbs on the steering wheel for the better part of the drive but stopped suddenly to use his blinker. "Here it is." They turned into a freshly paved driveway which led up to a sprawling ranch house with a wide front porch and windows everywhere. She spotted two chimney's in the roofline and a large double front door.

When they parked in front of one of four garage bays, she turned to him and smiled. "It's got King written all over it. It's beautiful, Declan."

He sighed. "It's a big damn house." He kissed the back of her hand. "Come on." He opened his door and she followed suit. When he reached her side of the pickup he took her hand again and led her up the porch steps. The space was covered and would provide shade all summer and protection from the elements in winter.

"Jason said we'd find the keys in the kitchen so it should be unlocked." He reached for the doorknob and pushed. A long entry greeted them, with a high enough ceiling to hang a chandelier, which there were two. Only they weren't made of crystal, but wrought iron and colored glass not unlike she'd seen in Julie's home. "I think they call it 'arts and crafts' style. What do you think?"

"Well if the rest of the house is anything like this I'm sure it's going to be great, Declan. You're going to be happy here, although you might need to hire someone to clean it."

"Four bedrooms, four bathrooms, a great room, your chocolate space and a humungous kitchen. Honestly, it's over the top."

I bet it is.

When he said the chocolate space was hers a warmth spread through her chest. They walked down the entry and sure enough, the back of the house was nothing but kitchen, dining and great room. "Holy moly," she whispered reverently at everything Camille and Josh had done in the kitchen.

"Your workspace is here." He opened a door, which she

thought led to a pantry but found a galley space big enough to start a whole chocolate making factory.

"Oh." She put her hands to her mouth and tears ran down her face. She couldn't stop them if she tried.

"Damn, honey. Please don't cry." He pulled her into his arms. "But please don't say no either."

She wasn't crying because of the space. She was crying because sitting on the counter was a black velvet box with a large diamond ring.

"Marguerite, you are the most intriguing, wonderful, special, and all around bratty woman I have ever met. I can't live without you, honey. Please make this old man happy and marry me."

When she could finally speak, she wrapped her arms around his neck. "You're not that old or I wouldn't be here with you right now." She kissed his cheek, then his lips. When he expanded the kiss she went with it and they stood there making out in the chocolate space for ten minutes.

"Don't leave me hangin', honey."

Feeling ornery, she pulled out of his arms and put the ring on her finger, which fit perfectly. "Well, I don't know, Declan. My reputation could damage yours—"

He reached for her and she squealed.

"Yes, yes, of course I'll marry you," she said on a laugh as he sat her butt on the counter and caged her in.

"That's more like it. And, I don't give a fig about your reputation. Besides, I don't really think it's as bad as you think it is."

No, it's worse. However, she didn't feel like arguing with him since he'd asked her to marry him and all. "What's the rest of the house look like?"

He chuckled and pulled her from the counter. They toured

the huge kitchen and when she opened a cupboard she found it full of dishes. She pulled open a drawer and found utensils and silverware. "Declan, did you know they were going to stock the house?" She opened every drawer and cupboard and found them full.

"Well," he put his arm behind his head and rubbed his neck, "when James brought me here to show me what was what, I got to thinkin' how hard it would be to furnish this place. When I expressed the thought to him later, he sent me to Camille, who told me not to worry about anything. Apparently, they're having some delivery trucks coming today, which is why I wanted to propose now. Baby, I need help puttin' everything in the right place."

She loved it when his twang came out because she knew he was either relaxed or really rattled. Looking at his expression, all she wanted to do was take away the lost look and help do anything he needed done. She had the day off, something she was getting more of lately because Dusty had hired not only a new waitress but another bartender for the days she was tired after coaching games, or working all night on chocolate recipes.

Looping her arm through his, she pulled him down the hallway on the other side of the 'great room' to look at the spaces down there. "I would love to help you put things in the right places." She stopped in the middle of the hallway, a thought occurring to her. "Declan, do you want a big wedding?"

He pushed a strand of hair behind her ear. "I want what you want, honey."

"I definitely *do not* want a big wedding."

A grin spread across is rugged, handsome face. "I'm relieved to hear it."

She smacked his bicep. "If you didn't want a big wedding, why didn't you just say so?"

"It's not the size of the wedding, but the time it will take to make you mine."

"Oh."

"Yes, oh. I want you sooner rather than later."

He pulled her down the hallway to the master suite but before she could explore the bathroom he pushed her up against the wall and caged her in again like he'd done in the chocolate room. "I think I want you now."

She was only too happy to oblige.

Chapter Twenty
REDEMPTION

Declan pulled into St. Anthony's in the early evening of the Harvest Festival Dinner. Marguerite's knee had finally stopped bouncing. She wasn't fooling him. She was nervous. Tonight was the big reveal of who'd been making the best chocolates around town, which had been dubbed "Theroux-ly Outrageous." He stared at the diamond on her ring finger. "You know, you're going to have to change the names of those chocolates now that you're a McKinley."

She soughed out a breath and turned to him. "Fine, but you get to tell Camille and Lauren you want the name changed." A Cheshire cat grin spread across her lips before she opened the door and climbed out.

God, he even loved it when she deflected. He got out and grabbed the containers they'd stacked in the bed of the truck. She went to take the top one, but he moved it out of her reach. "I've got it, honey. Go on in there and point me in the right direction."

Her hips swayed with her sexy gait and he grinned knowing she didn't do it on purpose. It was just *her*.

God, he loved his woman.

Instead of stopping in the main hall, she made a beeline for the church kitchen where prep on the buffet dinner was taking place. Julie, spearheading the whole thing, hugged Marguerite. "You made it. Great! I reserved this space for you to put together what you need for the cakes. Oh, hi Declan." She took the top bin off his pile and both women immediately dismissed him. With nothing left for him to do in the kitchen except deposit the rest on the counter, he wandered into the main hall where he ran into Josh.

"Hey man." He stuck his hand out, and Declan pumped it up and down a few times. "Marguerite getting set up?"

"Yeah, I've been dismissed."

"Figures. Here, you can help me rearrange these bales of hay. You're getting pretty familiar with them lately." His grin wasn't wicked, and he referred to his laid back position with his father.

"Sure am. What are we doing with them now?"

"Kiddie play area. The butcher paper is for them to draw on—here." Josh showed him where everything was supposed to be located and he got to work helping the King men and other church volunteers set up for the event.

Ever since their small wedding ceremony, Declan and Marguerite had been attending Mass regularly and he'd gotten to know a few folks. No one since the night of the fundraiser at Blue's spoke badly against Marguerite. In fact, he'd only heard the negative stuff from the few old biddies he'd found out had had a fancy for Dane Bainbridge and gotten nowhere with him. Of course, the rumors about what Marguerite had gone through on her undercover stint still came up from time to time, but it mostly had to do with what needed to be done to clear out the trouble in Timbisha Township.

Marguerite didn't know that most people already knew what she'd sacrificed and were willing to put all of it aside in order to make her feel like a welcomed person in their community. It didn't hurt that he'd also had a few discussions at Molly's—and other places—with people who liked to stir up the rumor mill. Plus, now that folks knew he worked for James King, it made all the difference in the world. If they gossiped, it was behind closed doors where it belonged.

Once all the tables had been arranged, and the food was laid out, Father O'Keefe gave the blessing and everyone got in line for the buffet. He noted the desert table had been set up but the deserts were covered and would be revealed once the kids had eaten a proper dinner.

Lauren explained the long table reserved on one side of the hall was for the King family, of which Declan and Marguerite were included. "James wants you with him as much as possible when we're out in public, but you probably already know that, don't you?"

"Yes, ma'am." Yeah, the man had enemies. Declan had read some of Bainbridge's files stored in James's office and the danger to James was a little more threatening than Declan liked. Unlike his mentor, though, Declan had brought all of those files to the sheriff, and together he and Jarod had interviewed quite a few people.

The harassment had dwindled down exponentially.

When he spied Davie and Lance who'd come into the hall with girlfriends on their arms and ornery expressions on their faces, he sighed. Timbisha Township would always have some sort of trouble going on and there'd be nothing anyone could do to stop it.

"What are you thinking about?" Marguerite's voice ripped him from his ruminations.

"Trouble."

"Oh, gosh, don't say that, sweetheart. I've had enough trouble to last a lifetime."

At her endearment, a mellow warmth spread throughout his chest, as it had done since the first time she'd used it on him. He leaned in and kissed her cheek. "You look beautiful tonight."

She narrowed her eyes. "Didn't you say I looked beautiful this morning?"

"I did."

"Huh." She deposited some pasta salad on her plate. "What's changed?"

"Not a damn thing."

He spied her smirk but she didn't say anything else even after they'd sat down to eat. Her knee began to bounce again and he knew she was nervous about the reveal. At this point, there was nothing to do but grin and bear whatever was going to happen when dessert was served.

"Aunt Marguerite, you don't need to worry." Jessica had finished her plate and stared directly at his wife.

"I'm not worried."

Jessica grinned. "You are but you don't need to be. All my friends loved your goodies, especially the hot chocolate bomb-things. They are *the best*."

He felt more than saw, her suck in a breath. "Thanks, Jessica."

Camille stood from the table and the sound level in the room lowered as the matriarch of Timbisha Township took the microphone off its cradle. "Ladies and gentlemen, thank you so much for coming to our annual Harvest Festival Dinner. As you know, this kicks off the holiday season and is one of my favorite family events. This year we have something special to reveal."

There were gasps around the room, mainly from children who already knew what was about to happen. Declan assumed Jessica had done her work well.

"For dessert this evening, we've asked our very own Marguerite Theroux-McKinley," she lowered the mic and smiled at Marguerite, "Honey, please stand up," then put the microphone back to her mouth again, "to provide her most popular treats. Having tried them all, I can tell you, they are simply the best chocolates I've ever tasted. They're so good, in fact, Mrs. McKinley has done me the great honor of accepting a contract with Cafe Armstrong! So, without further ado, I present *Theroux-ly Outrageous Chocolates*!"

Two people, volunteers Declan assumed, removed the cloth from the table to reveal a display to rival the best french chocolatier shops.

Applause broke out, and children dashed to the table, chased down by weary parents.

"Well, here goes." Marguerite relaxed back into her chair as if it were all a goof. But Declan knew better.

Within fifteen minutes, his wife was bombarded with people congratulating her on a job well done, shaking his hand as well, and asking when she could help with various parties and events from around the community.

Missy sat next to her and Declan stepped away to get his own chocolate bomb to dunk into his coffee cup. He leaned against the wall out of the way and surveyed the people gathering around his wife. Pride mixed with joy had him grinning from ear to ear.

"She's a natural, you know." Josh had sidled up beside him

and Declan braced himself for what the youngest King was about to say. "She's always held herself away from people at the same time listening to everything they had to say. It's a strange phenomenon. Being from this town, it's no wonder she accepted the job to get the hell out of here, and be a part of something other than this life."

Declan narrowed his eyes at Josh. "What the hell are you talking about? She didn't really like being out in the field. She was scared to death but never showed it because she didn't want to disappoint her uncle. You know that."

Josh nodded. "Yes, but I also know what she sacrificed in order to protect her sister from the vultures who live here. Missy's told me a lot, and we all misinterpreted Marguerite's behavior. I'm sorry for that, but I'm so damn happy she's discovered just how important she is to everyone of us, especially to our family."

Declan shook his head. "She hasn't really, but tonight is helping with that problem."

"Here, your mascara is running." Missy handed her a napkin to try and scrub at her non-waterproof mascara. She'd been out of practice in the make-up department and grabbed the wrong tube at the store.

"Sorry, I don't know why I'm crying. Has anyone noticed?"

"Pfft. Probably everyone, Ding Dong."

"Don't call me that."

Missy grinned, the brat. When did her little sister become so ornery? Oh, that's right. The minute she married the orneriest King.

"Did you tell Declan you were hyphenating your name?"

"No, but I'm only doing it for the chocolate business. Thankfully, Camille addressed me as Mrs. McKinley." God, she liked the sound of it. She hadn't wanted to hyphenate but the ladies had convinced her it would be good for the business.

Another family approached her to tell her how much they loved her desserts and asked for a flyer. Lauren created them with pricing and a list of the easiest items to make. No one had said a bad thing to her face and, in fact, some people went out of their way to shake her hand, or even give her a hug.

"See? Everyone loves you, Marguerite."

Another tear fell. She finally felt welcome in her hometown.

⁓

MARGUERITE STARED OUT THE KITCHEN WINDOW AT the barn sitting between her house and The Estate, and the mountains beyond. It was early November and dark clouds floated across the high desert sky trying to form together to make a little storm. In between, azure light peeked through, but Marguerite knew winter was around the corner.

She dipped another fortune cookie into chocolate before setting it on the rack to dry. The cookies had started out as little witches and ghosts for the King's Halloween bash a couple of weeks ago. Each treat had a note inside indicating to the children where a clue to the night's prize had been hidden.

Camille loved it so much, she thought why not do them like fortune cookies for Jarod's re-election celebration. Yes, he'd run unopposed, but the community still wanted to celebrate their favorite crime fighter.

Warm, strong hands wrapped around her from behind and

Declan nipped the back of her earlobe. "I thought you finished all those last night?"

"I did. These are special." She didn't elaborate because frankly she was nervous as hell to give Declan his fortune.

"Special like you?"

"Ha. Ha. No, they have customized notes in them." She took a deep breath.

He kissed her neck one last time and then moved to stand next to her. He tilted his head. "Oh, like you did at the Kings for the little kids? That was fun. The looks on their faces were nothing but pure joy." He kissed her cheek one last time, poured himself a cup of coffee and dropped a spicy chocolate bomb she'd made special for him into the mug.

He'd left her this morning to do his chores and picked up the mail on the way in. He took a ranching magazine out of the pile and sat at the counter to read and drink his mocha.

She continued her dipping and racking, watching the clouds drift, and the chocolate drip onto the wax paper beneath her drying rack.

I should be doing this in the other room.

But she couldn't resist the view from this window. It was idyllic.

"So, why are these special? Who're the messages for?"

"Well," she drew out, giving herself some courage, "the ones I made last night have generic fortunes in them. Lauren and I found a wholesaler online who sells them. They also sell blank strips for customizing. So, these are special for the family. Lauren and Julie are doing gender reveals for their spouses and for Camille and James because Julie really screwed them over when she had the twins."

That story was funny and it made her giggle.

"Oh, yeah, I was in town for that one. First time I met

everyone..." He trailed off as he read his magazine. Then he spoke up. "Wait, you know what they're all having?"

"Sorta," she hedged. "But yes I know what my sister, Lauren and Julie are having."

She turned to face him and he narrowed his eyes on her. She sucked in another breath and grabbed the one she'd made for Declan. There was no way in hell she was going to drop a bomb like this on him in public.

No.

Friggin.

Way.

When he saw she had one in her hand his eyes rounded and he swallowed hard, his Adam's apple bobbing up and down through his salt and pepper stubble since he hadn't bothered to shave this morning. "Holy shit."

She stood there waiting and he immediately broke the chocolate open.

He swallowed again before his warm, tobacco colored eyes glossed over. "Are ya sure, honey?"

She reached into her pocket, pulling out the stick saying she was most definitely pregnant.

When he continued to sit there staring at her, she felt the tell-tell dread of her past unfurling itself like a snake in her chest. "I know we've never discussed children, and frankly, I don't really know what to feel about it myself, but please know I didn't do this on purpose or anything—"

In a rush, he had her in his arms and was kissing her. When he came up for air all she saw was happiness, and love. "Marguerite, this," and he touched her abdomen making her cry, "is the best thing you coulda ever given me. I didn't know how life would be settlin' down but then I found you. I didn't think it could get any better but havin' a family of my own—with *you*

—is nothin' short of a miracle. I love you so, so much. I couldn't be happier."

She wrapped her arms around him.

"No, it's you who're the miracle. I was neck-deep in trouble until you moved here and wouldn't leave me alone. You proved I was worthy of a life filled with happiness. I love you, too, Declan McKinley."

Dear Reader,

Thank you so much for taking the time to read Marguerite and Declan's story. This one took me so long I thought it was never going to happen! Marguerite represents every woman who's set their personal needs aside to protect the people she loves, only to have it turn to tragedy. As they say, no good deed goes unpunished. And Declan, well, he made me swoon the minute he walked into the sheriff's station in *Josh's Challenge*. I hope you enjoyed their story.

If you don't mind, I'd love for you to leave a review, or a star rating, on your favorite platform. Also, I'd love to hear from you, so please feel free to reach out to me anytime on social media or my website.

Oh, and book five in the series is in the works...Dusty Boots has a story to tell, too.

Happy Reading,
Elise
www.elisemanion.com

PS: I'm no longer active on Facebook, however the page might still be up. If you're interested, you can read why there, or you can sign up for my monthly newsletter on my website and click on *Happy Distractions* in the menu. If you want to contact me via social media, you can still find me on Instagram.

Acknowledgments

A special note of gratitude to Lynda Bailey, my partner in crime and all things Indie. Thank you for your patience, criticism, advice, and most of all, friendship.

You're the *Naughty* to my *Nice* ;)

Also by Elise Manion

Trouble In Timbisha Township Series

Jason's Princess; King Brothers Book 1

Jarod's Heart; King Brothers Book 2

Josh's Challenge; King Brothers Book 3

Marguerite's Redemption; Book 4

Dusty's Girl; Book 5 (coming soon)

Applewood Series

Unwanted: Finding Where You're Loved